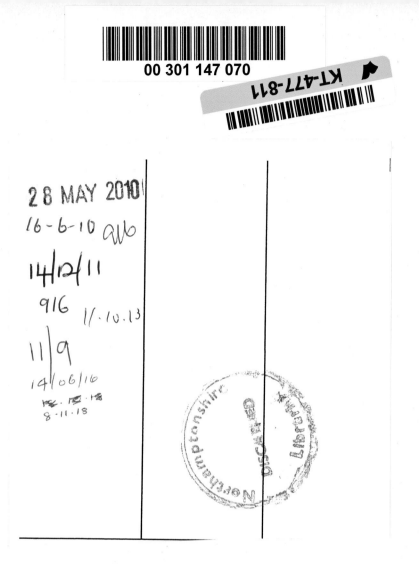

BEYOND THE SHORE

* available from Severn House

BEYOND THE SHORE

Connie Monk

This first world edition published 2010
in Great Britain and in the USA by
SEVERN HOUSE PUBLISHERS LTD of
9–15 High Street, Sutton, Surrey, England, SM1 1DF.
Trade paperback edition published
in Great Britain and the USA 2010 by
SEVERN HOUSE PUBLISHERS LTD

British Library Cataloguing in Publication Data

Monk, Connie.
 Beyond the Shore.
 1. Women artists – Fiction. 2. Widowers – Fiction. 3. Art
 galleries, Commercial – Management – Fiction. 4. Great
 Britain – History – George VI, 1936-1952 – Fiction. 5. Love
 stories.
 I. Title
 823.9'14-dc22

ISBN-13: 978-0-7278-6901-2   (cased)
ISBN-13: 978-1-84751-245-1   (trade paper)

All Severn House titles are printed on acid-free paper.

Severn House Publishers support The Forest Stewardship Council [FSC],
the leading international forest certification organisation. All our titles that
are printed on Greenpeace-approved FSC-certified paper carry the FSC logo.

Mixed Sources
Product group from well-managed
forests and other controlled sources
www.fsc.org Cert no. SA-COC-1565
© 1996 Forest Stewardship Council
FSC

Typeset by Palimpsest Book Production
Grangemouth, Stirlingshire, Scotland.
Printed and bound in Great Britain by
MPG Books Ltd., Bodmin, Cornwall.

One

'What a wonderful week,' James said as he held the car door open for Georgie. 'Have you any idea what being with you has done for me? You have helped me find a purpose again.'

Finding a purpose was one thing; falling in love another. Was that what had made her hesitate when, the previous evening, he had tried to persuade her to marry him?

'Yes, it was the best holiday I can remember. Dear James.' Once out of his car, she reached to kiss his cheek. 'Get your thinking cap on and find us somewhere exciting for the summer break. Mountain walking in Austria? Sailing down the canals in France? The lakes were lovely; they've whetted my appetite for bigger, more exciting things.'

'Make it a honeymoon. Georgie, can't you see how happy we could be?'

She made no effort to move towards the side of his house where she had left her own car parked while they were away. Instead, she stood with her hands on his shoulders.

'James, I've never had a friend like you. I am fonder of you than I can say. We were friends from the first day we met – and perhaps that's the problem.' There was something like embarrassment as she told him, 'We *liked* each other, but we didn't look at each other for the first time and *know.*'

He didn't answer immediately and she wished she hadn't said it. Was that how it had been for him when he had met Kathy, the wife he'd lost more than two years ago?

'Marriage is just the beginning. Georgie, we have a good foundation to build on; sharing all that we are would bring us even closer. Think about it; promise me you'll at least think about it.'

For eight days they had been together at a hotel in the Lake District. For one wild moment she faced the honest truth and before she could stop herself the words were spoken.

'We had rooms next to each other – *next to each other* – but they might have been miles apart. Is that a basis for marriage?'

He frowned, surprised by what she said. 'Do you think I wouldn't have preferred that we could have been together? But you have my complete respect; I hold you on a pedestal.'

Yes, she screamed silently, *but you don't hold me in your arms, you don't let passion override all your high-flown ideals.* And yet, wasn't it the way he clung to his principles that attracted her? That and his appearance, she answered honestly. He was handsome enough to turn any girl's head. Fifteen years her senior, at forty he had lost any look of boyishness he might once have had. His dark brown hair was always well cut and, like his moustache, it never gave the impression either of recently having been trimmed nor yet being due for a visit to the barber. The colour of his blue-grey eyes was emphasized by their fringe of thick, dark lashes; the bone structure of his face was as near perfect as she had ever seen away from the silver screen. Broad-shouldered, slim-hipped, he wore his well-cut clothes with distinction. She had met him just over a year ago when, recently appointed as Town Clerk of Winchford, he had been invited to open the annual fête at St Winifred's School on the outskirts of town, where Georgie was a housemistress.

'I must go,' she said now, 'or Muriel will think I've forgotten it's her birthday. Shall I call in and say hello on my way to school tomorrow week?'

'I'll be waiting for you.'

She held her face towards him, her mouth tantalizingly close to his. He ran his fingers through her boyishly cut, naturally curly hair, then dropped a light kiss on her forehead. She felt let down, conscious that he was restrained by the fact they were in the street where anything beyond a brotherly peck would be un-acceptable. She walked to her own car, a slight, slim figure, yet one that gave the impression of abundant energy. When she got into the driver's seat and put her hand to slam the door he was ahead of her, almost silently pressing it closed then making sure it was secure.

'Drive carefully,' he said. 'Remember you are very precious.' His words almost erased her feeling of disappointment.

★   ★   ★

That was on the first Saturday in May, her stepmother Muriel's forty-fifth birthday. Although Georgie had been only nine when her widowed father had remarried she had never called his new wife anything but Muriel. Not a motherly type of woman nor yet a glamorous one, Muriel Sharp's youth had been given to caring for her elderly parents and although she'd been only twenty-seven when they had died within months of each other, she had already felt that life had passed her by. Then along had come Cyril Franklyn, a widower with a nine-year-old daughter he adored and the need of a woman for her to turn to as she approached adolescence.

At Sycamore Cottage, where Cyril and Muriel Franklyn awaited Georgina's arrival, Muriel heard the click of the letter box. It was habit, rather than birthday anticipation, that made her hurry into the small square hall to pick the envelopes up from the mat. There were just two: one a card from Georgie bearing a Windermere postmark, even though she would be there in time for lunch, and the second an envelope from the bank.

While she was putting Georgie's card on the mantelpiece Cyril opened the one Muriel supposed to be the monthly bank statement. He took care of all the financial affairs except for the pound a week he gave her for groceries. Her mind was already on the preparation of lunch; she always liked to make it something special when Georgie was home.

'Christ!' Could she have misheard? It was out of character for Cyril to blaspheme and there could have been nothing from the bank that would upset him. And yet, just to look at his face told her that it was no ordinary bank statement he held in his hand.

'Is something wrong? Have they made a mistake?' Secure in the knowledge that they lived within the scope of his small pension from his final working years when he'd been engaged in the Housing Department at the Town Hall, she was ready to calm him down if a mistake had been made.

'You'd better read it. Bloody young swine. This sort of thing wouldn't have been allowed if Albert Small hadn't retired.'

She picked up the letter and read. 'Overdraft? It must be a mistake, Cyril. You'll have to drive into town and have a word with him. I expect this is his first appointment as a manager. He hasn't had Mr Small's years of experience.'

'Albert would never have written to me in that tone. By God, all the years I've been with that branch and to write a letter like that!'

'As if you'd let yourself get in the red! Silly young man. Wait until Monday, dear, and go in then. It's clearly a mistake. Let me give you another cup of coffee and then we'll think about what we're going to do with the day. So lovely of Georgie to come back in time for my birthday, when the school term doesn't start officially for more than another week.' She picked up the pair of white silk gloves that had been Cyril's gift. 'If we go out perhaps I'll wear my lovely new gloves.'

'For Christ's sake, stop your stupid chatter. How am I expected to think?'

'It's not stupid chatter to talk about Georgie coming for the rest of her holiday. Put the letter away till Monday. Or, if it makes you so angry, drive into town this morning and have it out with them. Why don't you slip over to see Mr Small and have a word with him? Surely you've been friends long enough for that.'

'Oh yes,' he sneered, 'we've stood next to each other in the choir for twenty years and more. He never charged me for going over my limit; he knew it would only be temporary. But he's retired now – no one's going to listen to him any more than they would to me. Once you're put out to grass you're useless.'

'Over your limit? You mean what they say is true? You have an overdraft?'

'I won't be questioned – not by *you*! And not by young Georgie when she comes either. Yes, Albert allowed me to have an over-draft, and yes, just lately it's got a bit out of hand—'

'Why didn't you tell me you were worried? Perhaps I could have cut down a bit on the housekeeping.'

'Stop talking such drivel. This is just a blip. I'll make it up. Perhaps Red Devil might romp home today in the two thirty. That'd give the young bugger something to chew on!'

Muriel looked at him in disbelief.

'Horses! You mean you've been wasting our money on horses?'

'Our money? *Our* money! Since when have you had anything except what I give you?'

Muriel sat very straight and looked him in the eye. If he expected her to cringe then he was disappointed.

'Yes, *our* money. The pension may be in your name but I earn every penny you give me – and more besides.' Hardly realizing it, they moved to stand facing each other.

By no stretch of the imagination could Muriel ever have been beautiful. Above average height, there was nothing willowy in her appearance; she looked strong despite her slim figure and hips that were as narrow as any lad's. Her legs were long and slender – in fact they would have been the envy of many a woman half her age – but considering she wore her straight skirts longer than most women, her legs went unadmired. The embarrassment of her entire adult life had been her bust. Even at school her huge breasts had been the butt of many a teasing joke. 'Puppy fat', her mother had said. But time had proved her wrong. With the years Muriel had learnt to disguise her top-heavy appearance as much as was humanly possible. Throughout the 1920s, when fashion had decreed it beautiful to have no more shape than a boy, she had encased her heavy burden tightly into submission, despite the discomfort, and with the passing of time she had become used to it. Muriel wasn't in the habit of running but, if she were to do so, there would have been no chance of so much as the slightest wobble in her heavy bosom. Like the rest of her body, her face was long and thin. Yet, a stranger looking at her might be drawn first of all to her luminous, dark eyes.

'You deserve more than I give you for housekeeping? How's that, then? You can't say I make marital demands on you. Call yourself a wife! Housekeeper, more like it.'

'No, not a housekeeper. If I were that, you'd have to pay me a wage. But then, of course, you couldn't do that or you wouldn't have money to throw away on the horses.' She seemed to stand apart from herself, miserable and ashamed at what she was saying but with no power to act differently. She wanted just to hurt him as he was hurting her. But they mustn't behave like this, especially not today, her birthday, and with Georgie due to arrive at any minute. 'Cyril,' she said, her dark eyes brimming with tears brought to the surface by emotion she hadn't been able to control. 'Cyril, we can't talk to each other like this. We're overwrought. I don't want more money, I told you, you can give me less if it helps. And why do you say you don't make demands on me? There never were demands; I was always there. You know I was.'

'Don't bring all that into it. You think I can't manage it, don't you? You think that's why I don't want you in my bed.' He leant close to her, his eyes half closed. Shame drove his anger. 'You can think what you like. Just look at yourself. At your age some women can set a man's pulses racing, oh yes, even an old sod like me. Why don't you smarten yourself up, for Christ's sake!' Then, in a high-pitched and unnatural voice, a poor mimicry of her own, he said, 'But how can I, when I don't have any spending money?' Then, normally – except that normally there was never this sort of venom in his tone – he went on, 'You, my dear Muriel, should be glad I've been fool enough to house and feed you. Most women at your age still have a spark of youth. But you, what are you but a dried-up old hag? Not that you've even been anything of a wife. As for having you in my bed, I'd have more fun with my maiden aunt – if I had one.'

'I'm not going to listen. You don't know what you're saying,' she told him coldly, determined to hang on to her control. 'I don't grieve that you've lost the ability to have sex, for you were always a selfish lover. You had no finesse, no thought for anything but yourself, even years ago. There was one thing I wanted, you knew what it was and you could have given it to me. I desperately wanted a child. If we'd had our own child would we be talking like this now? Would you have frittered money you couldn't afford lining some bookmaker's pocket? But you always refused; you always put that damned thing on so that you'd make sure I didn't conceive. Did you ever care that I was unhappy?'

'Unhappy be damned! What kept you here then? You had nowhere else to go, that's what kept you.'

'I would never have gone, even if I'd had somewhere to go to, because I loved Georgie.' What was happening to them? They never quarrelled. It was as if something inside them had been awaiting an opportunity to erupt. But Muriel hated scenes; they left a stain that could never be erased. 'Oh, Cyril, don't let's quarrel, not today of all days when she will be here any minute. Let's forget the letter until Monday.' She forced a smile, a smile that didn't appear as natural as she hoped, as she said, 'It's not the end of the world if you have to take some of the nest egg to straighten out the overdraft.'

'Don't you understand? If I'd still had that, there would have been no need for an overdraft.'

'You mean it's not just the month-to-month money you've overspent on? You mean we have *nothing*?'

The look he gave her bore neither hope nor affection and that was the only answer she had as he stormed out of the room. A minute later she heard him start the engine of his elderly car.

Driving round the bend of Addington Hill, Georgie had her first glimpse of the house. It was at that moment that her father's car turned out of the front garden and disappeared in a cloud of exhaust fumes towards the brow of the hill, travelling at a speed almost beyond its ability and far too high for safety on the narrow and twisting road. She pressed harder on the accelerator as she covered the final slope to Sycamore Cottage.

'Muriel,' she called as she opened the front door with the key they had insisted on her keeping when she'd left home. 'Why was Dad in such a hurry?' No answer. 'Is everything all right?'

'What a greeting for you,' Muriel Franklyn said as she came from the kitchen. 'I don't know what we're going to do, Georgie. God help us, I truly don't.' Her long, narrow nose looked pink as if she'd been crying. She might never have been a beauty, but to Georgie her appearance represented loyalty and stability. Nothing about her ever changed, with her deep auburn hair worn as it had been since childhood, simply cut and held back with a slide. She'd never known the natural spontaneity of youth, and in character she had become old ahead of her years. As Cyril had so cruelly reminded her, many women still retained a sparkle at forty-five, but it struck Georgie how tired and worn she looked.

'Do? Do about what?' Georgina planted the expected kiss on her stepmother's cheek, somehow thinking it would bring normality to the scene.

'Our little nest egg! To me it seemed a fortune – oh, perhaps not to you with a good wage coming in – but with Cyril's pension to live on, that superannuation was . . . it was . . . stability. Like a cushion to fall back on if we really *had* to. The stupid, *stupid* man, he's been wasting it, Georgie: horses, that's where it's gone, and those silly football pools. I knew he did the pools but I thought it was just his usual two lines like he used to before he retired. But no. He must have been drawing on the nest egg. Pounds and pounds, all wasted and never a word to me about what was happening. And why should he tell me? Who am I but a housekeeper in his home?'

'What made him tell you now?' Shocked by the words, Georgina rushed in with the first thing that came into her head.

As they'd talked they'd automatically been moving towards the kitchen of the Victorian house, a room heated by the old-fashioned range on which Muriel still cooked. Now she sat on a wooden chair by the table, biting hard on the corners of her mouth in an attempt to keep it steady. Then, taking a deep breath and with her eyes closed as if she were seeing the scene unfold before her, she told Georgie what had happened.

'But the bank knows him so well. He and Mr Small have been friends in the choir as long as I can remember.'

'Mr Small retired at the end of last month. There's some new young upstart as manager at the bank now. He said in the letter that he was amazed that the account had been allowed to continue and could only imagine it had been an oversight. Cyril's over-draft must be cleared. *Overdraft* – I tell you, Georgie, he's frittered it all away, and more too.' She gave up the battle and let the tears spill unchecked. 'Thank God you get a good salary; at least you'll not let us starve.'

Georgie's emotions were in a whirl: she ached with sympathy for the broken woman before her and yet it was as if the net were closing, making escape impossible. She was ashamed that at a moment like this she could be thinking about herself, and about that letter she had written in the bedroom of the hotel in Oxford where she and James had taken rooms the previous night on their drive home.

'We'll sort it out, Muriel.' To make amends for her straying thoughts she infused her voice with confidence. A few hours ago freedom had been within her grasp, her letter of resignation written and savings enough behind her to let her live while she worked on her paintings. Now Muriel's voice echoed in her brain. '*You get a good salary; you won't let us starve.*' Pulling her thoughts into line and concentrating on the new problem, she asked, 'Did this new manager say how much Dad is overdrawn? We must get that cleared and then he must smarten up and stop acting like a silly chump. There's only one winner when it comes to betting and that's the bookie.'

'It's not fair on you. You've always worked hard, winning a scholarship place at a fine boarding school. Then the bursary that saw you through university and with a good degree. Look at you now – fancy at your age being made a housemistress at St Winifred's. We've been so proud. And now we land this on you.'

'Once we know the exact situation we'll get it sorted. Dry your tears, Muriel, and wash your face. Today is a day for celebration.'

'We've never quarrelled before. Not that we've been close, and I dare say we don't live like most couples, but we've always shown respect. Not a cross word until now. I can't get it out of my mind. Don't even remember what I said to him; I seemed to go mad. I said cruel, hateful things, I know I did, anything to hurt him. And me, he said I was a –' her voice was almost swallowed in her sobs – 'a miserable, dried-up old hag, no companion, no comfort to him, hadn't been a wife for years. It wasn't fair.'

'He can't have meant it, any more than you really meant the things you said to him. He must have wanted to hit out at you because he was frightened and ashamed. When he comes home we'll all talk about it and work out what we can do. Go on, wash your face and put on your best dress. Today we have more to celebrate than to be miserable about.'

Fine words but they did little to cheer Muriel.

'You're a good girl. If *he* sees me as the things he called me, how must I seem to you? Don't remember ever feeling young and hopeful. I wasn't much older than you are now when I met Cyril. It seemed like a miracle. "Don't let yourself worry about finding a husband," my mother used to say, "there's plenty of room on the shelf." And that's where I expected to stay, like so many more after that dreadful war had taken its toll of the young men. For me there was no chance of anything else but living my life as a spinster with both my parents needing to be looked after.' Georgie had heard it all so many times that she could have made a duet of the tale. 'That was the way it used to be for many a young woman. Then, after I lost them both within months, into my life came Cyril. He used to see to the renting side of Millband and Stevens, the agents. With my parents gone I wrote asking to

go down on the books as the tenant; that's when he came to
meet me – I dare say to make sure I would be a reliable tenant
and not let the rent get behind. We'd had that house since the
day it was built and always looked after it as if it were our own.'

'Of course you had, Muriel,' Georgie said, right on cue.

'Twenty-seven, that's what I was, but I expect I looked more; I
never was anything to look at. There was no youth for women in
my position. But Cyril changed all that. We were married within
the year. It's like looking back at another life. I knew he asked me
to marry him because he'd lost his wife and didn't want you to
have to grow up without a woman in the house; he felt it wasn't
fair on you that there was no female to talk to if things worried
you. Not that you ever came to me for comfort and advice; you
had all the confidence I'd always lacked. But it was a happy home
– it *was*, wasn't it? It's not just that I forget what I don't want to
remember? I suppose the truth was that I married him as much
for convenience as he did me. But I wanted love; I *yearned* for love.'

'And you found love, Muriel. We both loved you; you know
that. Don't let today's quarrel spoil happy memories. I expect
Dad's driving out there somewhere feeling just the same as you
are. This has always been a *happy* home, and Dad knows that that
was largely due to you.'

'We *did* have happy times. We never quarrelled, not until today.
I said some wicked, cruel things to him, I know I did. And he
called me a . . . well, I told you. We had to hurt each other. It
was awful, like a nightmare. Just thinking about it makes me feel
quite sick,' Muriel croaked.

'You neither of you meant those things, Muriel. He must have
been embarrassed and cross with himself that he'd been such a
fool. But we'll sort out the overdraft, and then he must turn over
a new leaf and stop throwing money away. Hop off and get
changed and I'll help you pretty your face.'

'He *did* mean it, and so did I. It was as if it had been brewing
all these years. Why do you think when we needed a new bed
he insisted on two singles? Frightened I'd touch him, I expect,'
she snorted. 'If I lie very still he thinks I'm asleep. He's restless,
I hear him. I know what he's wanting. But it's not me. What
fantasies fill his head? Whatever he wants, he can't find it with
me. In the beginning he used to *use* me. That's how I always—'

Mid-sentence she broke off. As she'd rambled she'd sat with her eyes closed; she might have been talking to herself. Then, suddenly, she sat straighter, her eyes open as she realized what she'd been saying. 'Forget what I said, Georgie. Forgive me.'

'Go and get dressed, birthday girl. We'll make him eat his words, shall we?'

Left alone, Georgie opened her handbag and took out the letter addressed to the Chairman of the Board of Governors at St Winifred's School. She had taught there ever since she had gained her first-class history degree and, despite being younger than the rest of the staff, had been promoted to housemistress of West Wing at the beginning of Michaelmas term the previous year. Officially history was her subject, but her love was art, which she also taught, although at St Winifred's it was regarded as a subject of little relevance. Sometimes in the staff room she would look around at the other teachers – all good, well-meaning women but none giving any sign of feeling imprisoned by her narrow existence – and she would be gripped by fear. In the beginning had they had dreams not so different from her own? Was what they had become simply the outcome of years in the narrow confines of their all-female environment? So she had saved her money with the object of having enough behind her to live on until she could scrape a living with her art.

Was that the only reason she had decided last night that the time had come to write her letter? Or had James Bartlett had something to do with the timing? There was very little she couldn't talk about to James and yet instinct had prompted her not to tell him that she was resigning. Could that be because she was afraid he would jump to the wrong conclusion and see it as a sign she intended to accept his proposal? And what was stopping her? She was so fond of him and they enjoyed each other's company. Yet at the back of her mind was the fear of making a long-term commitment. A few hours ago she had had no doubt that at the end of the summer term, which was to begin in a few days, freedom would be hers. She would drive from St Winifred's for the last time into an unknown future. Now, gazing at the envelope, she felt trapped. Of course, the overdraft might be small; perhaps she would still have enough behind her to do what she wanted. She tried to cling on to hope.

A short while later she stood back and surveyed Muriel's trans-formation: with her face delicately made-up there was no sign of the earlier tears nor yet any hint of her dread of hearing Cyril's key in the door.

Lunch time passed without him. Slowly the afternoon dragged by. More than once Georgie was on the verge of announcing that she was resigning from St Winifred's; but how could she when she had no idea how much of her savings it would take to get her father out of debt?

'Wherever can he have got to?' Time and again Muriel said it, as the minutes slowly ticked by.

When just before five o'clock there was a loud knock on the front door, Georgie hurried to answer it. What she wasn't prepared for was the sight of the village policeman.

'I'm glad you're here, Miss Franklyn. Try and break it to her gently. There's been an accident – a nasty accident, according to what's been phoned through to the police house. Out there on Highleigh Ridge it was. No other car involved, just your father's. Fireman had to cut him free. He's in the County Hospital, badly hurt, they said in the message. No more than that.'

'Badly? How badly?' Muriel spoke from the back of the hall.

'No part of my job I like less than this, Mrs Franklyn. I wish I could tell you different, but the message was for you to get to the hospital as soon as you can.' The village constable felt out of his depth. He'd had little contact with the Franklyns; there had been no need. But he'd got used to seeing them in the village, and had always been sure of a friendly 'good morning'. They didn't deserve an upset like this.

'His car went over the ridge. Best brace yourself, Miss Franklyn. I see you've got a car out front. At least that's one blessing. I'll leave you to get on. I'm real sorry, ah, that I am.'

All thoughts of bank overdrafts and school resignations were forgotten as, less than five minutes later, Georgie drove with at least as much speed as her father had earlier over the brow of the hill and on towards the County Hospital. Believing she was shaping her life as she wanted, Georgie had set out that morning for Sycamore Cottage prepared to stand her ground against the arguments she knew she would face. Such a few hours later, everything had changed.

When they arrived, Cyril was still in the operating theatre, but from the Sister's solicitous manner when she spoke to them, any hope they'd been clinging to evaporated. They were brought tea, which they drank like obedient children even though neither of them wanted it.

'It was *my* fault,' Muriel muttered at intervals. 'The things I said to him upset him.'

'What really upset him was anger and shame for what he had let happen. You mustn't blame yourself, Muriel. We'll sort things out with the bank so that when he comes home he can start with a clean slate. You'll both have far more to think about than the things you said to each other today.'

And so they sat waiting, looking at their watches every few minutes as one hour, then two, went by. The hospital bustle of the day quietened until only the two of them were left. Then the kindly Sister called them into her room. Uninvited, the thought came to Georgie that there was just as much privacy in the empty waiting room as in the space little larger than a cubicle where they were taken.

'Your husband is in the recovery room, Mrs Franklyn, but it's too soon to let you see him. His injuries were extensive. I'm so sorry. Mr Osborne has done everything possible, but the outlook isn't good.' She believed it was always better to give bad news while the recipient was in a state of shock. 'He will need one-to-one nursing if he regains consciousness, but it may be a long wait for you. It might be wiser if you went home and rang us in the morning.'

Muriel shook her head. 'I'll wait. I don't mind how long.' And only after they had gone back to the hard bench in the waiting room did she say, perhaps to herself and perhaps to Georgie, 'I *must* speak to him. I have to make things right.'

It was past midnight when they were taken into a side ward where he was lying. The Night Sister was upright and starchy, with none of the gentle kindness of the woman who had talked to them earlier. But none of that mattered, for Muriel had only one thing on her mind: she must erase that dreadful scene, she must tell him she hadn't meant the things she had said. He was slipping out of life, of that she was certain, and the thought of their parting as they had that morning haunted her. Georgie's reaction was quite different: she wouldn't, *couldn't*, look to a future without him.

But events took their own course and he slipped out of life without regaining consciousness. While Muriel sat alone waiting, it was Georgie who collected the certificate signed by the doctor. Then, without returning to where Muriel waited, she went outside the hospital to the telephone kiosk and put a call through to James. That it was after midnight didn't occur to her; more than anything she needed to hear his voice.

'James, I'm calling you from the County Hospital—'

'Hospital? Are you all right?' Not a hint that it was an unconventional hour.

She found comfort in the fear she heard in his voice. And so she told him what had happened since she left him that morning. If she'd tried, she couldn't have held back the torrent of words. The accident, her father's death, Muriel's financial plight, her own feeling of misery and her shame that it should be tinged with self-pity for the blight cast on her own future. Even as the spoke she knew that later she would regret her honest outpouring.

'Are other family members there for you to call on?'

'No, there's only me. I must help her. She'll have nothing. My only hope is that Miss Shackleford will say she can move in with me at St Winifred's. If she could do that, just for a while, I could find somewhere to rent for her in Winchford. She must be frightened. She knows she can't afford to go on renting where we've always lived.' She heard the croak in her voice and was ashamed because she knew that apart from a grief that was too new for her accept, some of her misery came from the knowledge that she must tear up that letter of resignation.

'I don't want your stepmother to think I'm intruding.' James' voice broke through her shameful self-pity. 'But Georgie, you are never alone; you always have me. I'll arrange things in the offices here and come to you. How would that be? Is there an hotel in the village? I'll be there by Monday evening.' Then, after a pause that she might almost have imagined, 'Unless you don't want me; unless you think I'm interfering. Let me come, Georgie.'

'James, you don't know just how much I want you. I *must* talk to someone, someone who can see the whole picture. I can't believe Dad is gone. But there's so much else. The house is rented, but she won't be able to keep it on. She'll have nothing.'

James listened and knew she was beyond realizing she was repeating what she had already told him, grateful that she had turned to him for help and, despite himself, unable to get rid of the feeling that today's events might just be what was needed to tip the scales in his favour.

'Nothing is ever so bad that there is no way of dealing with it. You are a strong character, and to me you are dearer than I can tell you. We will sort things out. Do what is essential by way of arrangements but, until I get there, leave anything that can wait.'

'I can't see ahead, can't seem to think . . .'

'You can't see the wood for the trees; it's not to be wondered. Just get through each hour, Georgie, and without your realizing it the future will find a shape.'

Hearing him say it, Georgie felt comforted. Starting to walk back towards the hospital building she thought how fond she was of him – so what held her back from agreeing to marry him? She knew the answer even though she shied away from admitting it. He told her that their friendship was a firm basis for marriage, but friendship could never replace the miracle she had found with Malcolm all those years ago. But she couldn't base her life on *that*, could she? They'd been so young, and living in that beautiful city of dreaming spires they had both been on the brink of life. With heart and soul she had fallen in love, a love that could only have one outcome. Malcolm Durrant . . . Just to silently say his name brought back the wonder of what they'd shared in their student days. Both young, both inexperienced, but that had added to the wonder as they had lain together in the river meadow. The college clock had struck midnight; this was the day when finally they had to part. Looking back she had sometimes wondered that neither of them had suggested anything different. For three years they had studied, the degrees they attained were the key to their futures, or so she had imagined. But that night, lying under the starry sky, already they had been moving ahead. He had told her his plans: he had been given a chance to work in Rhodesia. It had disappointed his parents, but he wanted to see something of the world. He felt he couldn't spend his life

slowly climbing the ladder of success and knowing nothing else.
To her he was a hero above all others, and lying close to him,
feeling his hands on her bare skin under her blouse, guiding it
down to her groin, then opening her legs so that with his fingers
he caressed and probed, their excitement had mounted. They both
knew what would happen, what must happen. Above all else, it
was what they wanted. This hour would stay with them as long
as they lived. Half dressed and knowing nothing except what
instinct told them, this was nothing like they had expected from
their own exploratory experiences or even from the tender caresses
of his hand. As he entered her, he was wrapped in the warmth
of her body, so different from the adolescent dreams that woke
him. Arching her back, Georgie had pulled him closer, closer,
rejoicing in the pain of that first experience and feeling as if his
flesh was filling her body. She had known nothing like it before,
nor yet since. Could she find what she craved with James – dear,
kind, understanding James? He had lost his wife; he must have
found the way was to take each hour of each day at a time. But
it had been different for him; he had been climbing the ladder
of his profession, mixing with 'ordinary' people. Not like her,
surrounded by girls, her staff-room companions women all older
than herself, women who perhaps at one time had had dreams of
their own; but if they had, no one would think so to see them
now. Set in the comfortable rut of school life, enjoying long vaca-
tions of hill walking, museum visiting, sometimes alone, sometimes
together. Were they crushed by life? Well, she wouldn't let life crush
her, she *wouldn't*. Aware of where her thoughts were turning, she
was disgusted with herself. Only an hour or so ago her father had
died; Muriel was waiting for her in the hospital – and here she
was, letting herself be swamped by self-pity because of a hiccup
in her plans. Soon James would come, and some semblance of
order would appear.

Crossing the forecourt to the steps of the hospital she was ashamed.
James had said she was a strong character, yet she was looking to
him, a man, to deal with things as if the situation was beyond her
ability. She raised her chin, took a deep breath and marched up the
steps to the main entrance, putting her feet down firmly as befitted
a housemistress from St Winifred's.

★   ★   ★

It was Monday before Georgie could register the death and see the solicitor who held her father's Will. All he had was bequeathed to Muriel. But his estate amounted to no more than an overdraft at the bank, an ancient motor car, furniture that had made up their home for as long as Georgie could remember, a pocket watch that had been his father's, a few betting slips found in his jacket pocket, and his clothes, which would have to be sorted and divided between the Salvation Army and the dustbin.

'What an end to his life,' Muriel spoke aloud even though she was alone in the room taking his underwear from the drawer. 'I can see him now, that day I opened the door when the bell rang – and there he was. Those first months, getting to know him.' She shut her eyes tight, whether to imprint the image more firmly on her mind, to erase the bitter hurt of that final scene or to add passion to the plea as she said, 'If he's gone to the better land, please, *please*, give him peace and joy. Joy, deep down in his heart, that was what he wanted, that was why he chased his dreams with that silly gambling. Make him forgive me for the wicked things I said to him.' Then, silently, 'Hark, there's Georgie back. Goodness knows how I would have coped if I'd not had her here with me – her and her motor car. But what about the future? She'll be gone. I'll get a widow's pension – widow's mite more like it – but that won't cover the rent and rates, let alone put food on the table or pay the gas bill. I must look for a room in town, a bed-sitting room. Then I'll get a job. Although Lord knows what doing; all I've ever done is look after a home. A pity I hadn't been in the car with him.' And yet she knew the thought only came from a moment of weakness. She was forty-five; she had years of living ahead.

'I'm back, Muriel.'

'I'm just coming down, dear. The kettle's hot; I'll soon get us a cup of tea while you tell me how you got on.' There was nothing in her tone to hint at where her thoughts had been.

Georgie told her about James as she put some bags of shopping on the kitchen table.

'This Mr Bartlett who's coming,' Muriel said. 'You've never talked about him, Georgie. Is he your young man?'

Georgina's laugh was spontaneous. 'James is not my man, and

neither is he particularly young. But he is a very dear friend. He's the Town Clerk of Winchford.'

'Oh, I say, dear, that sounds very important.'

'You'll like him, Muriel. He's a solicitor. Well, Town Clerks mostly are I believe. I don't know why I expect him to be able to help us think straight about what we should do, but that's the feeling he gives you.'

'Did you ask him to come?'

'Now, can you imagine me doing that? No, of course I didn't. As soon as I told him about Dad he offered. Not just out of sympathy and kindness, but because he really wants to help. By next week I shall have to be back at school. This week we have a lot to get organized. But never mind about James. Muriel, I talked to the solicitor . . .' And so she reported the outcome of her appointment, nothing making the future any less bleak.

Driving north from Winchford, James' mind flitted between the council papers he had brought in his briefcase and what he imagined the scene would be when he reached Sycamore Cottage. He knew without having to be told that Georgie was frightened and uncertain of the future, and he liked to think that perhaps she wasn't as strong as the image she made herself present. Wasn't it feminine and natural that she needed a man to lean on? A smile played at the corners of his mouth as his thoughts went down that road. Then there was the stepmother. He knew nothing about her except that Georgie had been nine when her father had remarried, and considering that when he died he had been retired from the Town Hall a year or two, James imagined Muriel too must be in her sixties. Georgie had once said that she believed her father had remarried because he wanted a woman to run the house, and that slotted very neatly into the image he had of her: someone elderly and homely, someone Georgie would find it impossible to leave to fend for herself.

Turning up Maitland Hill, James smiled to himself. It seemed that Fate was playing into his hands.

It was only just six o'clock when the car turned in at the gateway, much earlier than Georgina had expected. She went out to greet him while, standing well back in the front room so that she wouldn't be seen peeping, Muriel watched them.

Not young, Georgie had described him. But neither was he old. Was he too old for Georgie? It would be nice to know she had a secure future with a husband, especially a husband in a good position. And he was really a very good-looking man: straight backed, dark hair, a fine figure of a man. 'But that doesn't mean a lot,' she told herself. 'Looks aren't everything.' She watched as the two outside greeted each other, then casually linked hands and turned towards the house. Was he really no more than a friend? If so, would he drop everything to come here to be with Georgie? Moving even further away from the window, Muriel half watched and half imagined the stepdaughter she loved as if she were her own. Perhaps not pretty in the accepted sense, indeed with her curly hair cut so short and her slim, straight build, she looked like a young lad. But her face was full of character, her greeny-grey eyes ready to sparkle with laughter, her teeth so even and white they looked almost too perfect to be real. Yes, Georgie was an attractive young woman if a person wasn't looking for the red lips and twin-peaked breasts promoted by Hollywood glamour. Her mouth was on the generous side but, when she smiled, the dimple in her left cheek came as a surprise. In Muriel's opinion it was a crying shame to think of her trapped in an all-female world like she was. What chance would she have of finding a husband stuck in an all girls' boarding school? Cyril had always been so keen on her teaching, but when they had driven the forty miles or so to St Winifred's for the annual fête the first summer Georgie had been there she had had her mind taken back to those lonely, empty years of her own single days, days when the future held no prospects except that each year she would be that much older and that much more firmly settled on the shelf. Surely Georgie must look at some of those ageing women and have the same dread. But Cyril clearly hadn't shared her feelings: he had seen the established staff as successfully secure and with good incomes. Surely there should be more to life than money. That had been Muriel's thought as they wandered around the extensive grounds of the school believing she and Cyril had enough to live on, with no frills but no worries either. Time had brought change beyond belief.

'James,' Georgie said as the three of them met in the narrow hallway, 'this is Muriel. James Bartlett, Muriel. He has checked in at the Crown and Anchor. And, guess what? He's booked a table for three for dinner. How's that for an unexpected treat?' And for Muriel, a treat it most certainly was. Little did she guess that it was *she* who created the biggest surprise of all as they were introduced. In that first moment James' preconception of the elderly, widowed stepmother melted. Had he met her a week before she might have slotted into place, but part of Georgie's birthday present for her had been a make-up bag containing the sort of things she could never have afforded to buy for herself – vanishing cream, powder, rouge, lipstick, and even mascara and an expensive moisturizing cream to use at night. Never in her life had she had such luxury. The other part had been an appointment with the hairdresser to have her hair shaped and the ends turned under something after the style of the pageboy bob. So far, except for that birthday midday when Georgie had titivated her while they waited expecting Cyril to return, she hadn't had the courage to wear the mascara, but she had perfected the art of applying just the right amount of rouge to disguise her sallow complexion.

'A treat indeed,' she answered in her soft contralto voice.

'The pleasure will be entirely mine,' James said to them both, accompanying his words with a formal bow of his head. Such olde worlde manners instantly endeared him to Muriel although Georgie hardly noticed; she had grown used to what she thought of as James' courtly mannerisms.

'It's kind of you to give up your time to come here; we both appreciate it,' Muriel replied in the same vein.

'I have no wish to intrude. I realize I am a complete outsider, albeit one who feels profound sympathy for the loss of your husband, Mrs Franklyn,' he said more than two hours later, as the waiter moved away with their used soup dishes.

'Intrude indeed! I can't tell you how much I appreciate it that you take the time in your busy life to help us see a way forward.'

'This evening all we'll say is that a way forward will be found. It is perhaps too soon for you to feel ready to face changes.'

'I have no choice. Cyril would be grieved to know the house will go. And yet . . .' Only silently did she finish the sentence, but Georgie guessed at its ending.

'Poor Dad,' she said. 'Oh, and poor you too – and being

practical I know as well as you do that none of this need have happened. But, Muriel, I bet my last pound that each time he put money he couldn't afford on some stupid bet, he was imagining the windfall that was about to come his way – his way and yours, too.'

Muriel nodded, her eyes reddening with tears she wouldn't shed – and mindful of the mascara Georgina had insisted on putting on for her. A fine thing if it ended smeared down her face!

'I know,' she said. 'And there's no emotion more wasteful than regret. I want just to remember all that was good. And so, like it or not, changes there must be.' She stopped what she was saying as the second course was brought and the vegetables were served, little realizing James' admiration for her lack of self-pity as he watched her. Then, the three of them alone again, she went on. 'I need to give two months' notice on the tenancy of the house and during that time I must find somewhere I shall be able to afford. As a widow I shall have a small state pension coming in once all the paperwork goes through. And I mean to look for work.'

'Tomorrow, by daylight, we will sit around the table and make our plans,' James said, with a warm smile that had little in common with his previous stiff formality.

Yes, Muriel decided, her thoughts shifting from her own problems, he would do more than nicely for Georgie. If only Cyril could have met him, she was sure he would have felt the same. All very well the way he had thought so much of those dowdy teachers, but that surely couldn't have been the sort of future he wanted for Georgie. Was James Bartlett the type of man Georgie would give herself to? Or, indeed, was that what he wanted? Then, as it had so many times during the last two days, her mind leapt back to what her own situation had been when Cyril had come along. Even though he'd been so much older than her, he had been attractive and she had believed she had found the meaning of falling in love. But supposing he'd been different, if she were honest she knew she would have grasped the chance of marriage at any price. But Georgie was different: she was a clever girl, she had a good degree and secure work; she must know the sort of independence a stay-at-home spinster could never have hoped for.

It was clear that despite making herself a rock to support her stepmother, Georgie's world had suffered a severe blow with the loss of her father. And as they ate their meal she seemed to need to bring him into the conversation, as if talking about him in a natural, affectionate way held him close.

'The truth was, he and my mother had wanted a son, then they got landed with me!' The affection in her voice told them she had never felt herself to be loved any the less for failing to be the wanted son. 'That's how I came to be Georgina – Georgie.'

'Oh, but Georgie dear, he loved you always,' Muriel put in, fearing that James might have been given the wrong impression.

'I know he did. I know they both did, although my memories of her are a bit hazy. But he made no secret that he was disappointed when I arrived. My mother was never really well after I was born – hopes of a son went out of the window. But I can see why he taught me cricket, made me understand the rules of soccer and rugger, taught me to row and to fish. We did all the things together that he would have done with a son. And remember, Muriel, how you used to come and watch us play tennis. It was a good thing I didn't turn out to be dainty and feminine, wanting to click away with my knitting needles.'

Muriel envied her; Georgie's love for him still held the security and innocence of childhood. Not for her the memory of the bitterness of the last parting. But wherever his spirit was, surely he must see beyond the cruel words. If he were really watching over them and knowing what was in their hearts (could he be?) he would know that she was having to make her mind move ahead, trying to make a new shape to her life. Suppose she couldn't get a job? There were plenty of men out of work, let alone women, and she had no experience in shops or offices. All she could do was look after a home, and being newly widowed wasn't the same on a job application as if she'd held down a good housekeeping job. She imagined herself spending the rest of her life struggling to make ends meet. She was middle-aged, plain, destined to spend the rest of her years alone. She was old – old in spirit, she told herself silently, just as she did so often, as if that way she could crush the need in her that sometimes pushed everything else from her mind. In their first years together Cyril used to make love to her, but even then he'd had no great sex drive, certainly none as demanding as her own. A few minutes of gentle penetration, quickening slightly as he managed to climax, and it would be over for the night. The night? The week? Sometimes for the month or even longer. And she would be left, every nerve in her alive with unfulfilled desire. For her there had been less satisfaction than she sometimes managed to reach by herself in her locked bedroom when he was out and she knew nothing could disturb her – or more recently in the stillness of the night since they had single beds. Yet nothing ever quietened the aching need in her for something always beyond her reach. In a young woman it might have led to a joyous union, but for her there was no hope.

Aware of where her thoughts had travelled she brought herself out of her reverie, feeling embarrassed as if her secret thoughts had been there for the other two to read.

'—kind of you,' she caught the end of James' sentence as he and Georgie talked. 'I shall have some telephoning to do in the morning, things that I wasn't able to finalize today before I left Winchford.'

'That's fine. I want to drive Muriel into town in the morning. So why don't you come over in the afternoon and we'll all sit around the table and thrash things out. Sometimes the view of a third person can be a help.'

James drove them home and when Georgie suggested his coming in he didn't hesitate.

'You may find a drop of whisky in the sideboard, but Cyril wasn't much of a drinker,' Muriel told them as they came into the narrow hallway. 'If not, I'm afraid it's just coffee. I'll leave you to it.' Her smile took in both of them. 'My bed is calling. Thank you more than I can say, James, for troubling about us as you have. It worries me that you have heavy responsibilities in Winchford that are being neglected.'

'Then you mustn't let it worry you,' he answered as Georgie went into the dining room to check the possibility of finding whisky. 'You probably guessed how dear Georgie is to me. Don't say it; I know I am too old for her. But affection takes no account of age.'

Muriel said nothing but her face broke into a warm smile as, resting her hand lightly on his arm for a second, she turned and left him. Through the open doorway of the sitting room he watched her climb the stairs, stepping as nimbly as she must have done all her life. Certainly this stepmother of Georgie's fitted none of his preconceived ideas.

'We're in luck,' Georgina said, returning with a tray carrying the half empty whisky bottle, two glasses and a jug of water. 'Sorry I can't say, "What will you have?" but alcohol was never important in this household.'

'And you know that had you been able to ask, this would have been my choice. And you? Can you take whisky?'

She nodded, putting the tray on the small table. 'You pour. I drink mine as it comes, no water.' She waited until he passed her a glass before she said, 'James, it looks as though Fate has taken my future in hand. I hadn't told you before because I thought you might have misunderstood why I was doing it, but I had a letter already written to give Miss Shackleford when I go back to school; I intended to leave at the end of term.'

'You mean . . .' As if to prove her point he turned to her in hope.

'There you are, you see! No, I'd saved hard all the time I'd been there so that one day I could have enough behind me to resign and be *free* while I decided on my next move. Free, James. Don't you ever long just for that? No commitments, no responsibilities?' How those memories crowded back into her mind! James may not understand, but she knew Malcolm would have.

James considered her question seriously before he answered.

'Perhaps at one time I might have agreed with you – mind you, I say *I might have* – but I had great happiness in my years with Kathy. I loved the responsibilities it brought me, I thrived on her pleasure in my professional progress. After I lost her I had all the freedom anyone could want and I found there is nothing more lonely.'

'And perhaps that's what I would have found. Anyway, it makes no difference now. I shall tear up my resignation and when I go back at the weekend I shall have to go and see Miss Shackleford and try to persuade her that, just as a temporary measure, Muriel can share my quarters while we find her somewhere to rent. Poor Dad, how he would have hated to see such a hole made in my savings to clear the overdraft.'

'Here,' he held his hand towards her and guided her to the settee, 'we can talk better sitting. Georgie – no, don't say anything.' He held a hand out as if to stop her words before she spoke them. 'This sounds like a practical, even businesslike suggestion, but you know that isn't the truth. I've told you often enough how I feel about you. You say Fate has taken a hand and, if it has, I believe it is to make us stop and take stock. Won't this change your answer to me?'

'James, I'm truly fonder of you than of any living person. But marriage . . .?'

'No, don't say anything. Just listen and trust me. Is there someone else, someone you have loved in the past and can't forget?'

She shook her head. The past was over, long ago. Her memories were her own and too precious to be shared with anyone.

Two

'It's an unnatural life, cloistered up with a bunch of women,' Georgie said as she picked up the bottle and poured another inch of whisky into the glass she had drained so quickly. 'I look at the few men I ever come in contact with, even you, dear James, and I can't imagine any of them could make me understand the miracle that surely must be what love is all about. I've always imagined you found it with your Kathy.'

'Yes, Kathy and I understood that miracle. The love I had – have – for her will stay with me as long as I live. But life goes on and one day I pray you and I will find the answer to that mystery together. But, Georgie, I give you my solemn promise that if you marry me I will never make demands on you that you're not prepared to give. Sometimes I've imagined you coming to me, wanting us to share our lives just as much as I do.'

'I do want us to be together. I love being with you; I can tell you my every thought. I'm not hiding from you that my body longs for love. But how can I be sure that's not because I'm scared of turning into the same sort of . . . of sad spinster as my colleagues at St Winifred's?'

His unexpected laugh was spontaneous. 'Not you, my darling Georgie. You say you've never met a man you've wanted to make love with.' ('Oh, but I didn't say that,' she replied silently.) 'And I'll tell you that I'm sure, positively sure, that those same men have looked at you and imagined you in their bed. I can feel the suppressed energy in you . . .' He held her chin and drew her face towards him. His mouth was only inches away from hers; despite herself it was she who made the final movement. With a smothered, hungry sound he covered her mouth with his. Under the bodice of her silk dress she wore nothing but a scarcely necessary satin bra. She could feel the excitement he tried to repress as his hand kneaded her small, firm breast, his thumb moving on her nipple, backwards and forwards, round and round. Her head was spinning . . .

Then, just as suddenly, he pulled away from her.

'How can you expect me to keep my word, when this is how I behave? This isn't how it will be.'

'Yes, James, it is; it must be. Never mind a silly promise. Yes, I'll marry you. And yes, we'll make it something wonderful. I don't want you to change how you feel for your Kathy, but we'll make a good life together.'

'Bless you. Yes, we will.' He held her tenderly. They both seemed lost for words.

Georgie was the first to get her feet firmly on the ground again.

'After I've given in my notice I shall have to work until the end of term. If they give permission for Muriel to share my accommodation until I leave, by that time we ought to have found her somewhere to rent. James, I want to be independent over this; I want to be able to pay her rent myself, just as I will Dad's overdraft.'

'I have an alternative suggestion, one I'd meant to make tomorrow when we talk together even if you still hadn't accepted me. Now, of course, it makes it all fall into place more neatly. I gave this a lot of thought after you phoned to tell me about your father's accident. So don't say anything, just hear me out. When Kathy was alive we lived in a three-bedroom house. After I lost her I felt I couldn't stay there; every room was full of ghosts and I was rattling around like a lost soul. The only thing that drove me, kept me sane, was professional advancement. I knew I had to move on. Then I applied for the Town Clerk post in Winchford. Before I took up the post I came down to look for accommodation, imagining I would buy something suitable for a bachelor. But when it came to the crunch I didn't want to part with the furniture we had chosen together. So that's why I bought Gregory House. And there I am, still rattling round in a place far too big, the only difference being that now I have even more garden than before.'

'That's no reason to marry, that and the fact that you want a woman in your—' Before she could say 'bed' he held up his hand to silence her.

'Just listen. You know how I've been hoping you'd change your mind and accept me, but when you told me something of the situation here my thoughts took another turn. The only thing that made me think the scheme might not work was that I imagined your stepmother to be more elderly, frailer, needing to be cared for. She may want to strike out and find somewhere for herself. But my thought was, perhaps if she were to come to Gregory House it might persuade you to change your mind – about us. Surely that would solve my problem of needing a woman's touch in the house, hers of needing a home – and I give you my word that as my wife, Georgie, you will have all the freedom you want. Perhaps you'll want to look for another post away from the female cloisters. Perhaps in a local school; it's up to you. Why are you laughing?'

'Why should I have been desperate to give up the job of housemistress at a fine place like St Winifred's and then take a post in some piffling little school in town? It's teaching I've done with, or I thought I had until all this happened. When I wrote that resignation letter I believed I knew just what I meant to do. I want to paint; I want to be able to call myself an artist. I ought to have stuck to my guns years ago but Dad was so keen that I followed what he called a "safe profession". What was the use of getting a good degree if I didn't use it to my advantage? That was his argument – and he could be very persuasive. Most of our battles gave him victory because deep down I couldn't bear to disappoint him. Even now I feel guilty. But I must do it, James, I *must*. Time races by and . . .' She pulled further back from him and met his gaze squarely. 'If you have a dream you should try and live it, even if it doesn't work out.'

'And that, my dear Georgie, is just what I intend to do; and for you and me I know it will work out.'

As a smile tugged at the corner of her mouth, the dimple in her left cheek got the message.

'And you understand that I'm serious about painting?'

He nodded. 'You forget I've seen one or two of your works, so I have no doubt of your talent. Work hard at it, Georgie, and when you have enough we'll organize an exhibition. Now, what do you think about my suggestion for Muriel?'

'If you knew Muriel that bit better you wouldn't even ask. She will relish the chance to have the responsibility. It had worried me that she would have hated to feel that I was paying her rent because she couldn't do it herself. And James, once we are married, we shall all be part of one family.'

Cyril's funeral was on the Friday morning and that same evening, driving separately, James and Georgina set out for Winchford. Although they left at the same time, Georgina had a head start as James had to call at the Crown and Anchor to collect his luggage and pay his bill.

She had gone about five miles when she picked up a nail in her tyre. It wasn't the first time she had changed a wheel but on that evening everything seemed to conspire against her. She wanted to have the job done and be on her way before James caught up with her, but as it turned out she was only just wriggling the spare wheel into position when he pulled in and parked behind her.

'Just look at the state you're in: hands, face and even your dress covered with oil. You should have waited, you knew I couldn't be long,' he told her, squatting down to fix the nuts. Then, looking at her in the fading light, he laughed. 'Time you had a man to look after you.'

'I'm not helpless.' She heard her answer as ungracious. 'Nothing special about changing a wheel; I've done it before. I don't usually get in this state.' Taking a rag from the open boot she cleaned her hands as best she could.

'You drive ahead,' he told her. 'I shall follow you back to the school to make sure it's all right. It's not as hard as it should be and there won't be a garage open at this time of evening. Clever girl.' He put the jack and spanner in the boot and moved to kiss her, but she drew back.

'I'm filthy.'

'Indeed you are. When we get to St Winifred's you can get straight in the bath.'

'I certainly shall. And while I get scrubbed up, you can make some coffee.'

'Will the ladies of St Winifred's approve?'

'The girls don't come back until Monday. The staff always need a couple of days to sort out the timetables and so forth. Anyway, we go straight into West Wing, so any who are back before me aren't likely even to know; and if they did, they would hardly

look on the Town Clerk as being less than a hundred per cent
honourable in his intentions.'

Dropping a light kiss on a clean patch by her ear, he chuckled.
'What a reputation to have to live up to! In you hop and lead
the way. At this rate it'll be dark before we get there.'

In fact they arrived back while there was still light enough for
Miss Hoskins, the Deputy Head, to see the two cars drive in just
as she crossed the quadrangle from Miss Shackleford's quarters
where they had been catching up on events of the Easter holiday
over a pleasant glass of sherry. She had been thinking how pleased
she was to be back, with summer term ahead and the prospect
of a very good entry for the School Certificate, when her attention was caught by the sound of an engine. Miss Franklyn was
back, and following her was another car. Pulling into the doorway
of East Wing she watched unseen. A man friend! Whatever was
the girl thinking? She knew the rules of the establishment perfectly
well, yet there she was at this time of night taking a man into
her rooms. Duty put Miss Amelia Hoskins on her guard. She very
seldom felt anything but the strongest approval for Miss
Shackleford's decisions, but they had come nearer to having words
about Miss Franklyn's promotion to housemistress than they had
before or since. Now the responsibility was hers. Hadn't the chit
of a girl told them in the Staff Room at the end of last term
that she and a friend were going to the Lake District? Well, Miss
Hoskins breathed down her nose, this would seem to be evidence
of what had been going on. Thank goodness the girls didn't return
until Monday; just imagine the sniggering and giggling that would
go on in the Upper School.

Once inside her rooms Georgie's greasy state seemed worse
than it had in the open air.

'You'll find the coffee in the right-hand cupboard and the
Cona on the bench; the matches for the meths lamp are in the
kitchen drawer. I'll leave you in charge while I get scrubbed up.
There are a few tins in the cupboard, see if there's anything we
can eat with no bread to help it.'

'Take your time. The coffee will keep warm and I'll read the
evening paper while I wait.'

Lying in the bath Georgie let her thoughts wander where they
would. She would leave school in July and by August or September

she would be married to James. For a moment, despite the warmth of the water, she shivered. What was it he'd asked her, about whether she had always refused him because there was someone else? Well, she'd not given a direct answer and yet after all this time surely she ought to have been able to say 'no'. It was four years since she'd seen Malcolm, both of them young and in love. She could understand why he wouldn't go from university straight into his parents' business; after all it wasn't so very different from what she too yearned for – freedom, no commitments. How clearly she recalled the day of their degree ceremony, both of them waiting to hear their names called, dressed in their gowns with ermine at the neck. She remembered her rush of sympathy and understanding when he'd told her he couldn't do as his parents had always expected; he had to be true to himself. There was a big world out there and he meant to see it, to *live*, and not to become just another cog in the professional wheel. And then their final hours together, hours that would stay with her as long as she lived. But she was marrying James, dear James. Malcolm was part of a dream, but James was reality . . .

The water was cooling but she couldn't keep her mind from slipping back to those last hours together. Every touch of his hand, every movement of his body pressed hard on hers . . . she wanted it never to fade. It was all so long ago and perhaps in memory it was now more wonderful than the reality; three glorious years of university life, and interwoven through it all was her first and only love.

Getting out of the bath, she pulled her thoughts to the present. Soon she would be James' wife and with him she would build a good and lasting union; they would have children, her life would be comfortable and orderly and their love would grow stronger as the years went on.

Her clothes were dirty, so she threw them all into the laundry basket and then, with the bath towel wrapped round her, she went through the living room to the bedroom. If James noticed he gave no indication and when, a minute later, she reappeared dressed in nothing but a satin dressing gown he gave her a welcoming smile and folded the paper away before getting up to pour the coffee. What a moment for someone to knock on her door.

'May I come in?' Amelia Hoskins called as she opened the door. 'I saw your light so I thought I'd slip in to say hello. Oh, I say, I've come at a bad moment. Oh dear, I am sorry.'

'James, this is Miss Hoskins, our Deputy Head. Amelia, let me introduce you to James Bartlett, my fiancé. You may remember he opened the fête for us last year.'

Amelia shook hands with James, muttered something about regretting she had disturbed them, and retreated.

Next morning she again knocked on Georgie's door, but this time she waited for it to be opened.

'I learnt my lesson last night; I didn't want to intrude again. Miss Shackleford has asked me to tell you she wants a word.'

'Right you are. Is she in her rooms?' For if it were to wish her well on her engagement it seemed to Georgie that it would be an informal chat. 'It must be telepathy,' she went on with a laugh. 'I want to see her too.'

'You'll find her in her study,' came the unsmiling reply.

Not for the first time Georgie thought how glad she would be to get away from the stifled atmosphere. It may be fine for the girls, they had their own lives, their own hopes, but how could any grown woman want no more than this?

'Miss Franklyn, come in and close the door,' Miss Shackleford said when Georgie knocked on her study door. 'I had no idea until this morning that you had returned.'

'I arrived last evening when it was almost dark. Too late to see anyone.'

'Humph.' It was no more than a grunt, but it told Georgie that all wasn't well. 'Too late for anyone to see you either, I imagine you believed. I am most disturbed by the word that has reached me – reached me and by this time I dare say every member of staff. I'm thankful the students hadn't returned or the place would be rife with gossip by this time. Really, your behaviour is beyond my comprehension. I had put my trust in you, Miss Franklyn, trust that you have betrayed.' Generally seen as austere (frightening, the girls might describe her), on that Saturday morning Miss Shackleford made no secret of her anger.

'Betrayed? I don't understand . . .'

'Then let me enlighten you. You are here as a teacher and on that score I have never been able to fault you. But that is only half your responsibility – indeed the responsibility of every member of staff. And until now, I thank God, none of my staff have ever put a foot wrong. We have a duty to the children entrusted to our care; we have to help them hold fast to a high moral code.'

'Of course we do.'

'And last night when Miss Hoskins chanced to call on you to welcome you back to the fold, what did she find? To bring a man into the premises at that time of night is something I *will not tolerate*. And please don't tell me that you considered the rules of St Winifred's only applied while the students are on the premises. And one rigid rule is that we do *not* bring men to our private rooms.'

'James Bartlett is my fiancé. I wonder Miss Hoskins didn't tell you.'

Ruth Shackleford's expression was one of disgust.

'It's a pity you couldn't keep your clothes on until after the wedding. Word has spread round the staff room that you were in nothing but your dressing gown – a dressing gown so thin, I understand, that it left little to the imagination . . . I am disgusted and ashamed, ashamed for the reputation of the school.'

Rather than feeling chastened, Georgie's anger was rising. She took the letter of resignation from her pocket and put it down in front of Ruth Shackleford.

'That is my letter of resignation. I shall leave at the end of term.'

'Indeed you will not! You will pack your bag and leave now, this very morning. And you can imagine the scene at lunchtime when before I say Grace I shall make a formal announcement to the staff for my reason for your sudden dismissal. St Winifred's has no place for anyone who behaves as you have. In this estab-lishment our aim is – and always will be – to ensure the girls entrusted to us grow into young ladies of high moral standards and gentle manners.' With that she tore up the letter and threw it into the waste-paper basket.

'Yes, I was in my dressing gown. I bathed because—'

The headmistress gave her a stony stare. 'Just leave.'

'Yes, I'll leave and be thankful to get away.' There was so much more she wanted to say. But in a few months time she would be

James' wife, James who was Town Clerk and held in respect locally. So she said no more; she simply left the room, slamming the door loudly behind her.

She had dreamt of the day she would be packing her worldly goods and driving away from the oppressively female world of St Winifred's, but in her imagination the timing of her departure had always been of her own choosing. As she took pictures off the wall and wrapped them in old newspapers she had collected from the unoccupied library and staff room, despite wanting nothing more than to get away, she was ashamed to see how her hands shook. It wasn't fear; it was anger. Instinct made her want to throw her things into cases and be gone; it took a good deal of willpower for her to pack carefully and make sure the few ornaments she possessed were protected between layers of clothes. As she worked she half listened for footsteps outside her door, perhaps a member of staff coming to say goodbye. But there was nothing but silence. The frightening thing was that she had no clear picture of what was ahead of her. Life with James, what would it be like? She always enjoyed being with him, for he was even tempered, unchanging. The days, months, years would all move along in the same way. Was he the man who would fulfil the hunger of her desires? If so, why had she never held him in her thoughts in those solitary moments in the silent darkness of her room as she'd found her own way to satisfy what she couldn't deny?

Today was the beginning of a new life. Her packing was done, so now the sooner she got away the better. She suspected word of her dismissal would have spread like wildfire, and if she needed confirmation that no details had been spared it came in the fact that no one came to bid her a friendly farewell. Well, see if she cared! She packed her worldly goods into her car and drove away without a backward glance, telling herself that she wasn't disappointed that not one person broke ranks to wish her well. Yes, she had wanted to resign and, yes, she longed for a future where she was free to be *herself* and not some paragon of moral goodness as a role model to those girls who, if truth were known, probably harboured the same longings to *live* as she did herself.

Following instinct she drove towards the coast, the nearest point of which was some twelve miles away at the small town of

Tarnmouth. There were many more beautiful resorts, places with stretches of golden sands and first-class hotels, but Georgie didn't look for a smart tourist centre with the elegance of Torquay or Bournemouth or the sophistication of Brighton. Tarnmouth was *real*. The Grand Pier catered for all tastes: anglers at the far end; a café with oilcloth covered tables and a hot water urn which belched out steam that covered the windows with condensation, the combination giving the café its own distinctive atmosphere; a theatre where racy comedians and inferior crooners packed the house during the summer season; housey-housey with soft toys or lurid tea sets to be won; then near the entry from the promenade a hall of penny-in-the-slot machines. Unlike so many seafronts there were no manicured flower beds, but on the opposite side of the road were various boarding houses, the larger ones calling themselves private hotels, and a row of ordinary shops such as would be found in any busy village and having no connection with the holiday trade. She parked her car in front of the pier then, carrying the two newspaper-wrapped pictures, waited for the oncoming trolleybus to pass before she crossed the road.

'I recognized your motor.' The man who called the greeting had come to meet her in the doorway of what originally had been a double-fronted cottage owned by a local fisherman but where the front rooms were now used as a gallery with local paintings for sale. The one on the left was home to a desk and this was where the business transactions took place; the one on the right was empty with the exception of the pictures on the walls and an easel by the window displaying a painting that Mr Adams, who ran the gallery, considered sufficiently eye-catching to tempt browsers inside. 'I'd been hoping you'd call in, Miss Franklyn. Got a bit of business to do with you; just you see the list I've made of the paintings of yours I've sold. And what's this you're bringing? Two more by the look of it.'

'Have you got room for them, Mr Adams? They're bigger than the others. I thought that now with summer starting might be the best time to bring them.'

'Come along in and let's have a look and see what you've got. I say, my dear, these ought to fetch you a bob or two. You know what I always say about your work when people come in here looking around at the pictures on show? What I say is no more than the truth; there aren't many people who can bring the sea to life like you do, bothered if there are. Some galleries, ah, galleries folk make a point of journeying to, where the works are by top-line artists, but their seas don't have that sparkle, like living water. Just you look there, the way you've got those waves breaking.'

'So you'll take them? If they take up too much space and don't sell, I'll collect them if you like and we'll try again next year.'

'Right now, Miss Franklyn, I'm not thinking about next year. No, bothered if I am. Who's to say whether I shall be here?'

She glanced at him quickly, uncertain what he was implying. She had never thought of him as an exceptionally old man; in fact she'd accepted him as he was without considering his age. Certainly youth was but a memory, but mostly what set him apart from the average men of the time was his old-fashioned appearance. His style of dress hadn't changed since he'd bought his first grown-up suit, and who but he in that year of 1937 was seen wearing a black frock coat, pin-stripe trousers, a stiff stand-up collar and wide black tie, the whole attire topped by a bowler hat? None of his outfit was in the first bloom of its youth any more than he was himself and the cloth that had originally been black had acquired a sheen that in some lights was almost green. But despite the age of his clothes, his trousers were always held in creases he ensured by laying them carefully under his mattress each night and he was fastidiously clean, his hands and nails a credit even to a man of leisure – which he most certainly was not. On one occasion Georgie had seen him on a Sunday evening coming out of church still in exactly the same style of dress, but his immaculate Sunday suit was as black as the day it had left the tailor's shop, as was his bowler hat.

Now, seeing her expression, he chuckled.

'Oh, I'm not expecting Saint Peter to be opening those pearly gates for me just yetawhile. No, I took a ten-year lease on this place back at the beginning of 1928 and I'd always expected to be able to renew it when it came to the end. But the landlord sold it on a year or so back. I've never met the new owner; it was all done through a solicitor and you know what it's like the way gossip spreads. Calls himself a boatman it seems, so I've heard, keeps his craft locally in the harbour. Never once has he been to see the place as far as I know – unless he came in pretending to be a customer.'

'But a change of owner doesn't mean he won't renew the lease, Mr Adams. If he isn't interested enough to come and visit, I'd imagine he bought it as an investment.'

'Ah, you may be right. But my Annie wants me to pack it in; time to stay home and keep her company, that's what she thinks. I haven't always done this, you know. I used to get around on my bicycle tuning pianos until I got caught up in an accident. After that, riding a cycle was out of the question but what I missed was having the people to have a talk with. I'd always had an interest in painting, but it was the folk to talk to I had in mind when I took this place. And that's the way it was in those days.'

And knowing how he loved to chatter, Georgie nodded.

'And are you ready to stay at home now? Won't you miss the trade here and the people?'

'Just between ourselves, Miss Franklyn, there's not the interest there used to be in pictures, too often I look at my day book before I lock up to go home and I've not so much as broken the ice. The only pictures folk are keen on these days are those in the Pavilion down the road there – the flicks, don't they call them? When I go home of an evening they're already starting to queue up. But many's the day I stand in this doorway and not a soul so much as stops to look at what I put on the easels in the two windows. Some good works in there, I can tell you. Over the weeks since you came by last all yours have found homes, but precious little else. Vases of flowers, pretty gardens, things of that sort, no one wants to know.'

'It's too early yet for many holidaymakers. You just wait a few weeks and the place will be buzzing.'

'Well, m'dear, I hope you're right. But for me, I reckon I shall hang my hat up when the lease comes to an end. There's some talk that the new owner is only waiting for me to go so that he can move in. It seems he's got a place down on Quay Hill – pokey little houses they are. It's not bad sized accommodation upstairs here, you know, and all going to waste. Well, we shall have to see. Perhaps you'll look in every now and then and see if these beauties have been sold – and I'll wager they won't be with me for long. If I decide to throw in the towel and I haven't seen you, I'll drop you a line at that school where you teach, shall I?'

'Actually I'm not there any more.' *Two hours ago I was, but no more, no more.* 'I'm getting married in a few weeks.'

He held out his right hand, an invitation for her to do the same, and then with his left he lifted his greening bowler respect-fully. 'Well now, that is good news. So you've done with being a schoolmarm?'

'I'll never go into a classroom again. I do hope you don't close the gallery, for after I'm married I shall have so much more time for painting.'

'Get yonder Mr Boatman taking the place over and I don't know where you'll find to put your work up for sale in Tarnmouth. But we'll worry about that when it happens. Perhaps it's no more than a rumour and when the time comes there'll be someone else wanting to take it over. Folk may not realize it, all chasing after all that Hollywood nonsense and wanting to outdo each other with their modern gadgets, but they need a place like this where they can just stop and *look*. If someone does take it on it'll never bring them a living, but it's a . . . it's a . . . what's the word I'm looking for?'

'A mission?'

'Ah, yes, that's about it. Five minutes in here opens their eyes to things that are worth appreciating, instead of always being in a rush chasing their own tails, wanting to be entertained. They crowd on to that pier right enough, but take five minutes to admire the work I have in here, not a hope with most of them. Now then, m'dear, let me get my cash book out and see what I owe you for the things I've shifted.'

A few minutes later she pocketed her money and wished him goodbye. 'I'm not the only one who would miss you, Mr Adams. The esplanade wouldn't be the same without you.'

He beamed with delight, then again removed his hat, this time with a courtly bow of his head, as he watched her cross the road to the car.

As she and James had arranged, they met in Winchford's Market Square then together went to Sydenham and Steward. Of all the jewellers in Winchford, Sydenham and Steward stood apart. When James had said she must have an engagement ring she had half expected he would produce the one he had bought years before for Kathy. Jewellery had never been high on her list of necessities, but she was glad when he led the way to the shop. Wearing another woman's ring would have indicated she would be stepping into her shoes, something that Georgie could never do.

This should have been the most exciting afternoon of her life; that's what she wanted to believe. Yet at the back of her mind (and often at the front of it, too) was the image of the one-time cottage on the esplanade with her old friend Mr Adams standing in the open doorway waiting to doff his hat to anyone he thought he might stand a chance of coaxing in.

'What time do you have to be back at school? Can we go back to my place first? My place . . . your place. Soon that's what it will be. Last night I lay awake thinking about how the three of us are going to slot in together. And, Georgie, if I had any doubts, they soon vanished. It will be up to you how much responsibility you want to give Muriel for running the house and how much you prefer to keep, but from the small amount I know of her I imagine it will be important for her to feel sure that she is there because we need her and not because we want to give her a home.'

'James, about the school. I gave Miss Shackleford my letter this morning and . . . and looking me straight in the eye, she tore it up. It seems I am not a fit person to be in charge of young and impressionable girls. I was given my marching orders there and then. My worldly possessions are in the car.'

'I don't understand. But that's ridiculous! What's the matter with the woman?'

Georgina started to laugh, suddenly feeling joyously free. 'It was the dressing gown that did it. It turned me into a scarlet woman. Enough of a sin to take a man into my rooms, but to take off my clothes and wear just a thin dressing gown put me completely beyond the pale.'

'But that's dreadful – and completely unjust. Didn't you explain? I shall go and see her myself.'

'You'll do no such thing. I like to fight my own battles. And you can't imagine how thankful I am to be free of the place. It stifled me.'

'But to think *that* of you . . .'

'Honestly, I don't care. I'm just thankful to be away from it all. There's nothing else to do in town, is there? You drive ahead and I'll follow back to your place.'

From the attic to the cellar he showed her round the house. Although she had been there before, she had never seen beyond the sitting room and the kitchen.

'As you said, it's hardly a bachelor establishment. And James, how clean and tidy it is.'

'I can't live in chaos. Mrs Delbridge cleans very thoroughly once a week, changes the bedding and takes all the laundry home. And except for making toast for breakfast, I seldom eat at home.'

'Will your Mrs Delbridge be out of a job once Muriel takes over or does she work for lots of people?'

'I've no idea. I've never discussed it with her. In any case I shall keep her on.'

Georgie frowned. 'Muriel will think you don't need a house-keeper – or a wife either. You really are Mr Self Sufficiency.'

'Oh no, I fear I'm not. No matter how well organized, this is a *house* not a *home*. I need a companion; I need you.'

'Do you? Do you truly?'

Standing at the head of the cellar steps she turned to face him, her hands first on his shoulders, then on the back of his head, pulling him towards her. She had had plenty of experience of desire; it was pure instinct that made her part her lips as his mouth came close to hers, just as it was to move the tip of her tongue around first her lips and then his.

'A few weeks and we shall be married,' she whispered, still so close that he could feel the warmth of her breath. 'I hate the thought of the smutty giggling there will be about us when the girls at school know. And they will know; it's sure to be in the local paper that the Town Clerk is to marry.'

It was less than a week since she had agreed to marry him. Yet now, it wasn't the romance of a honeymoon she yearned for, but a first night together set against an atmosphere of romance.

'I wish it could all be over,' she whispered urgently, 'the cere-mony, the reception, the innuendos. All my ex-colleagues, unmarried, all wondering, imagining. None of it would matter, it couldn't touch us, if we'd . . . if we'd already known each other, in the Biblical sense I mean. I don't know how else to say it without it sounding clinical and unemotional. I don't want a church wedding with a white dress and all the show of a virgin bride.'

At that he laughed. 'Funny girl you are. But I don't want that sort of wedding either. Kathy wore white – as indeed so she should.'

'When at St Winifred's they read the date of our wedding in the local paper, the girls will giggle and the staff will think their own thoughts. Perhaps they're happy with their lives; perhaps they haven't longed as I have for . . .' She left the sentence unfinished.

He drew her closer, his mouth against her hair as he whis-pered, 'We'll make a good life together. Holding you like this, I want to know you.' And she knew from his voice that he was smiling as he spoke. 'In the Biblical sense. I want to help you find the miracle you seek. But that's only part of the union we shall share. We've always been such good friends; the rest will simply be the missing link in the chain that binds us.'

In that moment she had complete confidence in their future; she looked back on the occasions when she had avoided giving him the answer he wanted and realized how blind she had been. She liked what he said about a chain binding them. A couple . . . coupling . . . if only instead of being dressed and standing at the head of the cellar stairs they could be in a dimly lit bedroom, glorying in their nakedness.

'Go and powder your nose or whatever you do, then we'll drive out into the country and find somewhere quiet for dinner.'

Just for a moment she hesitated, unsure how far the invitation went.

'Muriel has no telephone and if I have to drive back there before she puts the bolt on the door, I'll have to be on the road in a couple of hours.'

He held her away from him, looking at her closely. 'Is that what you want?'

She shook her head. 'You know it isn't. You know what I want.

This day is the first of the rest of our lives.' She laughed, a laugh that expressed her sudden rush of joy. 'What a day this has been!'

'And it's not over yet. What cases do you want brought in? All of them?

He drove them into the country where they found a restaurant that was everything she hoped: lit by candles, the waiter service efficient and discreet, the flowers in the vase on their table real, the food and wine excellent. Driving home as dusk gave way to darkness the air was filled with a cocktail of country smells. She felt removed from her everyday life – or could it have been that she wasn't accustomed to wine? Soon would follow the rich pageantry of nature. She mustn't let her thoughts go to that other evening – the hard ground, the aching longing, and the moment of fulfilment that had shone through her years like a beacon. But tonight must draw a line under it; her future was with James and anything she had touched on in that one adolescent experience would soon recede with so many distant memories of those university years. Tonight she and James would consummate their union not on damp grass but in a comfortable bed; not half dressed and horribly aware that they were on public ground and within sound of the college clock, but alone to explore their nakedness, to give themselves to each other and to the miracle she longed for. She imagined how they would undress together, undress each other, each action bringing them closer to the intimacy that lay ahead. But she was mistaken.

'You can use the bedroom; I'll undress in the bathroom. I want a quick shave.' And as if to prove the need, he raised her hand to his chin. 'I'll be quick.'

So, alone in the bedroom she took off her clothes. She could hardly wait for him naked, but the idea of wearing a nightdress didn't fit what she had in mind. So she dallied, thinking that he might join her before she took off her bra and pants – and any thought of night attire would be gone. It was such a glorious early summer night. She leant out of the window, breathing deeply of the soft air. And, just as she had hoped, he was back before she took off those final two items. In dark blue silk pyjamas he looked handsome enough to turn any girl's head and Georgie was desperate for hers to be turned. She unhooked her bra and stepped out of her French knickers, letting both fall to the floor. Following instinct she undid the buttons of his jacket and pushed it off his shoulders, then pulled the cord of his trousers, so his pyjamas ended up on the floor.

'Isn't that better?' she whispered, her heart pounding.

His answer was to hold her tightly against him then, picking her up, he carried her to the bed and immediately moved above her.

'Georgie,' he breathed, 'I'm almost bursting.' She reached to touch him, to clasp her hand around him. 'No, no, not like that. Oh God, I mustn't come, not yet. It's been so long. Don't touch me, Georgie. Just lie still a minute.' And in an attempt to hold on to his almost lost control he moved further from her and pushed his angry erection downwards. This wasn't the erotic and intimate preamble she had yearned for. After a moment's silence he raised himself over her once more. 'I'll try and be gentle,' he told her, his voice tender.

Gentleness was the last thing she wanted. She longed to feel his hands on her, exploring every inch of her, caressing her breast, moving on down so that he would know how her body cried out for him to penetrate deep into her.

'Don't be gentle,' she breathed, pulling his hand and pressing it to her small breast.

For one glorious second as she felt him enter her she knew that same exquisite fullness that she remembered, and then he started to move, his thrusting quickening beyond his control and in no time it was over. She felt nothing but the weight of him heavy on her.

She heard him murmur, 'ashamed', 'sorry', and even though every wild pulse in her body was screaming for what had been so close and then snatched from her, she made herself take his hand and say, 'Don't be, James. We have a lifetime ahead of us.' *Oh, but not like this, surely not like this.*

It rained on their final evening at Sycamore Cottage, and although by bedtime the clouds had rolled away the ground was still wet, and even though Georgie couldn't actually see the familiar puddle on the uneven garden path she knew just where it was. Leaning out of her bedroom window she closed her eyes, breathing deeply

of the familiar smell of the wet garden she had known all her
life. Always this had been her home, the place she'd returned to
– from boarding school, from university, from St Winifred's – and
always she had been sure of the way her father's face would light
up with pleasure when she arrived. Behind her closed lids she
felt the burning sting of tears. He had been her friend, her mentor
and her guiding light. Without question she understood and
forgave the way he'd frittered his 'nest egg'. Holding him close
in her mind she shared the hope he must have felt as he'd placed
each bet – hope and adventure too. Tomorrow she was to drive
away, taking Muriel to start their new life, but all that he had
been would be with her forever even though tonight was the
end of an era. That sounded affectedly dramatic, and she hated
affectation in any guise. Married to James she would have freedom
to do as she pleased with her days so, if she chose, she could
drive from Winchford and climb Maitland Hill and look at
Sycamore Cottage. But it would be no different from any other
house, bricks and mortar lived in by strangers. Life moves on;
much of the past got lost but there were some things which were
imprinted indelibly on her memory: she and her father in a canoe
as she learnt to paddle, the first time she beat him at tennis, the
laughter as they played croquet on the lawn (played it badly but
that didn't detract from the fun), the oak tree at the bottom of
the garden where, when she'd been about five, he had fixed her
swing from a strong branch; she could just see its outline against
the night sky. She mustn't let herself forget any of it or perhaps
he would be as distant and impersonal as the bricks and mortar.
Please, she begged silently, *make me be doing right. We have no choice
but to move from here – but what I mean is, make me be doing right
about James. He's a truly good man and I do love him. Imagine how
I would feel if he were in love with me – like he was with Kathy. Is
that what I want? I don't know, I just don't know. Perhaps if I filled
his heart and mind it would help me to . . . to what? To nurture the
love I have for him so that it became deep, wild, passionate, soul consuming?
Or am I letting myself behave like some silly adolescent – like the girl
I used to be?*

Across the corridor Muriel lay awake, her mind taking its own
journey. Was it wicked for a woman so recently widowed to feel
excited at the prospect of a new beginning? She had but one

real regret and that was the way she and Cyril had parted. Suppose
that hadn't happened, suppose he hadn't been blinded by anger
at her because she had discovered his secret life, and surely by
shame too, he might still have been here sleeping in that other
single bed. She was glad the landlord had been so accommo-
dating when she had gone to see him about giving up the house.
According to the terms of the agreement she was supposed to
give two months' notice, but taking into account the circumstances of her leaving and knowing she had to arrange the sale
of the contents of the house, he had suggested keeping the furniture and releasing her from the contract. She suspected he knew
of someone looking for just such accommodation but she was
grateful for the way everything was falling into place so easily.
So she was free to make a completely fresh start, unencumbered
by trappings of the past. Anything worth keeping from those
years would be held safely in her memory and, already, her
anger towards Cyril had been replaced by thoughts of happier
times . . . Was a future of overseeing the running of James' house
in return for her board and lodgings something to get excited
about? For most women probably not, but Muriel knew nothing
but thankfulness. Georgie had paid off Cyril's overdraft and taken
an up-to-date statement to the solicitor, so his secret addiction
– for that's what it must have been – had gone to the grave with
him. She ought to go down on her knees and send up a heartfelt prayer of thanks. Bed was comfortable, sleep was about to
overtake her, but her heartfelt thanks were sincere.

On that same night James was restless. He had no doubt that
he was doing the right thing. He wasn't a conceited man, but he
couldn't pretend that since he'd lost Kathy he had been unaware
that he'd been the object of more than one woman's hopes.
Georgie had been different. An independent young woman, she
had even gone so far as to tell him that she wasn't the marrying
kind. Yet right from the first he had recognized her need for
physical love. Just that one time he had made love to her and
even now, nearly four weeks later, he was frightened to let himself
remember how he had failed her. Yet, like it or not, memory
wouldn't be denied. That night had been so important; their only
time together before she drove back to Sycamore Cottage to help
Muriel. He took it for granted that for Georgie it must have

been her first experience and for him the first time with any woman but Kathy. Georgie had been desperately eager, arching her slender, agile body under him, holding him firmly between her strong legs. He thought of the moment when she had drawn his hand to hold her small, firm breast. That had been the moment when reality had stripped him of illusion. In the isolation of his bed, when night after night loneliness and desire had driven him, as his passion reached its climax clearly he imagined Kathy's breasts, so large and beautiful, the warm weight of them heavy in his hands. The memory never dimmed; he knew exactly the feeling of her hardened nipples between his thumb and finger. *Never will the memory fade, please God it never will.*

It surprised him that when Georgie had told Muriel of their premarital sleeping arrangements she had accepted with no qualms. For himself, he would have preferred that Georgie used the second spare room until after the wedding, but the way women's minds work was always something of a mystery to him and if that was the way she wanted it, then he didn't consider it important enough to argue. Dear Georgie. He harboured no illusion that she was in love with him or he with her. But for her father's death they would probably still have been in the same deadlock as over the previous months. Love as he'd known it was rooted in youth and could never happen twice in one lifetime, but he would do everything in his power to make her happy. Then his thoughts turned to Muriel, widowed only a month ago. It was said that everyone needed time to grieve before they were ready to build a new life. But how much time? More than poor Muriel had been given. And no matter how long, did time really dim the pain?

Just before the end of the school term there was a small paragraph in the *Winchford Times*. 'In June of last year when Mr James Bartlett, newly appointed Town Clerk, accepted an invitation to open St Winifred's annual fête in aid of the Whittington Home for Orphaned Girls, little did he suspect it was to be a day that would change his life. For that was when he met the school's history and art teacher, Miss Georgina Franklyn, who is to become his wife at a ceremony on Saturday next at the local Registry Office.' No mention was made of Georgie's dismissal – which probably meant the reporter hadn't heard the gossip the inmates of the school had enjoyed. With the wedding over even that small amount of interest vanished.

Returning from a round of golf one Saturday afternoon in October, James recognized Georgina's car parked by the hump bridge that crossed a narrow, fast-flowing stream about half a mile from where they lived. He pulled up just behind it by the stile that led to a path down to the water, then set off to join her. She must be walking, and who could blame her on such a perfect autumn day?

Instead he came across her just round the bend of the river sitting at her easel and so absorbed in what she was doing that she wasn't even aware someone was approaching.

'I'm glad to see you're out here painting. You didn't tell me you were working on a picture; I wondered if you might have decided to let it slide now that you're not teaching.' Then standing back the better to view what she had done, he said, 'I say, Georgie, that's really good; just look at the way that water ripples.'

'As if I'd give it up,' she answered, turning to smile up at him. 'Teaching those children, even the pretty hopeless job of teaching them to paint, was just a chore done for money. This is different. This is a labour of love. You like it?'

'Indeed I do. When it's finished, where shall we hang it? I remember those two fine pictures you had on your wall at the school; I was looking at them that evening while you were scrubbing up in the bath. When you didn't bring them with you, I assumed you'd lost interest and left them behind. It's good to see you're painting again.'

'Lost interest?' She laughed. 'If you can think I'd do that, you can't know me as well as I thought.'

He looked at her speculatively, but said nothing.

'If you wait while I put my things away, I'll follow you home. You can be the perfect gentleman and carry my easel.'

'Of course. But you didn't tell me what happened to the two paintings you had at the school. Under the circumstances I'm surprised if you left them.'

She chuckled. Any hurt she had felt about her instant dismissal had faded. 'Most surely I didn't.' Then, in what seemed to him like a complete change of subject, 'How well do you know Tarnmouth?'

'Not very well at all. I have been there just once, but it didn't have much to commend it so I didn't go again. Why do you ask?'

'I love it; it's an honest, down-to-earth sort of place. Anyway, if you don't know it well you may not have noticed a terrace cottage on the esplanade, used now as a sort of poor man's art gallery. Mr Adams, who runs it, is an old mate of mine. His pictures are all for sale and I took those two to him the day I left the school. They sold quickly. And that's where this one will go.'

James frowned. 'Georgie my dear, I remember you did once say you used to sell your pictures, but there's no need now that we're married. You must miss your salary; I should have thought. I suppose it didn't occur to me to give you spending money because it's something that hadn't arisen with Kathy. But of course in your case it's different because Muriel does the housekeeping. I'm sorry, Georgie. I'll put something into your account each month.'

'I don't want you to do that. And I've never sold my pictures because I was short of money; I sell them for the satisfaction of sharing them and knowing people other than *me* like what I do. I'll put these things in the car and you can fold the easel.'

As she started to move away from him he held her shoulder and turned her to face him. How serious he looked.

'Georgie, perhaps I'm old-fashioned, but in my book a husband should be responsible for providing. I may not be a wealthy man but there is no need, *absolutely no need*, for my wife to earn her own pocket money. I want you to promise me that this,' indicating the canvas on the easel, 'will hang in our own home.'

'I make no promises, James,' she answered with a bantering laugh. 'Suppose it turns out you are married to a budding Rembrandt, would you want to deprive the world?'

'I am serious. I know when you left the school your father's debts must have made a hole in your savings. But all that is over.'

'And so, James, am *I* serious. I have sold my pictures through Mr Adams' gallery for years. I used to drive all the way from home before I moved to St Winifred's. And so I shall continue.' There was no point in telling him the gallery might soon be no more than a memory. 'As I told you, I taught to earn a living; I paint because it's what I want to do. You say you may be old-fashioned. I say there is no *may be* about it. You are living in yesterday's world. No, even before that. Women are no longer men's chattels, in case you hadn't noticed.'

'When, before we were married, you talked about your painting, didn't I suggest to you that you should get together a collection, put on an exhibition? I would have no objection to your doing that; I would arrange to hire the Town Hall or wherever you wanted. But to hawk your wares and try to *raise money* on them is quite different. You know my feelings. Now we'll say no more.'

Just for a second she felt like a chastened child before temper took over.

'You go on home. The light is still good; I shall work for another hour or so. And one of these days, James Bartlett, you'll eat your words.' Purposely she didn't watch him as he walked back to the stile. Instead she returned to her stool and took up her brush, hoping her look of concentration – elaborate concentration – wasn't lost on him.

A minute later she heard the sound of the engine and knew he'd gone.

Afterwards neither of them referred to the incident but as the weeks of autumn went on they were both aware that it had created a sandy patch in the rock on which they intended to build their lasting relationship. She wished none of it had been said but had no thought of being influenced by James' opinion; in fact what she meant to do was put it right out of her mind. In the year and a half she'd known him, she had held him on a pedestal. That brief interlude by the river may have rocked the pedestal but she wasn't going to allow it to topple him.

When, on an afternoon in November, she set off to Tarnmouth with the finished picture she wished that things could have been different and she and James could have gone together. She wanted to open his eyes to the things she loved about the little town and, even more than that, she wanted him to see the gallery and meet Mr Adams and be proud that her work was held in respect. Then, with her memory stirred, so too was anger at the way he could casually disregard something so important to her. Why should she care what he thought? He knew nothing about art. She shouldn't let herself care, she should just be proud that dear old Mr Adams thought well of her.

As she parked near the pier she automatically glanced towards the gallery, and realized that whether winter or summer this was the first time she had seen the front door closed. Any second though her old friend would look out of the window and recognize her car. She looked forward to seeing him open the door and raise that ancient bowler with pleasure at the sight of her. Carefully lifting the picture from the back seat she closed the car and crossed the road. He must be showing someone around or even selling a picture. She approached the gallery hoping that between the time they'd last spoken and now he might have negotiated the extension of his lease and given up the idea of retiring.

But the front door was locked. At that moment Dennis Holbrook, the baker from next door but one, came out into the street. He liked to get out of his bakehouse and get a breath of air whenever he had the opportunity. And that's how it was that he was able to tell Georgie what had happened.

'He came in on the usual bus this morning, everything all right at home. But not much more than an hour or so later – well, it was when the ten thirty bus pulled up at the pier to be exact – I saw the conductor get out with a package and run over to the gallery with it. Call me nosey, but messages sent that way are always something too urgent to wait for a letter. So I just shut my door – the street was pretty empty, no sign of any customers coming – and popped along to see everything was all right. He was in there with a man I'd never seen before, he looked like he'd come straight off the beach with his tall sea boots. The poor old gent, he looked real shaken. "It's my wife," he said, "a neighbour's just sent to say she's had a fall and they're waiting for the doctor." Then the other one, the boatman, took up the tale. He said he was going to drive Mr Adams straight home and would be back later. Funny thing to say, *back later*, that's what I thought. Then I remembered the talk about someone with a boat in the harbour here having bought the property and kicking the old man out at the end of the year. Putting two and two together, I guessed that's who it must be. Maybe he had the garb on to look like a seaman, but this bloke could never fit comfy with the others down there among the working boats. Like so many of these la-di-da folk with time on their hands and money enough to buy a boat, they think they're Sinbad the Sailor. Must have been who it was; who else would Mr Adams have left a key with so he could get back in?'

'Is that all the note told him about his wife?'

'Yes. All done in a bit of a panic, I dare say. That's in part why I was looking out as often as I can, waiting to see Squire Sinbad's car come back. And bless my soul, talk of the devil, here he is now.'

A car drew up outside the gallery. The 'pretend sailor' got out. As he crossed the path he glanced along the esplanade to where Georgie and the baker were standing. Georgie clenched her hands until she felt her nails dig into her flesh, shaken by anger and resentment as she watched him open the door with her friend Mr Adams' key and enter the gallery.

Three

Georgie and the baker glanced at each other in silent agreement. Sinbad the Sailor, Mr La-di-da, call the stranger what he liked, his opinion couldn't be any less flattering than her first impression of the property's new owner. Still carrying her painting she hurried by Dennis's side, reaching the front door of the double-fronted building just as the seaman hung the *Closed* sign on the inside of the glass panel. Seeing they meant to enter, his frown was enough to stop the less determined in their tracks.

Pushing the door open, Georgie led the way in.

'Can't you read?' he said, his tone implying he was speaking to a complete fool. 'The gallery has finished trading, so it's no use bringing your work here.'

'I'm perfectly aware of that, although I came to Tarnmouth hoping Mr Adams had been able to extend his lease.'

'There was never any thought of that. But in any case, it's for family reasons he is unable to continue trading until the lease expires at end of the year.'

'What did you find out?' Dennis asked, his tone more agreeable than Georgie's had been. 'You say he won't be opening up again – does that mean she's done serious damage? I was here before you drove him home. Remember?'

'The news is not good. I took him to the hospital, driving behind the ambulance. They told him almost as soon as they looked at her that her hip is broken. It seems that at her age – she's older than him, not far off eighty, he told me – they can't try to do anything for her. Very probably they'll send her home tomorrow. She'll be bedridden of course. He wasn't allowed to stay with her, but he insisted on being nearby so that he can see her at half past six for the evening half-hour visiting. I'm going to collect him and take him back home at seven o'clock.'

Georgie forgot her previous anger.

'How awful,' she said more to herself than to him. 'Never to be able to stand, to know it's not going to change. What a dreadful, hopeless outlook. Not just for her, for both of them.'

'Indeed it is.'

With her antagonism if not receding at least taking a back seat to the other emotions the news had awoken, she looked at the stranger, a man so out of place in the gallery she loved. It was hard to guess his age; he had the weather-beaten look that had probably stolen his youthful complexion before its time. He could well still be in his twenties, although there was nothing boyish in either his appearance or manner. Tall and broad shouldered, he gave the impression of wiry strength. His brown hair was coarse and, she thought critically, it looked as though it needed a trim. Yet as is the way with hair of that type, as it grew to the nape of his neck so it curled. His beard was the same colour but neatly trimmed. He could probably do that himself, whereas a haircut meant a trip to the barber's shop.

Aware of her scrutiny, he raised his eyebrows enquiringly and she suspected she read mockery in his expression.

Dennis Holbrook cut through their thoughts. 'Well, I'm right sorry to hear news like that. The esplanade won't be the same without Mr Adams. I must get back to my ovens. Give the poor old boy my best, won't you?'

'Certainly I will.' And drawing a firm line under the interview, the stranger held the door open for both of them to leave.

'No, I want to speak to you before I go. Mr Adams must be so worried, about his wife of course, but about all the pictures he has here, too. You can't just put "closed" on the door of a place like this. The paintings belong to other people.'

'I'm perfectly aware of that. I have suggested to Mr Adams that if he notifies the various artists that their unsold work must be collected on a certain date, I will arrange to make myself available to be here.'

She opened the desk drawer and took out the writing pad, a pen and bottle of ink.

'You say you're collecting him from the hospital this evening. If I write him a note, will you give it to him? I have all the time in the world; I can easily look after the closing of the gallery for him.'

Did she imagine it or was he watching impatiently as she wrote? One way or the other, she gave no indication of being put off what she was doing. It was important that her old friend knew he could trust her to handle the closing just as he would have himself.

'I'll give it to him this evening, Perhaps we ought to introduce ourselves; it will give him more confidence in handing over the reins if I can give you a name when I deliver the letter. I am Dominic Fraser – or perhaps, since you say you are an old friend of his, he has already told you who it was bought the property?'

She shook her head. 'No, he simply said it had been bought by a boatman who lived on Quay Hill.'

At that Dominic gave an unexpected smile. 'And if you'd ever been inside one of those houses you would understand why I am keen to move in here. And you are . . .?'

'Georgie Bartlett. If I drive over to Tarnmouth in the morning, where can I find you to hear his reply? I'm sure he'll be happy for me to do it, but I don't want to ask you for the key until he says he agrees.'

'I certainly wouldn't part with it without his permission. Don't forget to take your picture,' he reminded her as again he moved towards the door to see her out.

'I shall leave it here. Once he gives the OK I can hang it and, who knows, it might sell between now and the end of the year.' As she spoke she took off the single sheet of wrapping paper and laid the framed picture on the desk. Then, forgetting her natural antipathy towards her arrogant new acquaintance, she smiled and for the first time he saw the dimple suddenly appear in her left cheek as she said, 'I'm not going to hang it yet, that might be tempting fate.'

Leaving the door open, he walked to the desk to see her work.

'Umph,' was his only comment, which might mean anything. She didn't care about his opinion, but, if he didn't like the picture, she would rather he said so. 'Umph' seemed to brush it aside as though it wasn't worth considering. So his next remark surprised her. 'I imagined you'd painted this yourself, but it's signed GF. You told me your name was Bartlett.'

'So it is. I used to be Franklyn. I've been bringing pictures here for ages, always signed GF. This is the first since I was married, but I prefer still to use the F.'

He nodded slowly, still looking at the painting.

'Back in the summer I was passing and I noticed in each of these front windows was a seascape – clearly here in Tarnmouth. GF they were signed. Yours?'

She nodded. 'I brought them in as a pair at the beginning of summer.'

'On the first of January I shall be bringing them back here. I bought them to hang them in the booking office here.'

She was disappointed. By her standards to enhance the walls of an office was no reason for buying paintings.

'I wish they'd gone to a home, to people who had bought them because they wanted to live with them.'

'I'll see Mr Adams reads your letter and sends his reply. How early can you get here in the morning? Nine o'clock?'

'If I'm to run the gallery, I shall always be here at nine o'clock. Where shall I find you?'

'Here at nine. Don't be late; I am taking a fishing party out on the tide and want to leave harbour at nine thirty.' Then, holding the door wide open, he said, 'Until the morning, goodbye, Mrs Bartlett.'

'Goodbye Mr . . . I can't remember what you said your name was. But goodbye anyway.' She remembered his name perfectly well, but it gave her childish pleasure to imply that she hadn't been interested. Had she looked back as she got into her car on the opposite side of the road, she would have been surprised to see the broad – and boyish – smile.

Driving home she faced the next stage in her plan. James had objected to her taking her work to the gallery, so his reaction to what she planned to do promised an uncomfortable evening ahead.

'Hello dear,' Muriel greeted her, 'so you left your picture for sale. Perhaps James won't notice that it's not with your painting things. Best not to look for trouble. Did Mr Adams like it? Well, of course he did.'

So Georgie told her about her afternoon.

'You've actually offered? Oh, but, Georgie, you ought to have asked James first. He won't like it.'

'Asked permission how I spend my time? Why, that's ridiculous. It'll only be on Saturday afternoons that he'll be home while I'm there.'

'I know, dear. But he's a proud man; he won't like to think of his wife serving in a shop. Call it a gallery if you like, but bring it down to brass tacks and it's a shop.'

Soon after six o'clock they heard James putting the car in the garage.

'I'll go and look at the vegetables. It's best I'm not there when you tell him about the gallery.'

Her warning only confirmed what had been in Georgie's mind.

Never one to shy from what has to be faced, she told him almost as he came into the room. He listened, saying nothing, and she wished he would interrupt her, even with the argument she was anticipating. Yet he didn't look angry. Indeed, he was watching her with affection.

'So I'm going in at nine o'clock tomorrow and this man who has bought the property will give me Mr Adams' reply. Maybe he'll refuse my offer.'

'Of course he won't. You say you've known him for years, he must know you can be trusted. You really don't mind doing it? You'll be tied up right through the run-up to Christmas and beyond.'

'So will anyone who has a job of work.'

That brought about a quick frown. 'Job of work? You didn't mention being paid.'

She laughed. 'Of course I shan't be paid. I shall do it because I'm fond of Mr Adams, but even more than that because I have always loved the gallery. It makes me really angry to think of that wretched boatman having the power to turn him out.'

'I fear this Mr Adams has worse troubles on his hands than closing down the shop – or gallery as you like to call it.'

'And you don't mind, James? You won't get hoity-toity and say you won't have your wife working in a shop?'

From outside in the hallway Muriel heard his laugh and breathed a sigh of relief. She had really feared that what Georgie meant to do would make him angry, but worse than that, would hurt him that she could go against his wishes. They were so happy here, but Georgie, bless her, she always rushed at things and didn't look ahead and see the outcome of her actions. When she'd been single and with independent means it hadn't mattered, but now she was his wife she really ought to refer to him before she carried on as if she were still free and single. Muriel crept nearer the door and heard him say, 'Mind? What sort of a man do you think I am? If you're prepared to give up your time to help a friend in trouble, then how could I possibly feel anything but pride in your decision?'

With her hand on the door handle Muriel was held back by instinct. They weren't speaking. In her mind's eye she could see the way James would be drawing Georgie into his arms, holding her close against him. Muriel crossed her arms and hugged her firmly encased voluminous bust tightly to her, with eyes closed as if that way she would escape the aching loneliness that suddenly gripped her.

On the surface the winter evening passed as they usually did when James wasn't at a Council meeting in the Town Hall and the three of them were together. Music on the radiogram, Muriel sewing and Georgie reading while James did *The Times* crossword.

'Bedtime, young lady,' James said later as he folded his paper in his usual neat manner. 'I'll just go and do the shoes, then I'm ready too.' Shoe cleaning was all part of his evening ritual, something that Muriel had felt uncomfortable with in the beginning. Why should he clean her shoes for her? It was something that Cyril had never done even though he'd been her husband; instead it had been she who had cleaned his more often than not. But James had been insistent and each night before he went to bed those which had been worn that day were collected up so that, in the scullery, he could clean and polish them – hers, Georgie's and his own. Nightly rituals never varied: while he did the shoes, Muriel set the table for breakfast and put the milk bottles on the doorstep for the morning.

Even before James joined her in the bedroom, Georgie's mind was already moving ahead to tomorrow.

'I'm sure Mr Adams will be glad for me to take over,' she told him as he came into the room. Better not to sound too excited at the prospect, she reminded herself. 'I have to be there at nine in the morning because Mr – Mr Whatever-his-name-is, I can't remember – is taking a fishing party out on the tide and he'll give me the key. It's going to be a really busy day. I have to check the names and addresses of the owners of all the pictures, then write to each one explaining what's happened.'

'Hand write? Don't do that, Georgie. In the morning, scribble down the gist of what you have to tell them and I'll dictate something to Miss Corbett. You can hand write the name on each one – it looks more personal anyway. She can cut a copy for the duplicator and run off however many copies you need. You'd want to post everyone's at the same time so you wouldn't get them off until the day after if you had to write them by hand. It'll be just as quick to let Miss Corbett do them.'

'Would you do that? That would be a huge help. The rest is plain sailing, but I didn't like the thought of having to explain it over and over again.' Then, with a chuckle, 'Imagine my writing getting worse and worse with each one.' She held her hand towards him as he came to the bed. 'You were a long time coming up.' He'd been no longer than usual but recognized the invitation in her words.

'You ought to go straight to sleep,' he said softly a few seconds later as she nuzzled close to him. 'You have to be away early in the morning.'

'The morning is hours away. And sleep is miles away.'

He would have been less than human if he hadn't responded as she pulled the cord and undid his pyjama trousers. And if he hadn't responded to that, he certainly would to the caress of her hand as it encircled him. But when with her other hand she drew his to her small breast some of his fast rising excitement receded; the difference between her almost boyish figure and the way his mind had been turning as his passion mounted frightened him. He loved her, she was his wife. He mustn't let her guess.

'Georgie, Georgie,' he whispered, moving his hand from her breast and covering hers that fondled and caressed him, frightened that she would realize that her underdeveloped body had momentarily halted his rising passion. 'Yes, oh yes,' he whispered, his covering hand tight on hers, forcing it to move on him. Thankfully he felt his pulses pound, his excitement mounted. With no further preamble he raised himself above her. With her lips parted and her eyes closed Georgie strained to reach the goal that was so tantalizingly close; tonight it must be good, for him, for her, it must, it *must*. She felt she was racing to catch up with him and for a second she believed she would succeed. Then his voice stripped her of hope. Damn him, damn him, why couldn't he wait for her?

'Come on,' he whispered urgently, 'with me, Georgie, yes, yes, come on, *come on*, now, Georgie.' She felt his quickening pace, and so soon she felt the still, heavy weight of him. 'Thought . . . you were going to . . . you couldn't—' So breathless that he could hardly speak, he rolled off her. She knew that, for him, the episode was over. 'Get to sleep, darling,' he said softly a minute or so later, his voice full of affection. 'You have an early start in the morning.'

'Not tired.' She sounded like a sulky child. But whatever she'd answered would have been lost on him as he slipped peacefully into sleep.

At the far end of the landing behind her closed door, Muriel turned her pillow and made another attempt to settle. Although she had been at Gregory House no more than five months, her life before that seemed like another world. It was a strange situation, keeping house for Georgie and James, living as one family even though there were moments when she felt lonelier than if she were employed by strangers. Did they mind having her always with them? If she were in employment she would either have had a sitting room of her own or would spend her evenings in the kitchen.

She and Georgie had always had a happy relationship; she and James got on very well. But three is an awkward number. Take this evening for instance; Georgie must have been as aware as she was herself of the way James' thoughts were turning. An early night, he'd said. If Georgie read his mind she gave no indication – at least, not while the three of them were together. But now that the enforced trio had broken up, while she was here alone, they were together. She remembered the early days of her marriage to Cyril – but even in those days Cyril had never looked at her with the devotion that was clear to read in James' expression when he talked to Georgie. And quite right too, of course he loved her. What would they be doing now? In Muriel's imagination nothing they did could be wrong between two people who were in love. Pushing her voluminous nightgown almost to her shoulders, she held those much despised breasts in her capable hands. She kneaded them, her fingers working on them almost as if they had a life apart from the rest of her body – and free at last after a long day being crushed almost out of existence, that wasn't far from the truth. Was James doing this? Or this? Or this? With no one to watch her, no occupant in a second bed in the room, she followed every natural inclination.

Before long, like James, Muriel slept. Only Georgie lay awake. Purposely she turned her mind to the events of the day that was gone and let her imagination carry her forward to the one that lay ahead.

At two minutes to nine she drew up outside the gallery just as Dominic, seeing the car, came out to greet her.

'I'm glad you're on time,' he said as he opened the door and passed her the key. 'I gave Mr Adams your note.'

'What was his reaction?'

'He's grateful.' Then after a brief pause, 'No, damn it, he was more than grateful. I dare say the day had taken its toll. Poor old chap. He took off his hat and wiped away tears of relief. "Miss Franklyn is an old friend, I'd trust her with my life." That's what he said as he mopped up.'

'I won't let him down.'

'This is it then.' Dominic Fraser held out his hand. 'I doubt if we shall see each other again. You'll be cleared out by the end of December and I'll start moving in on the first of January. Goodbye, Mrs Bartlett.'

'Can you tell me where Mr Adams lives? I'd rather take money to him than post it.' She took a notebook and pen out of her handbag and was ready to write.

'Not off hand. I'll let you have it but I want to get away now.'

Immediately, she heard his tone as arrogant, confirming her first impression even though he had spoken kindly of Mr Adams.

'I won't keep you. Goodbye Mr . . .' Again she took childish pleasure in letting him see that she had forgotten his name, but if she'd intended to knock him off his perch it was clear she hadn't succeeded. Turning away, he started along the esplanade towards the harbour. She even saw arrogance in his walk, in the set of his straight shoulders and the way he held his head. In that second, into her mind flashed memories of how over the years she had spent plenty of time talking to the boatmen, a friendly fraternity, lacking in riches but with an abundance of appreciation for their lives. As if Mr Sinbad could ever fit in with them! But she had no time to waste on him; ahead of her was a day in the gallery and she meant to enjoy every moment of it.

Surprisingly, her thoughts weren't on the troubles that had befallen Mr and Mrs Adams; they were centred wholly on herself, and the weeks before her when the gallery would be her responsibility. Then something else penetrated her awareness: on a cold November morning there was no heating. She was in the front room to the left of the entrance door from the road. Behind that, reached by an open doorway, was a second, smaller room. She'd heard Mr Adams refer to it as the hideaway for his clutter. Perhaps there would be a stove in there. What she found wasn't a stove; it was the remains of dead ashes in the grate and a few pieces of coal in a green baize bag. She imagined the elderly man arriving each winter morning, getting off the trolleybus by the pier and crossing the road clutching his worn green baize bag with firing for the day. And looking around she saw that it wasn't just firing he brought, for by the sink there was a brown paper bag which, on inspection, she found to contain two plates, one covering the other and containing two slices of beef, a lump of cheese, and a slice of bread. Such a small thing to make her eyes sting with unshed tears.

'I'll look after it all for you,' she whispered. 'We all ought to be like you; we expect to get things easily. Makes me ashamed.' Scraping the food into the paper bag she rinsed the plates under cold water from the tap. Well, she wasn't doing him any good standing here feeling guilty for her easy life; she had a gallery to sort out. But she couldn't work if she was cold. There was an electric power point by the side of the fireplace but no sign of an electric fire. So, locking the door behind her she walked to the far end of the esplanade to Seward's Electrical Shop. Was it really worth spending all that money just for six weeks? She didn't let herself listen to the question. She wrote a cheque and gave it to Eric Seward then went back to await delivery of a two-bar radiant heat fire.

There was a woman looking in the window of the gallery and as Georgie came close, hoping it might be a customer, she gave her a cheery 'Good morning'.

'The door's still locked,' the woman told her. 'That's two days. The old gent is here in the doorway as regular as clockwork as a rule. I hope he's not ill. Perhaps he'll come on the next bus.'

'No, he's not ill. But I'm looking after closing the gallery for him – it finishes at the end of the year.'

The woman's crestfallen expression wasn't lost on her.

'You mean he's not taking anything for sale?'

Georgie sized up the situation and knew that this woman's work was more than a hobby; clearly she wanted the money.

'Come inside out of the cold while we talk,' she invited, careful to hide her only half-understood rush of sympathy. 'You have pictures here? There's no other outlet around here.' Then, as they closed the door on the bitter wind that blew in from the sea, Georgie told her visitor about Mrs Adams' fall.

'Isn't it awful the way something can happen in a second? One minute life is ticking along nicely – then nothing can ever be the same.' As the stranger spoke Georgie had a good chance to look at her. A tall, angular woman, big boned and yet thin. The fur collar at the neck of her black overcoat gave no illusion of affluence, rather it looked like some mangy fox found by the roadside.

'Yes, none of us should take anything for granted, should we? If you want to leave your pictures until the end of December, there's always hope that people will come in looking for something special for a Christmas present. I have one there, see, propped against the wall. I shall keep my fingers crossed that someone might like it.'

'Fancy being able to do work like that! I don't paint. But I just wondered . . . I expect he would have said he only did paintings . . . but I just wondered if with Christmas coming he might have been able to sell some of these things my husband and I have made. But it's too late, I can see that.'

'Not necessarily. Let me have a look at what you've brought.' Georgie had no idea what made her say it, except that there was something about the woman that touched a chord in her. 'We ought to introduce ourselves. I'm Georgie Bartlett. And you?'

'Alice Soames. Mrs Bartlett, you'll probably think I have an awful cheek bringing stuff along like this – I mean, I've only ever made things for pleasure; I've never been taught. And anyway, the gallery just sells paintings.' Although she had undone her case, she kept her hand firmly on top of it so that it couldn't be opened.

'Yes, I know the gallery is for paintings,' Georgie agreed, telling herself that was a loophole if whatever Alice had brought was amateurish and useless. 'But please let me see what you've brought. If you've been making things for pleasure, then perhaps what you've done might give pleasure to other people.'

Gingerly Alice opened the lid of the old leather suitcase, exposing a number of carefully wrapped packages. Without so much as a 'May I?' Georgie took one out carefully and unwrapped it to reveal a casket that looked like an oversized egg. She'd never seen anything like it.

'It looks real, it's eggshell thin. Why, it's exquisite. You lift it out of the tissue; I'm scared to touch it.'

'I used an ostrich egg for this one. The others are all the same principle, but they're smaller – chicken, ducks, geese. But this one I thought was large enough to make into a trinket box.' The eggshell had been cut into two halves, then opened on two minute hinges. The outside had been painted first with a pale blue wash, and then decorated with gold leaf, whilst both halves of the inside were lined with dark blue velvet. In the base was resting a wooden tray, cut to the exact shape and made into sections to take trinkets. The whole thing fitted on a delicately carved wooden stand.

'I've never seen anything like it,' Georgie said softly. 'So delicate. However did you come by an ostrich egg?'

'In the beginning I don't really know. Barry, that's my husband, he had a great aunt who went to live in South Africa. It came from her, that much he does know, and he thinks she came back to England when his parents were married. Aunt Margaret he's always heard her called, but she died ages ago. Whether she brought it as an actual egg, or whether it was blown first, I couldn't tell you. But he says it had been in the attic of his family home all his life. It wasn't until I'd made some of the smaller ones that he suggested I should have a go with this one. And you know what? It was actually less fiddly than working on the little ones.'

'How can you bear to part with it?'

'Needs must, if I can find a way of selling it. I wouldn't have suggested it to him – after all, it belonged to his family, so it was his until I got my hands on it – but it was his idea. What do you think?'

'I told you what I think. It's quite beautiful. Not just the egg, but the wonderful fretwork of the stand, the perfect fit of the tray. And you say you've never been taught?'

'Oh, I didn't do any of that. That was Barry. Woodwork was always his life – not plain sailing sort of stuff. He did church work, repairing ancient carvings, and all that sort of thing. But it's been years since he's been able to work. He had a fall when he was on a ladder doing something to our guttering. I was out shopping or I'd never have let him go up there without me holding the ladder steady. When I came home the ambulance was there taking him off to the hospital. His back was broken; they said he'd never walk again. They sent him home from hospital, and the doctor said he'd never be any better.'

'And he did this intricate woodwork?'

'It's his salvation. If he had to sit in his chair all day long not doing anything except read the paper, he would get miserable and bitter. Well, who wouldn't? But while he's working he forgets his troubles. Nothing like being busy. He's done the filigree work on the small stands, too. We sent away and bought the silver wire.' As she talked she had unwrapped a specimen of her selection. Eggs of different sizes, painted and decorated in a variety of pastel colours, they were all undone and stood on Mr Adams' desk.

'I'll tell you what we'll do, Mrs Soames – or may I call you Alice as it looks as though we'll be seeing plenty more of each other until the gallery closes? I'm Georgie. There's a table in the back room, we'll cover it with velvet – I have some at home.' It was a lie, but Alice would never guess that she meant to stop on the way home to buy it. 'Then if you come in tomorrow morning we'll make a display and stand the table by the window. We'll spend an hour or two pricing them and I bet you, with Christmas just around the corner, they'll not only sell but will bring people in and perhaps help sell a picture.'

It was too much for Alice Soames.

'Don't take any notice,' she gulped as she reached for her snow-white handkerchief to wipe her wet cheeks. 'It's just it's been so long since things were going right. I can't wait to get home and tell Barry. But tomorrow's Wednesday and I've got a cleaning job for two hours every Wednesday morning.'

'When could you come?' Georgie asked, surprising herself that she should be going out of her way to make things easier for someone she had only just met.

'I could come this afternoon, or tomorrow afternoon. Once I know Barry is comfy in his chair he'll busy himself with his woodwork while I'm out.'

Georgie imagined the ease and comfort in her own life; she thought of James, dear James, and knew there was so much she had to be thankful for.

'Until they're priced we'd better put these out of sight in the back room. Let's say tomorrow afternoon, shall we, for the pricing? Does Barry have a wheelchair?'

'Oh yes, I couldn't leave him just sitting otherwise. He can wheel himself anywhere in the downstairs rooms. It's wonderful how well he's done. I'll start carrying them through, shall I?'

Unobserved, Georgie watched her carrying the ostrich egg into the back room. Her lisle stockings had lost their grip after a multitude of washes, the heel of each had been neatly darned; the shine on her well-polished shoes told of brushing as vigorous as James brought to bear on his last job of each day; her cloche hat would have been fashionable a decade ago.

Picking up two smaller eggs, Georgie followed her to the back room.

'I was thinking,' she said, their job done. 'Do you ever take Barry out in his chair?'

'Come rain or shine, we always have half an hour's walk in the evening. It's good for him to have another man to speak to for five minutes. He used to play darts in the Barley Mow – in their team he was – and sometimes if his old pals are down there I wheel him in and leave him. A glass of ale and a bit of man's talk takes him out of himself. I notice he always has a better night when he's been "with the boys" as he calls them. Boys! None of them will see fifty again. Now, Mrs Bart – Georgie – if we put prices on, does that go to Mr Adams and he – or you if you're in change till the place shuts down – does he or do you give me what you think?'

'We'll do it the same as the pictures, except that he always prices those and with the eggs I want you and Barry to decide how much we should ask. Then ten per cent goes to Mr Adams. You two work out the prices tonight and we'll do the display together tomorrow afternoon.'

Alice nodded. 'Don't know what to say, how to thank you.' The corners of her mouth were twitching dangerously. 'Must fly. I do an hour at the Parish Hall on the way home. There was a barn dance there yesterday evening, so you may be sure there'll be a right pickle to get cleaned up. Not my favourite place to clean – the hall's not so bad, but I wish they'd treat the lavatory the same as they would at home. Oh well, needs must when the devil drives.' About to open the door to leave, she turned back, her long face seeming transformed by the sudden happiness that swept through her. 'Fancy, if Barry and I could earn enough so that I could stay home with him, we could have a sort of cottage industry. Still, if he can put up with what's happened to him, I can put up with a bit of polishing and cleaning. See you tomorrow – and thank you, thank you more than I have the words for.'

Georgie's first encounter with Alice Soames made a lasting impression on her. She found herself looking back to her sheltered existence at St Winifred's and thought about her fellow teachers, wondering, perhaps not for the first time, but certainly with new clarity of vision, whether the impression they gave of enjoying full and satisfying lives wasn't a face-saving performance, exaggerated to hide an emptiness they wouldn't admit. Who was the happier, they or Alice with all the hardships Fate had doled out to her? Never had Georgie seen such a look of hope and thankfulness as she had from Alice at the thought of what might lay ahead for herself and her husband.

That night she told James and Muriel about her visitor and about her decision to try to sell the eggs.

'Would Mr Adams approve?' That was Muriel's immediate reaction. 'Bringing different work in will change the character of an art gallery.'

But James gave his wholehearted support. 'If you can help

them, then it must be the right thing to do. There but for the grace of God . . . And, being practical, in the economic climate of the country today I'd say the average working people are more inclined to hang on to any spare money rather than lash out on oil paintings. But things such as you described might well sell with Christmas coming.'

'That's what I thought, James. I do hope they will. I'd love to be able to help them. She's an educated woman, a woman who I'm sure wasn't brought up to . . .' Then with a mischievous twinkle as she caught his eye, 'To hawk her wares. You're happy about what I'm doing, James?' Not that she would stop doing it if he answered in the negative.

'I'm extremely proud of what you're doing. I have always made it clear to you that I have no objection to your working – whether teaching, which was your profession, or as you are doing now, out of kindness committing yourself to running the gallery until it closes. If you were rushing off to do some menial task and getting paid each Friday my feelings would be very different.'

'Oh, James.' She laughed. 'I never realized my friend James was such a snob. There's nothing wrong with people who sell their labours – you do it yourself.'

'I do what I was trained for, just as you were trained in history and in the ability to pass on your knowledge. Important work, Georgie, none more so.' His words sounded pompous but not the way he spoke them, nor yet the affectionate expression as he looked at her. Her mind took a leap to the home she imagined Alice must have gone back to (after she'd cleaned the Parish Hall), where her husband waited, a man of talent and so dependent on her.

'Poor woman,' Muriel said, as if she had followed her thoughts. 'How a person's life can change in a second!'

But not at Gregory House, where the evening proceeded on its usual course: Muriel cleared away the meal, Georgie dried the dishes, James did the crossword then went to his study for half an hour while Muriel sewed and Georgie read; then it was time for Muriel to put out the milk bottles and James to clean the shoes. Would their lives ever change, or was this the rut they would continue to move in as the years rolled on?

★　　★　　★

Next afternoon Georgie held the front door wide open so that Barry's wheelchair could be brought in. During the morning she had covered the display table with the midnight-blue velvet she had bought on the way home the previous evening and now it was standing in position inside the window of what had once been the parlour before Mr Adams had given it new life as part of the gallery. Carefully, one by one, she had brought the eggs out from the back room and now they had to be priced.

'You know how many hours you spent on them, so I shall leave the pricing to you,' she told the couple. 'I've made a sign to stand behind the table on an easel.' She made herself sound efficient and businesslike, but somehow couldn't hold back from saying, 'Isn't this exciting?'

'The best day we've had for a long time,' Barry agreed. 'It never does to let yourself get down about things. We none of us know what tomorrow will bring, be it good or bad. And by Jove, this is *good*. That's a splendid sign you've done.'

And so it was; she had brought all her talent to bear on writing it. EVERYTHING HANDMADE BY LOCAL CRAFTSMEN. When the tags were all written she listed the items and booked them down just as Mr Adams would have done himself. The display was surely eye-catching, so now all they needed were customers.

As she was about to hold the door wide for Alice and Barry to leave, she felt that he wanted to say something else but was hesitating. Perhaps he was uncertain about asking how they should collect any money due to them.

'I'm here every day, except Sunday of course, so look in when you like and see whether anything's been sold,' she told him. But still he hesitated, raising a hand to indicate to Alice that he wasn't ready to be pushed.

'It's just a thought, and I don't want you to feel we're taking advantage of the kindness you're already doing us—'

'There's no kindness in taking those exquisite little things. They will attract more people in than any notice I could put outside telling people this is their last chance to buy a picture.'

'As far as we're concerned it's kindness beyond our dreams. That's why I didn't tell Alice about this; she would have said I was taking advantage. I want an honest refusal if you think it's no good.' And wriggling with difficulty to reach down into his coat pocket, he brought out a carved wooden dog. Not just a dog, it was a Scottie terrier, of that there was no doubt. 'You don't have to say yes to it.'

Alice looked embarrassed. 'Oh, Barry, you're putting her on the spot. You shouldn't have brought anything else.'

Georgie took the carving in her hand. 'You made this?'

'That's what he does when I'm out,' Alice said. 'Whittles away at his wood all day long. A lot of the wood I find when I go beachcombing.'

'I made up my mind when I got well enough to be in my chair that I wasn't going to give up my work. Wood, it's like a living thing to work on. It's helped me to hang on to . . . to . . . to what? Eh, Alice?'

'To hope, I believe that's the most important thing it's done. Just to sit and do nothing would have sent him on a downward spiral even with the best will in the world.' Alice rested her hand on his shoulder, her momentary annoyance gone.

'When I first came home from the hospital after they'd told me I wouldn't walk, I was dead set on proving them wrong. I made up my mind that nothing was going to make me helpless. One day I'd be back at my work. In my book, there's no more rewarding work in this world than restoring church carvings, replacing what time has rotted with something that matches up to what those craftsmen did so long ago.'

Georgie nodded. 'Yes, I can understand that. And . . .?' she prompted him to continue.

'I had to come to terms. It wasn't easy. But from somewhere I found some sort of inner resource. Alice, bless her, she started collecting wood off the beach and I learnt that there is the same satisfaction in making a little fellow like you're holding as there is in restoring some ancient reredos.'

'So you have more at home? If you want to try and sell some, there's only six weeks – less until Christmas. Bring them in as soon as you can. This is . . . well, it's almost unbelievable that anyone can create something like this from a lump of wood.'

Alice had never pushed that chair so fast or with such deter-mination as she did on the journey home. Within an hour she was back, on her own and with her suitcase.

★ ★ ★

That was the beginning of new life being breathed into the gallery that had become so familiar to most of the locals that they hardly glanced as they walked past. The sign announcing work HAND-MADE BY LOCAL CRAFTSMEN caught their eyes and, in some cases, gave them ideas. The vicar's wife arrived with a pile of handmade Christmas cards produced by the St Luke's Ladies Group and left over from the Christmas Bazaar, an event only ever patronized by regular churchgoers.

'They may not sell, even here, but they are really well made,' she said persuasively to Georgie. 'Anything you can get for them will go into the Church Roof Fund.'

Clemmy Durrant, whose dentist husband had run off with his secretary, leaving her on her own to bring up their two young children, brought sets of crocheted chairbacks; Deirdre Fuller, from the manor house on the hill behind town, brought in a set of six embroidered seat covers for dining chairs with instructions that if they sold the money was to be sent to the orphanage in Winchford.

'It's the best thing I could have done,' Georgie said as she reported her progress to Muriel and James. 'I sold two carvings and the ostrich egg jewellery box today, apart from one set of chairbacks and one or two Christmas cards. It might not be great trade if I were in business, but it's all grist to the mill and I'm looking forward to seeing the Soames' expression when I hand over their share.'

'Embroidered dining chair seat covers, you say? But imagine the hours and hours of work in six of those. How generous to say the money is to go to the orphanage.' Muriel couldn't have been more interested in the happenings in the gallery if she had been running it herself.

'Does it tell you anything, Georgie?' James prompted. 'That she should try and sell them in Tarnmouth for the orphanage here in Winchford? Is Fate giving you a nudge?'

'Should it?'

'I shall buy them. We all owe a good deal to that orphanage; it changed the course of all our lives in this house. I'll make out a cheque and leave you to fill in the amount, then post it off tomorrow.'

Muriel nodded. 'Amen to that. Our lives might have been so different had you not been asked to open that fête.'

'You two really are the limit,' Georgie chuckled. 'Next thing, you'll be wanting to donate to St Winifred's to pay our debt of gratitude.'

'Most unlikely.' His gaze met hers and, not for the first time, she was aware of just what a handsome man he was. 'My feelings on St Winifred's are better not delved into.'

'James Bartlett, you are an exceedingly nice man.' It was said quietly. Muriel felt a message passing between the two of them and was glad to stack the dessert plates and escape to the kitchen.

There were moments when she longed to be anywhere but where she was, a third person they must always be aware of. They included her in everything, and she was never made to feel that she was in the way, but married less than six months they must long for time alone when they could speak without her hearing. She leant against the porcelain sink, her eyes closed. When she was in the room with them he had never taken Georgie's hand, never momentarily put his arm around her. It wasn't fair on them that she was always there – and it wasn't fair on her either. Ah now, that was coming nearer the truth. Leaving the dishes piled up waiting to be washed she dropped to sit on the kitchen chair, her arms folded in front of her, her hands pressing against her tightly encased breasts. When they had suggested her living with them she had had no premonition of what would happen. It was imagination, she told herself angrily. He was such a handsome man – handsome in appearance and in character – and what was she but a sex-starved, ageing woman? What was it Cyril had called her? No she wouldn't let herself remember. She might be ageing but she wasn't old and she longed, yearned, ached, for a fulfilling love every bit as much now as she had twenty years ago.

She ought not to stay here; she ought to look for a housekeeping post away somewhere. Nothing would quieten the needs of her lonely body, but staying here was making it impossible to drive out the image of him . . . Georgie's husband . . . her stepson-in-law. Before she had married Cyril and over the last decade of her marriage she had tried to satisfy her own desires. But even that had changed lately. It wasn't of her doing that as she strained towards a goal that so often was out of reach, it was James' image she saw behind her closed lids; *her* hands became *his* hands.

Georgie's husband, the man Georgie loved and who made no secret of his love for her.

'Are you all right, Muriel?' Georgie's voice surprised her. She felt her face grow hot and felt it must be obvious. Would Georgie guess where her mind had been?

'Yes, I'm better,' she lied. 'Was suddenly so hot, couldn't seem to breathe. I'll just stand by the back door a moment.'

'You poor thing. You should have called.'

Pulling herself back to normal and ready to play her role to the full, Muriel stood by the open door, taking in deep breaths.

'It was nothing. It's the way it happens sometimes.' She needed to say it, in her mind making herself into an ageing woman, removed from the other two. 'You wait twenty years, it'll catch up with you. I used to think my mother made it up to attract attention, but it hits you – so hot that you feel you can't breathe. Better now. Leave the dishes, dear. I'll wash; you can dry if you want. Truly I'm all right now.'

'You're too young for the menopause, aren't you?'

'Women vary, I believe. It's only happened once or twice. I've probably got years of it to put up with before it finally relegates me to old age.'

'Old age? You seem – and look – years younger now than you used to.'

'Surface dressing,' Muriel said with a laugh. 'I have a pension coming in and no one but myself to spend it on. I've never had such nice things to wear.'

And so the incident passed off and she was assured that if Georgie had noticed her flushed face she would have put it down to natural causes and not suspected it had anything to do with the journey Muriel's imagination had been leading her on.

Business at the gallery was having a boost as the winter weeks passed by. An extra sign on the door invited passers-by to come in and browse, and often a casual look led to a sale of one or other of the craft items.

Even so, with only three days to go before Christmas, there was still an attractive display and not much hope of moving it at the last minute. She knew Barry had more at home, just as she knew that Clemmy Durrant had been struggling to finish crocheting a tablecloth, but now that the schools had broken up for the holiday she had little hope of getting it done. But Georgie had other reasons for not wanting to lock the door on the gallery than a need to help those who were down on their luck. It had given her life a new purpose.

'The days are going so fast. When I think how I looked forward to giving up teaching – and yet I dread closing the gallery,' she said to Muriel.

'James has been very good about it. But I'm sure he'll be glad when you settle down at home again. If you want more to do, dear, I ought to look for a job somewhere else and leave you to take care of things.'

'Perish the thought! Don't get ideas like that, Muriel. You're happy here, aren't you?'

'Of course I am. But if you had the responsibility of looking after the house you wouldn't have the urge to rush about all the time.'

'You know me better than to believe that!' Georgie laughed. Then she promptly forgot the suggestion.

Next morning she was alone in the gallery when she heard the front door open and hoped it was a purchaser and not just a browser. It was neither, she realized, as Dominic Fraser walked in.

'You don't seem to have sold many pictures; the walls look pretty full,' he observed, looking around.

'I didn't really expect to,' she answered coldly. 'You don't buy a picture as if it were no more important than . . . than . . . than a fishing rod. At least, you don't unless you want to decorate the wall of an office.'

Holding her gaze, he raised his eyebrows. She knew he was laughing at her.

'Believe me, Mrs Bartlett, I choose carefully, even for an office.'

'In fact,' she said, 'some of the pictures have already been collected by their owners. I have brought everything in here now. This time of year no one is going to want to wander about in an unheated room and there's no stove in there.'

'You shouldn't use that radiant heater where you have customers. You ought to have an electric radiator. I have one in the cottage; I'll fetch it over. If a customer got burnt you'd be responsible.'

'You don't have to do that. I can buy—'

'For little more than a week? I'll go and fetch mine. One thing less to bring when I move across.'

'If you think this is dangerous, then thank you.' But there was no gratitude in her voice.

After he'd gone she sat behind Mr Adams' table and looked around her, his words echoing in her mind. '*For little more than a week.*' This place had been important to her for so long, even before she went to university, and then in the years she'd been teaching when her painting had been the only part of her life she'd really cared about. Now there was not much more than a week to go . . .

When she heard Dominic's car draw up outside she moved to the window where the Soames' artefacts were displayed, and watched him unload the radiator. She would use it for the remaining days and then this place would be filled with fishing gear, the walls bearing notices about day trips on the sea. She felt empty, numb; the future had no shape. Perhaps it is true that when your spirit is low the only way to go is up. Certainly that's what happened to her. Suddenly, she knew exactly what she meant to do. She knew there would be obstacles, but she was ready to fight – and to win.

Four

'I'll change these round,' Dominic said, carrying the radiator in. 'It will take a while before you feel the benefit of it, I'm afraid. Set the temperature you want and leave it on permanently to maintain the heat. Where do you want the other one put?'

'I'll plug it in in the little back room. Or . . .' An idea sprang into her mind, one that might help her win Round One of the battle she knew loomed. 'Or, why don't you take it into the room on the other side of the entrance? It's already cleared; remember I told you I'd brought all the pictures in here. If you want to, you could start getting your things in place in there, then when the moving day comes you'll be able to concentrate on your furniture for upstairs.'

She suspected he knew she had some ulterior motive for the suggestion, but couldn't decide what it was. He gazed at her thoughtfully before he answered.

'Do I detect a change of heart? Are you tired of being tied to this place every day and want to speed your departure?'

'You're wrong on both counts. I could never have a change of heart about this place. It's been an important part of my life for too long, Mr Fraser.' And as soon as she said his name she recognized the teasing expression in his eyes and knew she had fallen into a pit of her own making. 'All right, so I know your name, I always did know it. But you made me so angry. I wanted to take you down a peg.'

He shrugged his broad shoulders. 'That was your privilege.' Even though he said it without a smile, she knew that inside he was laughing.

'I know you refused to extend Mr Adams' lease—'

'In fact he never asked me, but you're right in believing that I had – and still have – no intention. I need these premises. And if you saw the cottage on Quay Hill you would understand. But I'll be honest and tell you that, had he wanted an extension, even though I would have refused him, I would have felt very bad about it.'

'I'm glad. I should hate to think this house belonged to someone who could treat him like that without even caring. But that's not what I want to talk about. It's *me*.'

'My answer is the same; it has to be.'

'Of course I can understand your wanting to live here and run a booking office here. I don't see how you'll manage when you're out on the water, but I expect you've got it all worked out.' She would sink her pride; there was no other way. 'Just listen to what I've been thinking, that's all I ask.'

'I'm listening.'

'I can't see why you need all this space to take bookings for sea trips.'

He believed he saw the way her mind was working. 'That, and store gear for *Tight Lines*, my fishing boat.'

'What I want,' she said, wanting to sound cool and businesslike but the facade soon slipped, 'what I want more than anything, is a chance to carry on what I've started here. I offered to close down the gallery, but somehow rather than getting rid of things I have brought in . . . brought in . . .' She indicated the items displayed on both the table in the window and on Mr Adams' desk. 'And if by some miracle I could sell it all before the end of the year, the people who have made all these things can bring more.'

'There is some beautiful work,' he said thoughtfully, then, 'Especially the wood carving,' he added, taking one in his hand.

She nodded. Then, unable to stop herself, she launched into the story of Alice and Barry Soames. 'If there were an empty shop along here, or if anyone already trading had the sort of trade that might take all these things, then I wouldn't feel so bad about shutting the door here. But I must be honest,' she added, realizing that what she had said must have sounded like a plea for his sympathy, 'it's not just for the Soames and the others who have their own reasons for needing to sell their talent, it's for *me* too. I wake up each morning keen for the day.'

'And so you should, a bride of only a few months.'

'Yes, of course.' She brushed his answer aside. 'Marriage is fine and we're completely happy.' Whatever gave her the need to say that? 'But nothing will ever make me a domestic sort of person and, in any case, I don't run the home.' He was giving her his full attention, but more than that he was looking at her as though he could see into her mind. 'But that's beside the point. My suggestion is that you let me rent this side of the downstairs – not lease, just rent month by month, so that if it doesn't work out you can turn me out – that's this room and the little kitchen-cum-everything-else behind. I'd pay you rent and in addition I would take your bookings when you were out. What do you think?'

'I ought to refuse. I can easily engage someone to cover the hours I can't be here to take bookings. You have as good as told me how desperate your local craft people are to make a few shillings; it couldn't be difficult to fill a post like that.'

She nodded, holding his gaze. 'Surely you won't always be able to know in advance when you have other things to do. Boats need maintenance, don't they? And to engage someone to sit in there all day when I could do what you want with no effort to anyone – and no wages. Doesn't that tempt you?'

'Not particularly. Anything I would expect to pay you in wages will be deducted from your rent. Will be? *Would be*. I haven't agreed yet.'

'Yet?' She picked up on the word. Her dark eyes were shining with hope, her face couldn't hold back its smile. So, for the first time he noticed the dimple in her left cheek.

'You think we could work together?' Until that moment it had never entered her head that his first impression of her might have been as unpromising as hers of him.

'How can we tell? We haven't even started to know each other. But it's surely not necessary to be bosom friends with a working colleague.'

'OK,' he said after another moment's thought. 'We'll give it a try. This time of year you won't be bothered too much by my side of things; there are usually just one or two fishing trips in *Tight Lines* although even then I sometimes take the boat out on my own. It wasn't what I had in mind for the place, but you seem to have given yourself extra clout by taking in these things for sale. Just look at the minute hinges on the small eggs! The talent and patience of that man—'

'And his wife's talent and determination too,' she added. 'But for that, goodness knows how they would have kept afloat.'

'This model lugger he has made, I'll buy that.' He took out his wallet and passed her a ten-shilling note. 'Can you put it somewhere safe for me, and when you see him, ask him if he could make a case for it. A wooden box – cabinet – with a glass door, something I can fix on the wall. It would look well between the two pictures – your two pictures. What do you think?'

At that precise moment her thoughts might have surprised him, but all she said was, 'I'm sure he could do it. He looks in almost every day, so I'll ask him. And I can tell them that I'm not closing at the end of the year?'

'The truth is, you have Barry Soames to thank for it. Damn it, but how many men would find his sort of courage? Would you? Would I? May we never be put to the test.'

'So this is a sort of sop to Fate? Belt and braces protection: by trying to help him – and the others – we are making sure we don't hit bad times?'

'Put like that, it doesn't sound good, does it?' His face broke into an unexpected smile. 'And it's not entirely true. You want to run this place for your own sake as well as theirs, and I find myself with a ready-made booking clerk. Once the move is over and you understand the system I work, we shan't be falling over each other. If I'm in the room through on the other side of the corridor there will be no need for you to keep an eye on the place – and if I'm not in there it will mean I'm right out of your way. Now to discuss rent and wages . . .'

While she and Dominic had been setting out their arrangements for running the two businesses separately and yet so closely connected, nothing had been further from Georgie's thoughts than home or how Muriel was spending her day. If she could have seen her in Bingham and Wrights, the premier departmental store, she might have been surprised but she would certainly have been delighted. For Muriel was in the fitting room, being helped by a fitter while she tried on dresses. She had been saving her widow's pension for more than a month and was there to buy something smart and modern. For nearly six months she had had no expenses, so every penny of her pension had gone on her wardrobe.

'Try this one, madam; the colour would look lovely on you,'

the helpful assistant suggested. The dress was tawny brown, slim fitting to emphasize her flat stomach and narrow hips.

'It's beautiful.' Then, feeling her face flush with embarrassment, she rushed on. 'It's my top half, though, it's out of proportion.'

The assistant laughed. 'I think you go wrong by trying to flatten it. Look how the Hollywood beauties glory in large bosoms. Why don't you take off the bodice you hold yourself in with and I'll go and get a selection of good, uplift brassieres.' And she was gone before Muriel had time to argue.

Left alone she took off the uncomfortable casing that had become so much part of her life and looked at herself in the mirror. A good uplift brassiere – like the Hollywood beauties. Her heart was pounding. What was she doing here, buying clothes to flaunt her body, pretending that at her age she could find the youth she'd missed out on? Hearing the assistant returning she automatically folded her arms in an attempt to hide the offending part of her anatomy.

'I've brought Miss Davies with me; she is our professional corsetière.'

'Now then, madam, if you'll hold your arms out to your side . . .' and Miss Davies put her tape measure around Muriel. 'Now straight up, reach as high as you can.' And another measurement was taken, this time from under each breast to above it. 'You may be on the large side, madam, but many women would envy you. Your breasts are a good shape. You will find yourself so much more comfortable in a well-fitting brassiere and, apart from that, clothes are designed for the female form. First of all let's try this one.' And so it went on. For the first time in her life Muriel felt at ease with the 'encumbrance' she'd carried all her adult life. At last Miss Davies was satisfied – while Muriel's feelings were a cocktail of embarrassment and excitement. She felt that all eyes would be turned on her as her twin peaks stood out proudly in front of her. But there was no doubt that the tawny dress hung better; and there was no doubt, either, that the transformation had taken years from her.

'I think I'll keep it all on,' she said as she smoothed her long, capable hands down her slim waist. Quickly working out the cost she made another decision. 'I'll have three of the brassieres if you can pack the things all into one bag.'

Mrs Muriel Franklyn, dependent widow, had walked into the store; Muriel Franklyn, a woman to be reckoned with, emerged on to the High Street. She wished Georgie were at home; she was looking forward to seeing her reaction. But the house would be empty, and there would be no one to see the transformation. So she made another decision: she would go to the restaurant above the Olde Tudor Inn and have her lunch.

As she studied the menu she was aware that someone had come to the next table, but she didn't look up.

'Muriel, this is a delightful surprise.'

At the sound of James' voice she forgot the menu and felt like a child being caught out, dressing up in her mother's clothes – except that her own mother would never have flaunted her figure as Muriel felt she was doing. She wished she had kept her over-coat on; she even wished she had let them pack her new clothes so that she was still encased in the suit of armour that had been her defence for so long. Whatever must he be thinking? There was nothing new in her feeling old beyond her years, old and plain, but this was far worse.

'I'd been shopping and as there's no one at home to make lunch for, I thought I'd get something here. I didn't expect to see you.'

'This is where I always come. The food's reasonably good. You'll be glad when Georgie closes the gallery and is at home with you. But I tell you what, Muriel, say if you don't like the idea, if it makes more work for you, but how about if I drive back home at midday? I'd not have long in the house but it would be much more pleasant from my point of view than eating alone here.'

'More work? What rubbish. If you have a long enough break, it's a lovely idea. And soon Georgie will be there soon too.'

'Starting tomorrow, then,' he smiled. 'Meantime, did you come in here for peace and quiet or may I join you?'

As he sat down opposite her, she realized she was sitting a little straighter, and looking down it seemed to her that the twin points of her uplifted breasts must be apparent to everyone in the restaurant.

They had finished eating and were waiting for their coffee when he leant a little towards her and said quietly, 'You should wear that dress more often. I've not seen it before. You look lovely.'

This time there was no doubting the flush on her face; her whole body seemed to be on fire with embarrassment.

'Silly,' she growled, ashamed that she hadn't the grace to accept a compliment. What must he be thinking of her, a grown woman with so little self-confidence? So she rushed on, 'You've not seen it because this is its first airing; it's new.' Now why had she told him that? 'I came to town to buy a new frock, something to wear over Christmas. But when I tried it on I liked it so much that I asked the girl to wrap up my old one so that I could wear it straight away. Silly really; when Christmas comes I shall wish I'd waited.'

There was something about the honest way she talked that touched him. It was impossible not to compare today's Muriel with the dowdy creature who had just lost her husband. And yet there had been such dignity in her manner on that first acquaintance. Now, he added to her confusion by covering her hand with his when she started to open her purse to pay for her lunch.

'Please, allow me. The only thing that has been less than perfect about the surprise of our having lunch together is that the time has gone too fast.' Then, as the waiter took the note he passed and they stood up from the table, James took her coat from the stand (a coat with which he was familiar) and held it for her to put on. He looked her up and down, noting the shorter length of her skirt and the slim legs. 'I wish I had time to drive you home but I'm afraid I haven't. I have an appointment at two o'clock.'

'The walk will do me good after that lunch. Thank you, James. After my exciting morning, it really was the icing on the cake. Just wait until we tell Georgie this evening that you are planning to come home to lunch each day. She will be so glad. After her busy life at the school she must have found time hanging heavy with only me for company.'

'I look forward to it, too. Goodbye. See you around six o'clock.' With that he turned towards the council offices and she set out for her walk home. There would be a bus in twenty minutes or so, but she wanted the walk, she wanted to be by herself and indulge in reliving the last hour. It was as if she lived a dual role:

on the one hand she was Georgie's stepmother and James' efficient housekeeper, grateful for her part in the threesome; on the
other hand she was a love-starved, middle-aged woman, living
on dreams – dreams which bore no likeness to reality. Dreams
were safe; nothing could take them from her. Yet she wished he
hadn't said – and she seemed to hear his voice again as she strode
homeward – 'You look lovely.' The James who lived in her im-
aginary world might have spoken like that, but she didn't want
to hear it from Georgie's husband.

This would be the third time Georgie had driven home from
Tarnmouth ready to face an argument when she told James what
she meant to do. The first had been when she'd offered to take
over the closing of the shop; the second when she'd taken more
items for sale and decided to keep the doors open for trade until
the last day of the year. But this time was different; this was more
than just a few weeks.

'Another change of plans,' she announced to James and Muriel
while they were eating steak and kidney pie. Always a good cook,
this was something at which Muriel excelled. 'You remember that
Mr Fraser – he's the owner – intended to use both front rooms
of the property for his booking office? But this morning he called
in and when he saw some of the beautiful craftwork I could see
he was uneasy about there being no outlet for such talent, especially when the people who bring things for sale do so need the
money. I suggested to him that I should rent – not lease, just rent,
so that either of us could terminate the agreement at any time –
the rooms on the ground floor to the left of the entrance. That
leaves him a booking office and a small room behind where he
can keep his rods, nets and all his other clobber.'

Muriel looked uneasy. Whatever was the silly girl thinking
about? She seemed to forget she was a married woman now and
couldn't just make arrangements to live as though she had no
one to consider except herself. James had been so tolerant, but
surely now he would put his foot down. And what about his
decision to come home for lunch each day? She had been so
looking forward to that, but if Georgie weren't going to be here
then surely he wouldn't bother. It was selfish and naughty of
Georgie. She ought not to expect it of him; it wasn't fair.

After Georgie had dropped her bombshell, for a moment there was silence. Then James said, 'If that's what you want, then of course you must do it. But you can't think of it as a career to spend your days in a shop – for that's what it is, Georgie, and you'll find that more and more of your trade will come from handmade fancy goods and not paintings.'

'I expect that's true. But James, darling, I'm not looking for a career; if I were I wouldn't have got married. Anyway, I love it there.'

'The choice must be yours, of course, but you have a first-class brain and to my mind it'll be wasted. Looking after the place to help Mr Adams was one thing, but renting a shop for the benefit of these outworkers is something quite different.' Yet he didn't sound angry, something that surprised both Georgie and Muriel.

'I was telling you when you came in,' Muriel said persuasively to Georgie, 'James had suggested coming home for lunch each day. He was looking forward to it. You really ought to be here, dear.' She felt James' gaze was on her, but she avoided meeting his eyes.

Georgie's laugh was spontaneous. 'Oh, Muriel, as if James wants me to spoon-feed him his lunch. You don't mind, James, do you?'

'The truthful answer is no, I don't mind. The idea that you should arrange your day around the half-hour or so I shall be able to be in the house at lunchtime hadn't occurred to me.' Then, turning to Muriel with a friendly smile, he said, 'You'll feed me, won't you?'

'Silly man,' Muriel chuckled. 'But it's not *you* I was really thinking about, it was Georgie. Now that she's married she ought to want to spend her time in her home.' There! She'd made herself say it, made herself sound as if that's what she really wanted. But the truth was there in her mind, impossible to ignore. The thought of the lunchtime breaks she and James would share filled her with excitement laced with fear; they could be a dangerous combination of dreams and reality. With no one there but themselves there might be days when he would have time to stay and dry the dishes – or perhaps he would drive her into town to buy groceries. For a moment her imagination ran wild until she pulled it back into line.

What a miserable specimen of a woman she was, that the prospect of half an hour alone with her son-in-law (for that's what he was and she wasn't going to let herself forget it) could threaten to become the highlight of her days. If Georgie were home to make a third none of that would happen, for Georgie (*Bless her*, Muriel said to herself, trying to guide her thoughts back into line) would have her car and they would shop together. And what about those afternoons when she went to her room, locking the door behind her even though the house was empty? An afternoon rest was what she called it, but . . . No, no, she mustn't let her thoughts go down that road, not now, sitting at the table with him, and with Georgie there too. *Concentrate on the love they have for each other; be happy and thankful that dear Georgie fell in love with him — and he with her.*

When Georgie had arrived back from Tarnmouth, Muriel's new dress had been entirely covered with an overall, the kind that resembled a crossover sleeveless coat that tied securely around the waist. That's how she always dressed when she was cooking or cleaning. So that evening when Georgie followed her into the kitchen she was just about to slip her arms into it.

'Wait! Let me look at you. Muriel, you've bought a new dress — it's gorgeous. I didn't notice when we were out here before James came home, and I didn't mention it in front of him. Turn around. It's perfect. Perfect colour, perfect fit. You look so different. Is it the cut of the bodice or have you bought a really good bra?'

'Bra?' The abbreviation was new to Muriel.

'Brassiere. Gosh, you've got a figure like a film star.'

Muriel automatically held her arms in front of her chest. The habit of years died hard.

'I wanted to buy something to wear at Christmas. But when I got to the shop, the assistant was so helpful.' Then, her long face breaking into a smile that refused to be held back, she said, 'Oh, I wish you'd been there too. It was such fun. I've thrown my old bodices away. This is so comfortable I don't even know I'm wearing it.' Once started there was no stopping her. Automatically running the water for the dishes, she described the way the corsetière had measured her; she even confessed shame-facedly how much she had spent on her new undergarments.

'And worth every penny. You look lovely. It wouldn't be worth it for me, though,' Georgie chuckled. 'I've got almost nothing to put in it.'

'You don't know the times I've envied you. I have enough for both of us. All my adult life it has felt like an ugly great weight strapped to me. But, wearing this, it's like being free of it – until I look in the mirror and see a stranger. Anyway, I was telling you about my morning. I came out of the shop feeling like a new woman. That's when I decided to make the outing a real treat and go to the Olde Tudor and have some lunch. Coming back here to an empty house would have been a let down.'

'The Olde Tudor, surely that's where James eats at midday?'

'I didn't know that – not until he came in.' Was she apologizing?

'So you were able to have company. I bet he thought you looked pretty splendid. *One* dress is no good though; you'll have to go shopping again now we've seen this new transformed you. I wish I could come with you.'

'What about if I came over to your gallery? There must be a dress shop in Tarnmouth. And I'd love to see where you spend your days, see the craft things you have told us about.'

'I can understand why you love it here, Georgie.' Standing in the middle of the one-room gallery a few days later, Muriel slowly turned around as if that way she would absorb everything she saw. 'So much work, all of it done lovingly.'

'There's not much chance of anyone buying an oil painting with all the expense of Christmas, but these small things are shifting well. I tell you one thing, Muriel, it really takes the crow out of one to see what such ordinary people can do. Most of them have had no real training – but you just said it all, so much exquisite work and all done by people who love what they do.'

'And need the money, I'm sure. I really ought to buy something.'

Georgie laughed, looking at her with affection. 'Indeed you ought – but not here. You've come to Tarnmouth so that we can look at the dress shops. There are only two, and neither of them selling the quality of what you're wearing.' For nothing less than the tawny creation would have done for this outing. 'But we'll keep looking until we find what you want. Did you say you wanted to help me in here?'

'I'd love to. What can I do?'

'Can you dust each item carefully? When we have a wind like we did yesterday everything gets covered with dust even with the door and window closed. I'll see to the floors.'

It was an hour or so later – an hour in which they had sold a Christmas table centre decoration and three lace-edged handkerchiefs – when Muriel stood gazing out of the window where the Soames' work was displayed. Suddenly she shivered.

'Are you cold?'

'Not a bit. It's comfortably warm in here. A goose on my grave, isn't that what they say? Do you feel sometimes that everything is so good, so full of hope somehow, that it's not right, that it can't last?'

'Too introspective for me at this time of day,' Georgie answered with a laugh. 'Anyway there's no cloud on the horizon. And, Muriel, if Dad can see us now, I'm sure he must be happy. Perhaps it was Fate that you had to give up the old house. Just imagine if it had been his, not rented, and he had left it to you. You would have lived there trying to keep everything as it had been. No, I'm sure he must be glad that things worked out as they did. So just chase that goose away.'

Muriel nodded, shame and guilt almost bursting her bubble of happiness. Cyril had been gone no more than half a year and here she was with her mind taken up with her new image – and her secret dreams never including him.

'How about if you mind the shop for five minutes while I pop along to Mr Roberts? We need more coffee. If anyone comes to see if their things are sold, this is the book to look it up in. Or, if they bring anything for sale – well, you can size it up as well as I can. They usually decide how much they want to ask. I shan't be five minutes.'

It was a new experience for Muriel. When she heard the jangle of the bell on the outside door she had a moment's panic but by the time the customer came into the gallery she was composed and ready. The sale was only one last-minute Christmas card but it gave a boost to her confidence. Just imagine if someone should come in to buy a picture while Georgie was out! Of course, no one did. But she made up her mind that she would do her best to persuade James to come in on Saturday afternoon. If he could see the place he would feel so proud of what Georgie was doing, and it worried Muriel that he seemed to avoid coming to Tarnmouth. He really ought to take an interest; if he didn't it might drive a wedge between them. Today he had agreed to have his lunch as he used to at the Olde Tudor, but tomorrow he would come home and they'd eat together, just the two of them. She would have a talk to him and suggest that they made a surprise visit on Georgie. Pleased with the idea, she felt some of her earlier guilt fading.

But apparently James had other plans and had arranged a round of golf with a colleague from the Council on Saturday. So the idea faded and Muriel told herself she had no need to worry; it wasn't as if James wasn't proud and interested in the progress of the gallery.

So the old year ended and the new one started with Dominic moving into the rooms on the first floor and attic. Georgie heard the move going on, but she kept to her own quarters and the first she saw of Dominic was in the afternoon when he came out of the front door to find her on a pair of steps fixing a sign to the lintel over the window of the front room on her side of the property.

'Here, let me do that. You should have called me; you knew I was indoors somewhere.'

'I can manage. I like to do things for myself.'

'Maybe you do,' he answered, 'but one false move and you could find yourself starting off your business with a broken leg – or neck.' She hesitated, not wanting to admit that the weight of the sign was making her task well nigh impossible. 'Come on now, Mrs Bartlett. I'm a lot taller than you are.'

She knew he was right, but there was little grace in the way she gave in. 'The steps weren't high enough.'

'True,' he said, his eyes shining with laughter. Then, taking the sign from her and giving it his full attention, he said, 'This is a good sign. Where did you get it done? I didn't think there was a signwriter in Tarnmouth.'

'Where?' she repeated. 'In the room behind the gallery. Is it all right, really?

'You did it yourself? Of course, I might have guessed. I forgot you're an artist. Although this is a different talent. Now then, can you pass me the first screw? We must be sure we get it absolutely central and straight.'

'I've marked where the screws have to go,' she answered in a voice that brooked no argument. Then, telling herself that at least she had scored one small point, she did as he said; but some of the excitement she'd felt at the success of the sign had evaporated. He'd bought two of her pictures and through the window of his side of the building she had seen where he had hung them behind his desk and yet he seemed to have forgotten that it was she who had painted them.

The job was soon done and he folded the steps and started back into the room behind the gallery, the obvious and only place they could be kept.

Then he turned to her with a smile that told her it had nothing to do with politeness and everything to do with enjoyment. 'Mrs Bartlett,' he said, 'how about we do a bit of bartering?'

'Bartering? You mean about me working for you taking bookings? But I though we had that sorted.'

'Indeed we have. This is something that has just come to me. Not true – actually it came to me outside when you told me you had made your own sign. How many fish suppers would it be worth for you to do something along the same lines for the booking office? This time of year I fish most days when the sea conditions permit.'

'I don't need you to catch our supper. If you want a sign like the one we've just put up, yes, I'll happily do it for you. In fact I'd rather do it and know they were a proper pair than have you find a signwriter who might put my effort into the shade.'

'Would the lady be looking for compliments?'

They were two adult people, people who had never met except on a business level. Yet, standing in that little kitchen-cum-workroom-cum-everything else, they held each other's gaze and both laughed. It had nothing to do with anything that had been said, and everything to do with sudden and inexplicable happiness. For both of them it was the beginning of something new and, in that moment, she knew her initial animosity towards him had gone and that even though they would probably see very little of each other, they would have a comfortable association from now on.

'You must tell me what you want put on it. It's no use simply saying Booking Office.'

'Sounds like a theatre,' he agreed, the laughter still lingering behind his eyes. 'What about simply putting my name, then underneath in smaller lettering "Book Here for All Day Pleasure or Fishing Trips"? Too many words? Could you do that? What was the exact size of your wood? I'll get something cut just the same. Sure you don't mind?'

'You seem to forget I have a personal interest. Part of my rent is in the work I do for the booking office.' Then, realizing what he might understand from her words, she felt every bit as hot and embarrassed as poor Muriel sometimes did. 'I didn't mean that the way it sounded. I meant I want to feel the two businesses can run comfortably in harness.' Was that better or worse? Would he think that despite her being married she was chasing after him for friendship? 'I mean . . .'

Why did she feel he was enjoying her discomfort? He didn't smile as he assured her, 'I know just what you mean,' in an understanding voice, and yet she could see from his eyes that he was enjoying the situation.

'Anyway,' she tried to change the subject, turning away from him to write something down, 'this is the size of the wood. Get that cut and I'll do my best.'

'And I promise you I'll remember those fish suppers. Just you and your husband, or have you any family?'

She wished he hadn't asked. Wasn't he even interested enough to remember that when he commented on her name being Bartlett yet she signed her pictures GF she had explained that she had only been married a few months?

'My stepmother lives with us, so there are three. But you don't have to give me fish you catch. Out of season, when you can't be getting much trade, you'd be better to take your catch to the local fishmonger.' She knew it wasn't said out of kindness so much as her need to take him down a peg or two. Only a few minutes ago they had been working together amicably, talking like friends. Now she felt she understood exactly why the boatmen at the harbour didn't accept him as one of them. Did he realize it, she wondered, or had he so much self-confidence that it would never occur to him? 'I must get on, I have some letters to write,' she lied by way of escape. 'Thank you, Mr Fraser, for putting up my sign.'

'My pleasure, Mrs Bartlett. I say, if we are to work side by side wouldn't it be better if we dispensed with all this Mr and Mrs rubbish? I'm Dominic and you're . . .?'

'Georgie.'

'That's very masculine, surely, for someone so feminine?'

Why couldn't she simply smile her thanks at the compliment? Instead she needed to talk, to hide her unease from him in chatter.

'My parents were dead set on having a boy — George Samuel he was to be called. Instead, they got me, Georgina Samantha. I've always been just Georgie.'

'I was only pulling your leg about it sounding masculine. Georgie suits you remarkably well,' he said, his gaze taking in her short curly hair and boyish figure. 'So, my friend Georgie, you know what to do if anyone comes in to book a fishing trip? The price lists are self-explanatory — a price for the trip, then additional charges if they rent equipment. OK? Seas permitting, I go out on turn of the tide — the Tide Table is on the desk.'

'It's all perfectly clear. Are you taking anyone this morning?'

'No. There's seldom much doing at this time of year, but I like to get out there anyway. In fact — don't tell the punters — but I prefer it on my own. Get a bit of a swell on and some of them can't take it. How are you on the water?'

'I learnt the rudiments of sailing, but never on the sea. We lived inland, so it was on the river. Dad taught me to sail. He loved the water and, with Mum having died, he had to look after me. We did everything together, even after he remarried. I was nine then. Soon after that, our little boat had to be laid to rest. It needed more work on it than we could afford so our sailing days came to an end.'

'What you learn as a child you never forget. Maybe you'd like to come out and cast a line some time?'

'I would love to. But, you forget I have a gallery to run — and a booking office, too.'

'There are Sundays.'

'I have a very tolerant husband, but our Sundays are precious.'

He was gazing at her thoughtfully, but what his thoughts were she couldn't guess. 'Yes, of course. I should have remembered you have a husband. Not many married women would want to leave home each morning as early as you must have to, then spend the entire day here. But how about this, my friend Georgie: in January most folk haven't money for non-essentials, so for you it must be a slack period just as it is for me. We'll pick a calm day then lock the place up and play hooky. What do you say?'

'We'll play it as it comes. But I don't possess anything suitable to wear for fishing at sea.'

'You must familiarize yourself with the stock I have in the back room for hiring out. Probably too big for you, but the oilskins will keep the cold and wet out. Now I must get togged out and get on the water. I may look in later. You're OK about everything?'

'I doubt if I shall get any bookings for you; the place seems dead.'

And so it remained for the whole of that day. Neither the butcher nor the fishmonger opened on a Monday and the gulls looked like getting a supper of buns which by morning would have become rock hard.

Tempted by a morning of calm water and winter sunshine, when a few days later she saw Dominic pass her front window on his way to the main door, involuntarily she felt a rush of excitement. Would he suggest that this was the day? She waited, listening for the sound of his step in the passage.

Instead, she heard him say, 'Let me help. I'll hold the door wide open. You must be Mr and Mrs Soames; I've been looking forward to meeting you.'

Georgie's spontaneous reaction was disappointment, quickly followed by shame as she imagined her friends' never failing pleasure in coming. Sometimes she had some money for them, but since Christmas there had been almost no trade. Either way, they never let their disappointment show. Now Dominic opened the inner door to the gallery and ushered Alice in.

'Friends for you, Georgie. But I'm borrowing Mr Soames for five minutes. I want to see if he can help me over a case for my little boat.'

As the door closed on them, Georgie glanced at Alice then quickly away again. The look of joy and hope wasn't for the world to see.

'Mr Fraser saw us coming and waited to speak to us outside. That carved boat Barry made, he says he wants a showcase to hang on the wall between your two pictures. He told us they were yours. Just think, Georgie, what it will do for Barry if he can take on an outside job like that. I know he loves doing his carvings, but they are always a reminder that he can't earn what you'd call "outside money" like he used to when he worked.'

'You never know, Alice, one job might lead to another.' Georgie wanted to keep the spirit of hope alive, but how many people would be likely to bring work his way? 'I've had almost no one even browsing in here since Christmas, so there's nothing waiting for you, I'm afraid.'

'Not to worry.' It was said with a little too much brightness. 'The sunshine is free and just look at the morning!'

That's just what Georgie had been doing as she'd decided to lock the gallery if Dominic suggested a fishing trip. Before she had a chance to answer, however, Dominic threw open the door, a broad smile on his face.

'Get kitted out, friend Georgie. Barry has agreed to man the booking office – in the unlikely event of anyone being tempted by the calm forecast. If Mrs Soames – or Alice if I may? – will do the same in here . . .'

'Will you, Alice? I don't know what Dominic has arranged with Barry, but my terms are the same for the gallery. If anyone brings anything in, use your discretion – or your tact if it's not suitable – and make sure they name their own price. If anyone buys anything book it down in that exercise book. It's unlikely that you'll get any callers at all; the place is dead. Will you do that for me?'

Alice had felt that today was going to be special, but whatever she'd envisaged it hadn't been that she and Barry would be left in charge. Her long, thin face lost its normal worried expression as it broke into a smile that took years off her.

'You leave it to us. You've explained to Barry about the booking side, Mr Fraser?'

'Dominic, not Mr Fraser. Yes, he's quite happy. Off you go, Georgie, and get kitted out. It's just gone ten thirty; we'll be on the water before eleven. A couple of hours and then, how about if, when we've got *Tight Lines* moored in the harbour, we stop off at Bert Crisp's and pick up fish and chips for our lunch? Can you get the table ready upstairs, Alice?'

'That's very kind, but . . .' Glancing at the door into the passageway to make sure Barry was out of earshot, she said, 'Not stairs.'

'Ah! No, of course. Then what about the room behind here, can that be sorted so that four of us can get round the little table? Bring down anything you want from upstairs.'

The morning was taking on a party atmosphere and by the time he and Georgie left the Soames in charge and set off towards the harbour they felt as excited as a pair of children offered a sudden treat. And treat it proved to be. Her understanding of the sails remained the same whether on the river or the sea, but nothing she had experienced in her childhood had the thrill of cutting through the waves and hearing the sharp slap of canvas in the breeze. Although at a glance the sea looked calm, there was quite a swell and Dominic kept a wary eye on her; so many of those he took out started well until the boat was stationary. But Georgie proved to be different. She loved every second; she baited her own hooks and her skill in casting was evidence that her father had taught her well. She played the fish as well as anyone Dominic had taken out and then, having retrieved the hook, either threw the catch back if it was too small or despatched it with one sharp and positive knock.

'You're no novice,' Dominic said with admiration.

'*On* the sea, I am. But I used to fish with Dad from the pier.' She chuckled, remembering. 'What the other fishermen must have made of us, I can't imagine. My mother died when I was very young, as I told you, so there was just Dad and me. Before I even started school we always had a week in Hastings at the beginning of September for the fishing competitions; all I was capable of was holding the rod and hoping, but you've no idea how proud I was to be there doing the same as him. He taught me how to thread a worm on to the hook; how to get the hook out of a fish's mouth and put it out of its misery if it was big enough to eat, or throw it back if it wasn't. I wish you could have known him. He really taught me all I know – well, all the important things I know.'

'Is your husband a fisherman? Would he be interested in coming out?'

The question came as a surprise to her. 'Isn't that strange? I've no idea.'

At that moment there was a tug on Dominic's line and he started to reel the fish towards the boat.

'Feels like a good fish,' he said. 'Can you hold the net ready?'

She did as he said, memories crowding back of just such occasions on Hastings pier. She guided the net under the fish with a slick movement that showed she'd done it plenty of times before.

'A bass,' she shouted, 'a lovely bass.'

They both had the idea at the same moment: lunch for four.

'I'll gut and fillet it,' Dominic said, getting to work as he spoke. 'I reckon Bert Crisp will fry it for us. What do you think?'

'I think we have a cheek to ask it of him, but this is Tarnmouth – it's not like other places.' Watching the deft way he worked, listening to the screech of the gulls as they swooped to catch the tasty morsels he was throwing back into the sea, she gave an involuntary shiver.

'Not cold, are you?'

She shook her head. 'No. It just hit me. All this: the gentle motion of the boat, the sound of the gulls, the nostalgic smell that belongs to fishing. This has been a very special morning.'

He nodded. 'Do you wonder that this is where I escape to at every opportunity? We'll do it again, Georgie.'

She nodded. Yes, she was sure they would. But nothing could hit her with the impact of this first time.

'There, the bass is ready for cooking. Let's make for the shore and see if we can persuade Bert Crisp to do the honours. He ought to be glad we are supplying our own fish, all he needs to do is add the batter and fry it.'

They sailed back into the harbour, tied up *Tight Lines* then deposited all their gear in Dominic's large shed before making their way to the fish and chip shop.

'He might refuse to cook what we bring for ourselves,' she ventured.

'Bet you a pound to a penny he won't. You go on back and tell them that they are about to have a fresh-from-the-sea lunch. There's no oven in that back room of yours, so go up to the kitchen and warm four plates. Then put the "closed" sign on the door so that we can eat undisturbed. Let's hope the Soames enjoyed their morning; then they might like to do it again.'

Half an hour later it struck Georgie how different this lunchtime was from the way it would be at Gregory House. Even though James would be at home for no more than about three quarters of an hour yet because Muriel would have everything prepared to time with his arrival, their meal would be eaten in a tranquil atmosphere. The table would be set with the same care as she always showed – cutlery placed precisely, white damask napkins in silver rings, cut-glass tumblers that radiated shafts of lights as the sun shone on them.

In the little room behind the gallery the scene couldn't have been more different. Georgie had heated the plates in the oven of Dominic's kitchen, then, holding them in a cloth to save burning her hands, had run down the stairs with them as soon as she heard Dominic arrive. Wearing its golden overcoat of batter the bass looked as appetizing as it smelt as it was served direct from its wrapping of greaseproof with a thick outer covering of newspaper.

'I found this in your cupboard,' Georgie said, putting a bottle of ordinary malt vinegar on the table. 'You don't mind, do you?'

'Good girl,' Dominic said approvingly. 'I'll fetch two more chairs. You'd rather sit to table on an ordinary one than stay in your own, I expect, Barry?'

'I usually stay in this one, but if you'll give me a lift I'd really like to get my knees under the table the same as the rest of you to enjoy this treat. My, but it makes you hungry just to smell it.'

From the eager way they took up their knives and forks, it was clear they all agreed with him. Looking round the little room with its assortment of picture frames stacked against one wall, an empty easel next to them and a second easel bearing a canvas with Georgie's half finished painting of the beach and pier, Georgie was aware of an unfamiliar feeling of contentment. There was nothing phoney about these people or this place. As if by contrast she remembered her years at St Winifred's. Her glance met Alice's and she knew the moment was leaving its indelible mark on her, too. These three were comparative strangers and yet she was completely relaxed and comfortable with them. Unexpectedly she seemed to feel her father's presence. *That's stupid*, she told herself. Or was it? *Just imagine if he were here with us, he'd be talking, laughing, delighting in the adventure of such a makeshift meal; and this morning, out there on the boat, how he would have loved that.*

Alice had already put a kettle on the gas ring, and while Dominic lifted Barry back into his wheelchair and the two of them returned to the booking office, she insisted on washing up. Georgie took the 'closed' sign down from the front door then opened it to look along the esplanade, smiling to herself to find that she was following in Mr Adams' footsteps. Just as he had, she hoped to see a customer bearing down on her. The morning sunshine had given way to the raw cold of a dull January after-noon and, although she looked in both directions, there was no one in sight.

'I must tell you about my day,' she said as Muriel put the soup tureen on the table that evening. 'It was such a bright morning, I was really tempted when Dominic Fraser suggested I should go with him on his fishing boat. And at that very moment the Soames arrived . . .' And so the whole day was described, her story ending with, 'He – Dominic Fraser – asked if you enjoyed fishing, James. He thought another time you might like to catch our supper.'

'That's most kind of him. But fishing has never appealed to me. Of course, I like the end product. But I'll leave you to do the honours and bring it from the sea. Will the Soames hold the fort for you again, do you suppose?'

No wonder she beamed at him across the table. There wasn't a jealous or possessive thought in James' head; not that there was any cause for one, but some husbands would have resented a wife wanting to do more with her days than make a home. Glancing at Muriel, the question came into her head: *more* or would it be seen as *less*? There must be thousands of women, just like Muriel, who thrived in caring for their families and who would hate to rush off each morning, forsaking the ordered routine of home.

Winter gales blew from the north-east, the angry sea crashed across the esplanade. Even on the end of the pier no one fished. *Tight Lines* stayed safely moored in the shelter of the harbour while Dominic spent his days working on *Blue Horizon*, his pleasure boat. One thing about cold winter days, it gave the craft workers a chance to build a stock to be taken to the gallery ready for Easter and the first influx of day trippers. With only one room for pictures and craft goods alike, Georgie climbed the ladder and put in more tacks so that the paintings could be hung in two rows instead of one. She had finished her picture of Tarnmouth beach and pier and, with her easel set up in the centre of the floor of the gallery in the hope that anyone passing might see her at work and be tempted in, she started work on a scene created from her memory of her morning fishing on *Tight Lines*. Her initial sketches were on the pad lying on the desk.

She was at her easel one morning in early March, when a stranger entered.

'I've come in the wrong half, but the other side looks empty. Do you know when Dominic will be back? Ought I to have gone down to the harbour?' There was something about the woman that reminded Georgie of Dominic – yet that must be nonsense, she told herself. How could this tall, sophisticated, expensively dressed woman have anything in common with bearded, casually scruffy Dominic Fraser? Perhaps it was in her manner, or her well-modulated voice.

'I look after the booking office for him when he's out. But, with seas like this I'm afraid the boat can't go out.'

The stranger laughed. 'And, if it could, you wouldn't get me riding the waves,' she said. 'You must be Mrs Bartlett; he has told me about you and the gallery. I'm Priscilla Fraser, Dominic's mother.' She held out her hand.

Georgie took it in her own, first checking to see hers had no spatters or smears of paint. A formal greeting, but they were instantly at ease with each other.

'I'm disturbing your work.'

'I'm here to be disturbed. To be truthful I planted myself where I was visible through the window in the hope that someone might come in. I'm so sorry Dominic isn't here; he hasn't been in much since the weather broke. I think he's working on *Blue Horizon*.'

'I spent the night near Winchford with one of my authors—'

'Your authors?'

'We're publishers. Didn't he tell you? It never appealed to him. I make pretence of being disappointed, but to be truthful he wouldn't have been happy. He's a free spirit, he always has been.'

'A free spirit . . . not many people have the opportunity. Have you time for a coffee? I was thinking of making one when you came.'

'I'd like that. While you're making it can I look around in here? He tells me you have some very lovely wood carvings.'

Five minutes later, Georgie came back with a tray carrying a percolator of aromatic coffee, two cups and saucers and a plate of biscuits.

'I've been enjoying myself prowling around. It amazes me how much talent there must be around us without our realizing. Tarnmouth is an ordinary enough little town, so I suspect most places must be the same. This crocheted tablecloth is like gossamer. Imagine the hours someone has sat making it. I'd like to buy it, if I may. But Mrs Bartlett – when Dominic phones he refers to you as Georgie, so may I do the same?' As Georgie murmured her smiling consent, she went on, 'But, Georgie, I'll tell you what has really taken my eye. On the desk here you have your sketch pad.' She started to laugh as she gazed at it. 'This caricature of Dominic, it is *so good*. What does he think of it?'

'I've not shown it to him. I just do them for fun. If you look back you'll see all sorts – people who have brought their work in for sale.'

'Umph.' She gazed at the pad, deep in thought. Her next words took Georgie by surprise.

Five

'I was telling you, my husband and I are involved in publishing. I handle the children's section and, as you can imagine, pictures are as important as the written word for small children. Have you a family?'

'No. I've not long been married.'

'So I don't expect you've come across the *Freddie the Fisherman* series. Freddie has endeared himself to today's generation of under-fives with his escapades, in no small way due to the illustrations. Unfortunately the artist has decided to give up his career and go into the Church. I tried to talk him out of it, but there is no greater lost cause than a man who believes he has a mission. These caricatures have life. I wonder, Georgie, if I were to send you a copy of the manuscript of Freddie's latest adventures – and one or two of the little books already published so that you can see the sort of thing that's needed – would you consider taking on the drawings?'

'Why, of course I'd love to do it – if you think I'd be good enough. I've only ever done things like that –' she indicated the drawings in her pad – 'just for fun.'

'And that's what it should be – fun. Make the characters people the young will enjoy. You'll give it a go? The manuscript is short, of course, so if you'll read it and do some specimen drawings for me to show Maurice Crawford, the writer, then we'll go from there.'

'I had no idea Dominic came from a publishing background,' Georgie mused as they sipped their coffee in easy companion-ship. 'But then, why should he have told me? I've never talked to him about my past either.'

'I called him a free spirit. Well, that's just a part of it. He has never been indolent. He worked well at school, read English at Cambridge, then, just when his father and I were thinking he'd soon join us in the business, he dropped his bombshell that he had heard the call of freedom.' She said it with affection. 'Luckily for him my father had left him quite comfortably off, money that had been held in trust until he was twenty-one. By the time he finished at Cambridge he was able to get his hands on it. And who can blame him for listening to that silent voice telling him there was a wide world out there waiting to be conquered?'

'Taking day-trippers to sea or on fishing trips from Tarnmouth is hardly what I'd describe as answering the call of the wide world. Surely you must have been disappointed?'

'One lesson I have learnt is never to think I know best when it comes to how folk like to organize their lives. He was just twenty-two when he sailed off into the unknown. We had letters from wherever he put into port – Marseilles, Aden, Port Elizabeth – then nothing until something arrived from Goa. He wasn't just escaping work; he did all sorts of jobs. He was away a couple of years that time and when he came back, as his father said, he stayed just about long enough to change his shirt. Then off he went again. He bought a sailing boat and hired a crew of three, crossed the Atlantic, got a job working off Newfoundland with the cod fishermen for a season, then sailed down the eastern coast, through the Panama Canal and into the Pacific.'

'Still with the same crew? They must have felt like family after so long.' But why had he never told her any of this? She felt surprisingly hurt even though reason told her that his life was no more her concern than hers was his.

'No. His crew were just hired for the trip out; they left him when they reached Newfoundland. I think he took on a couple of men for the next leg of the trip, but I don't know. He sold the boat in Vancouver and trained northward to some remote place whose name escapes me, but still in British Columbia. Timber country, you know. He worked in the lumber trade; he must have been there about nine months, right through a northern winter. I can't imagine anything worse! But when spring came he bought a truck and drove east beyond the Rockies into prairie country where he got agricultural work in the wheat lands. Then a couple of years ago he took us by surprise and just walked in on us. He had come home as part of the crew on a merchant ship.'

'Did he think he was ready to join the business?' But how could he ever be? The sea was in his blood.

'We waited and said nothing, giving him space. Then he drove off early one morning and didn't get back until midnight. He'd set the wheels in motion for his next project: he'd arranged to buy this property and he'd fallen in love with a pleasure boat that was for sale in Tarnmouth Harbour. If he'd not been sure of his next move until that day, suddenly stumbling on this little town made it crystal clear to him.'

'You must be the world's most understanding mother,' Georgie said, topping up their cups. It took a conscious effort to keep her tone light. He never stayed anywhere, so how soon would it be before he announced he had his sight fixed on far horizons?

'The dearer a person is to you, the more willing you are to stand back and keep your words of advice to yourself. We none of us know what is right for someone else.' Then, her change of tone putting Dominic's affairs behind them, 'And it seems this place is right for you – or so I understand.'

So it was Georgie's turn to talk of the past and what had brought her to where she now was. There were some things better not said, so she didn't mention the lead-up to her father's accident or her fears that even the strongest friendship could never be the right base for marriage. Of course those fears had been groundless; she and James had a wonderful relationship . . . Dear James. As a friend she had loved him; now, as a husband, her love had widened as their intimate understanding of each other grew.

'—go to the harbour and find him,' Priscilla was saying.

'He won't be back yet. He was going to the timber merchant this morning with a list of measurements. He is replacing some of the fitments in *Blue Horizon* to smarten it up ready for the season.'

'Then, my dear, I'll get on the road. I thought I'd make a detour and pop in to see Maurice Crawford and tell him the good news that I believe I have found just the talent he needs to bring his stories to life. I'm sorry not to have seen Dominic. But it's my own fault; I ought to have let him know I was coming. But I wanted just to arrive and see what everyday life in Tarnmouth is like.' She paid for the crocheted cloth, which Georgie had wrapped ready. 'On my way out can I just go up and see his rooms? I'm not trying to see whether he makes his bed properly – if at all. I'd just like to have a picture of it in my mind.' She was gone a minute or two, then when she came down she opened the door of the booking office and glanced around, nodding approvingly. 'You know something, Georgie?' she said as the two of them stood in the open front doorway. 'I've been in London for getting on for forty years; I'm a hard-nosed business woman, yet I can understand the appeal of this little town. What is it, do you think?'

'For me it's its honesty; it doesn't pander to trippers with ice-cream kiosks, shops selling 'presents from Tarnmouth' and spades and buckets. If you want an ice cream you go to the general shop where Mrs Briggs makes her own, or else you wait for the ice-cream man on his tricycle to come on his round. Look along the esplanade and what do you see? The local butcher, the baker, a draper's shop and, next to that, a wet fish shop, Mrs Briggs' general store with a post office counter, Mr Haynes the barber with his pole over the front door, a fish and chip shop and then, in the other direction, an ordinary greengrocery with its crates on the pavement, and beyond that a funny little cinema where every evening a certain Miss Hunt plays the piano in the interval just as she has since the days when it showed silent films. It's an unpretentious, living small town high street, except that on the other side of the road is the beach.'

Priscilla was watching her as she talked but her expression gave no hint of what was in her mind as she looked at the young woman who had made Dominic change his plans about what he had intended to do with the property.

The remainder of the day was as uneventful as might be expected, for no one ventured out during a winter storm unless it was essential. So promptly at five o'clock, Georgie locked the door and went home, keen to tell her news about the new string to her bow in the form of Fisherman Freddie and his friends.

'My dear, that's splendid!' James looked at her with pride. 'Who knows where it might lead; there may be other writers out there who will want you to cooperate with them. There's no doubt you have talent. This person is Mr Fraser's mother, you say? If she finds your work is well received, other things may come your way.'

Georgie took his hand, her fingers gripping his, her eyes shining with excitement as she looked up at him. Dear James, his pride and pleasure in her accomplishment was plain to see. Muriel looked from one to the other, nodding approvingly. Then without warning or encouragement, into Georgie's memory came the story of where Dominic's free spirit had led him. And so it would tempt him away again. Surely she ought to hope that that would be the way it would go, for then he would let her rent the whole of the ground floor for her gallery. Wasn't that exactly what she had wanted in the first place? So why did the thought of the future suddenly leave her with such an empty feeling? While he followed where his free spirit led him, she would become just one more person he had encountered on his travels, left behind to create illustrations for someone else's stories, to paint her seascapes and sell handmade crafts. Three months ago if she had been told that 'Sinbad the Sailor' never stayed anywhere long enough to take roots, she would have been filled with hope that that would be exactly how the future would be. Where was the logic in his wanderlust giving her this feeling of hopelessness – or was it jealousy? In the weeks she had been at the gallery her life had held purpose. It was nothing to do with Dominic, not Dominic as a person, she told herself. *If it were I'd soon pull myself out of it.* As if one could compare feckless, fun-loving Dominic with James. No, it had nothing to do with Dominic as a person, but everything to do with freedom, being able to follow where the spirit beckoned. Then her mind took a sideways leap and she imagined Alice and Barry Soames; materially they had so little, yet really they had everything. She was ashamed, and to assuage some of her guilt she carried James' hand to her lips.

'You're a lucky girl,' Muriel said to her later while James was in the study going through some papers he'd brought home and handwriting the agenda for the monthly council meeting so that it could be typed and put out to the members the next day. 'So much of your thought goes to the gallery and now there is this extra work. You know what I wish, Georgie? I wish you could tell me you were pregnant. Just think what a difference that would make to your life; you wouldn't need always to be chasing around outside the home.'

Georgie laughed. 'I don't think James sees me as a stay-at-home mother. Or, if he does, he's in for a disappointment.'

'I would have given my eye teeth to have a baby when Cyril and I got married. But he made sure it didn't happen.' Was James making equally sure, she wondered, half expecting Georgie to follow the subject. But Georgie said nothing.

With the first hint of spring in the air the first trickle of Sunday visitors came to Tarnmouth. The shopkeepers had to look on as people wandered the length of the esplanade where the only establishment to be open was Mrs Huntley's Tearoom at the far end where the esplanade sloped away into Quay Hill. But Kitty Huntley wasn't the only trader to make the most of the opportunity. At the top of Quay Hill was a board announcing: THIS WAY TO THE HARBOUR WHERE *FAR HORIZON* WILL SAIL FOR A TWO-HOUR TRIP AT TWO P.M. FARES PAYABLE ON-BOARD.

'The first trip of the season yesterday,' Dominic told Georgie when he looked in to see if there were any bookings for *Tight Lines*. 'Only eight people so it was hardly worth the fuel, but summer's on its way, Georgie. How are the illustrations going?'

'If you can hold the fort for me for five minutes, I'll post them off to your mother. Do you think they look OK?'

He looked through the pile of pictures, chuckling at the expressions on some of the faces.

'Not being on familiar terms with Fisherman Freddie and his mates, I can't give an opinion. But there's personality in each of those faces. My bet is the author will be delighted. You've worked fast.'

'I like to work fast.'

He nodded. 'You and me, both. Take too much time, get too comfortable, and the rut gets deeper.'

'Are you in a rut?' She wished she hadn't asked. Supposing he said he was, supposing he said that he had to get out of it before it got too deep. But what if he did? They had learnt to work comfortably enough together ('comfortably' – there was that threatening word again), but she must never let herself overlook his arrogant assurance that his life must take no account of anyone except himself and his own desires.

He considered her question, but when he answered his tone was casual. 'So-so,' he said with a shrug. 'Mother tells me she gave you an account of my travels. A rolling stone gathering no moss, is that what you think?'

'No,' she answered. If he was waiting for her to try to persuade him to ignore his wanderlust and stay where he was, then he would find himself disappointed. 'Is it moss or cobwebs we gather if we stay forever in one place, looking ahead and knowing what next week, next month or even next year will bring?'

Perching on the edge of the table-cum-desk he gazed at her, his eyes shining with mischief. 'Come, come, now. Can that be the voice of a bride of only months? You know what, my friend Georgie? I believe you and I have one thing in common: staying power isn't amongst our virtues – if, indeed, it is a virtue. Just look out of that window, see how high the sky is this morning. Life is a gift that should be *lived*; it's not a series of months and years to be got through while we count our blessings for the material wealth we accrue.'

'You make it sound so simple. We all have responsibilities to other people. Don't we? And if you choose to spend your life chasing rainbows, how will you end up? Probably alone and lonely.'

He laughed. 'Now take a deep breath and say all that again sounding as if you believe it. Have you never felt the urge to escape, to wander lonely as a cloud? The truth, now.'

'Often. I know solitude isn't the same as loneliness. I love solitude; I believe anyone who paints must do. But would I love it if I were really alone, no one at home with a welcome, no one to want to hear how my day has been?'

'Ah, but my dear Georgie, you have a husband.'

Georgie realized it hadn't been James she had in mind, but Muriel.

'Anyway, no doubt you will follow your inclination one of these days,' she said, choosing to ignore his reference to her marriage. 'In the meantime, I must take advantage of your being here and slip along to the post office.' As she talked she put her letter and the sketches into a stout envelope. 'Weather permitting you have two takers for a fishing trip tomorrow. You'll see it in the book.'

The post office was empty, so she was back in a couple of minutes.

'OK, I'm back,' she called through the open doorway to the booking office.

'You know, Georgie, I've been thinking: those drawings you've sent off were good – good for the children's book they are to illustrate, but more than that. So, I'll put my thoughts to you to mull over. Another few weeks and there will be the usual influx of holidaymakers – and there is damn all for them to do in the evenings. Not warm enough to sit in the deck chairs, if the tide's up there's nowhere to walk except the street. When you close, why don't you put your easel up in front of the pier? That's about the only place for visitors to go – although once they've seen the show there's precious little for them to do.'

'There's housey-housey.'

'Three cheers! Listen to my idea and tell me what you think. Folk aren't that flush with money nor yet are they confident to spend their savings, with the way things are going on the Continent.'

She frowned. 'Adolf Hitler, you mean? You don't honestly believe he's got his sights set on England?'

It was out of character for Dominic to look so serious.

'Do you ever listen to the wireless, hear the ranting and raving of his speeches and hear the wild, almost hysterical, excitement of the people? It's been building for ages, like a . . . a boil. Festering, growing bigger; it will never die down of its own accord, it will have to be lanced. This year, next year, five years time? I don't know, Georgie, but I'm sure it's at the back of folks' minds. And human nature being what it is, they try to hang on to their material security as if that will protect them. Anyway, I was talking about my idea.' But Georgie couldn't so easily put behind her what he had said. 'The B & B houses will fill up like they do every year, but if you're looking to sell oil paintings I fear you will be disappointed. Now sketches, caricatures, something that costs no more than a shilling or two, that would be something for them to take home and show their friends, something that would always evoke the spirit of their holiday.'

'You think so?' It was impossible not to get a buzz of excitement. 'I could put a sign on the window.'

'Better than that! You could set up your easel in front of the
pier in the evenings; that's when people are just wandering like
lost souls. I bet you a pound to a penny you'd get your first sitter
in minutes. Get one, and others would follow. I'd even sit for you
myself to start the ball rolling. Mr Sinbad, eh?'

She felt hot and embarrassed and sure he was aware and
enjoying the situation. All her old animosity came to the surface.
Renting his rooms didn't give him the right to pry into her
things!

'You've been looking at my sketch pad,' she accused him, imagining her sketch with the words Mr Sinbad below and finding
no humour in the situation.

'Guilty ma'am,' he chuckled, seemingly unaware of her
displeasure. 'Don't imagine I didn't know that's what they call me
down in the harbour. Ought I to mind? I'm afraid I don't. They're
good chaps, every last man of them, all of them local. They're a
close-knit community, I'm an outsider, and I don't expect them
to draw me into their circle. If I decide to stay a while here, I
hope that after they know me better they will come to see I'm
no different from the rest of them.'

'It's partly your own fault, you know. You can have a very arrogant manner. And because you don't speak like they do they think
you are giving yourself airs and graces and consider yourself too
good for them.'

He shrugged. 'Anyway, it's not me we're discussing; it's you. Is
your husband sitting at home waiting for you in the evenings?
Do you have to forget Tarnmouth and be a good housewife
preparing his dinner? The delights of married life are outside my
ken.'

'Clearly,' she answered coldly. 'If I were to tell James that that's
what I wanted to do, then he would give me his support. Just as
he has for everything I've done here.' *No, not everything*, came the
silent reminder; *there was no support when I wanted to bring my
pictures for Mr Adams to try and sell in the first instance.* Owning the
business herself had made it acceptable. 'Summer is weeks away
yet. The only visitors are those who drive out for the day on
Sundays.'

'Food for thought though, don't you agree?'

'Why should I want to start something else, having spent the day in the gallery? Would you want to take a second boatload out in the evening? It's the same thing.'

Again he shrugged his shoulders, as if to indicate he was bored with the topic.

'I'll go and check the bookings, and then I'm off for an hour or two on *Tight Lines*. Not such a bad life, is it?'

With a shingle beach and no more than a few feet of sand even during spring tides there was little to attract families with children to Tarnmouth. So, while some popular resorts had to wait until the school holidays for their season to start, this unpretentious little town welcomed a small but steady stream from about the beginning of June onwards. Trade at the gallery picked up and Georgie decided to stay open until six o'clock instead of five.

It was towards the end of that first June week that, as she turned the sign on the outer door to read *Closed*, she noticed how, as people came away from an afternoon sitting on the pier, they seemed uncertain what to do. A couple went to the trolley-bus stop; three or four more looked up and down the esplanade uncertain how to spend their evening. Her decision was made. She went into the booking office and took up the earpiece of the telephone which Dominic had had installed. A moment later she heard Muriel's voice.

'Is James home yet, Muriel?'

'Not yet. He told me at lunchtime that he couldn't get here until after seven. It seems the Mayor was going in to discuss plans for some sort of civil defence scheme. You know, I do believe there are those who are enjoying the feeling of unrest. If you ask me it gives them a feeling of importance. Not James – I mean the men who run the town. Civil defence, indeed! Where could be safer than here in England?'

'I'm just ringing to say that I shall be late. Tell him not to worry, but I may not be home until ten or thereabouts.'

'Why, dear? Is something wrong?'

'No. It's really quite exciting – at least it might be. I'll explain when I get home.' She replaced the receiver before there could be any more questions.

And five minutes later she was setting up her easel in front of the pier. Unbeknown to anyone, a few weeks ago she had prepared a sign that read: *What better souvenir of a holiday than to take home a caricature? Six by eight inches: two shillings, or twelve by fifteen inches: seven shillings and sixpence.*

Dominic had come home just as she was crossing towards the pier but instead of following her he went up to his rooms and watched from the front window. If she was sitting there waiting for her first customer, he would go over. The first was important. He smiled to himself, watching her set up her stall. After the morning he had made the suggestion to her, neither of them had referred to it again and he had supposed she had run into trouble at home. At the thought anger and frustration overcame the pleasure he had been taking in watching her. He was a fool, he told himself. Married less than a year, she was still in the early throes of romance; and even if she'd been married for ten years, what difference could it make? She loved her husband; she had made a lifelong commitment. If he had any sense – or, more truthfully, if he had the courage – he would let her rent the whole building as she had wanted and move off. He could ply his trade in some south-west resort; there had never been any logic in setting up in Tarnmouth. But he had never followed the course of logic; he had always followed some inner spirit. And where was his inner spirit guiding him now? The answer was clear: he wanted to be *here*, fool that he was. He wanted to stay where he could see her every day, be there for her if she needed him. Ah, but now those women who had been watching her set up her easel had made a decision and the four of them were approaching Georgie.

Trade was brisk; she made as much in that one evening as her profit in more than a week in the gallery. Just as an elderly man was settling himself in the model's chair and running a comb through his thinning hair having taken off his cap, Georgie saw Dominic approaching.

'What good ideas you have,' she called in a laughing greeting.

'My head's full of them,' he answered in the same vein. 'When you are free can you do me? I'd like a twelve by fifteen to hang in the office. What do you think?'

'Give me a quarter of an hour and I'll be ready for you.' She had never known the minutes and hours of an evening fly so fast. When he reappeared the best of the daylight was fading.

'Pack it in for tonight,' he suggested. 'I'll be your first tomorrow. I spent my waiting time buying our supper from Bert up the road. It's in the oven keeping warm until you were free. You must be starved by this time.'

'I'm not as hungry as you'd think. The time has just flown. I ought to go home; Muriel will have kept my supper for me.' As if to prove that she was lying, her tummy gave a loud rumble of emptiness.

'What a dull world it would be if we only ever did what we ought. I'll carry your easel and this,' he said, folding the model's chair.

'I hadn't expected to stay on this evening, so I didn't have much to eat at midday. Now I know it's worth my while – and good fun, too – I shall start to have a proper meal when I shut at one o'clock. But, Dominic, I shall have to gobble up and get going or James will begin to worry. I didn't tell them what I was doing.'

'And the good James will approve?'

It hadn't occurred to her that he wouldn't.

There was an atmosphere of casual companionship as they ate their cod and chips in the kitchen-cum-living room above the gallery. She meant to go home the moment she had finished, yet when the last chip was eaten and Dominic offered her a cigarette, she took one and leant across the table to put it to the flame of his gold lighter.

'That's a remarkably posh lighter for Mr Sinbad,' she teased.

'A twenty-first-birthday present. It was from an uncle who had always been very special to me, but unfortunately he was ill at the time of my birthday and died soon after.'

'I'm sorry. You usually use matches.'

'Indeed I do. I wouldn't call myself a sentimentalist, but I'd hate to lose this so I don't take it when I'm working – neither did I take it on my trips abroad. I'm a bit like a man who gets a gold watch on his retirement and only gets it out of its case on high days and holidays.'

'From my viewpoint this has been a long working day.'

'Ah, but this is the first time we have shared supper in my humble abode. I see that as cause for celebration. Do you want to telephone your home and reassure them that you haven't come to any harm? Then you could stay and make us both some coffee.'

'Don't tempt me. Coffee would be lovely but—'

'And the company?'

'It's been fun, Dominic, and thank you for my supper. I mustn't do it again though. It's not fair on James to stay out so late – especially if I'm going to set up shop over the way often during the season. He and Muriel get on well together, but it's not right to expect him to spend his evenings with only his mother-in-law for company.'

She felt a change in Dominic's mood. His easy, bantering manner was gone as he answered, 'Of course. I understand. Did you suggest to him that you both should come out for a fishing trip? You remember you said you didn't know if he fished.'

'I did ask him. He's never been an angler and didn't seem keen.'

'Ah.' Hardly a word at all, but it spoke volumes.

'Well, you'd better get on your way. Good girls aren't allowed out in the dark by themselves.'

It had been such a happy, relaxed hour, yet quite suddenly it had gone sour. She hated to leave on that note so, stubbing out her cigarette, she started to stack the plates.

'I'll do the dishes before I go. Woman's job.'

'You're no ordinary woman, Georgie, my dear friend; you are an artist. Sinbad is but a humble seaman, so he will do the dishes.' Then, before he could stop himself he took both her hands in his, his flippant manner gone. 'Thank you for the last hour. I don't usually entertain married ladies in my room but . . . but . . .' he was silent for a moment, knowing he ought to finish the evening on a light note yet not able to stop himself as he said, 'These last months have meant more to me than I can put into words . . . the friendship between us . . . the . . . the . . . pulling together . . .'

'Yes.' She drew her hands away from his. 'Yes, we work well together. I didn't think we were going to when we first met.' She said the first thing that came into her head, anything to put a brake on the serious turn his words threatened to take. She must get away; she must be by herself; she couldn't think clearly while they were tottering on the edge of such seriousness.

'I'll come down with you and lock up.' The moment had passed, even though it had taken some of their easy camaraderie with it. And so the evening ended as the clock on the church at the other end of the esplanade chimed the hour and struck ten.

Automatically she drove out of town, taking the road towards Winchford. Her mind was in turmoil; she couldn't go home feeling like this. She must think. She must chase away the devils that were trying to lead her down a road she wouldn't let herself contemplate. It was a quiet drive through a farming area, so she drove the car on to a grass verge and switched off the engine. Now there was nothing to take her attention, she would look squarely at the situation.

It was almost a year since she and James had married, a year in which he hadn't changed one iota from the man she loved. She had loved him then and she loved him now, today, tomorrow and always. With that firmly established in her mind she felt more able to face this latest complication. '*My dear friend Georgie.*' She heard the echo of his words. But was that all she was, was that all he wanted of her? However he felt, it was all she had to give. Friendship. She had believed that that was all she needed for a full and fulfilling marriage. But this year had taught her just how wrong she had been. Friendship could never be enough. A marriage without friendship might have no hope – wasn't that what James had said when he'd been trying to persuade her? But what of a marriage without the consuming need of two people to share all they were – to laugh together at jokes not obvious to anyone but themselves, to talk and to listen to each other's viewpoints, but, surely above all, to know a burning need of the fulfilment that must come from a true union of bodies and souls. Right from when they had first met, she and James had had a perfect and easy companionship. In this last year they had made love often – he was gentle with her, he was considerate, sometimes she reached the physical climax she strained for, sometimes it remained out of reach and she was thankful when she felt his movements quicken and knew he had reached the point of no return. Was that normal? Was that how it was with every couple? And where was that miracle of union she had yearned for? Perhaps it was always no more than a pipe dream based on ignorance.

Of its own volition her mind took her in another direction.

She imagined lying with Dominic. Her mouth felt dry; she put her tongue around her lips. Alone in the dark night she raised her hands to cup her small breasts. What was the matter with her that she could feel like this when their relationship had gone no further than sharing the premises, one or two fishing trips – and this evening. Her mind was racing out of control. Then, with a sudden, jerky movement she pulled her hands away and folded her arms tightly in front of her, raising her chin. *It's nothing to do with Dominic that I feel like this; it's nothing to do with James either. It's just . . . just . . . I don't know what's the matter with me. I ought to be ashamed. I have a devoted husband, a good home, I love what I do at the gallery – and this evening by the pier, I loved that too. I have everything, everything. Think of the Soames, whatever sort of love life they have – and probably all they have is memories – that miracle of union is theirs forever.*

I must go home, James will be worried. Dear James. Tonight perhaps we'll find that miracle ourselves. He is my life just as I am his. If I can't find the high passion I've yearned for, what we have is still solid and unchanging. That's how it will always be, year after year, when youth is no more than a memory. Marriage is for as long as we both shall live. What more could I ever want than to be safe in his love as long as I have life?

I must go home; they'll be worried. She pulled the ignition knob and as she steered the car from the grass verge on to the empty road she sent up a fervent, silent plea. *Please help me to know that what I've done is right; please make me worthy of James. Truly I know it's my own fault that I can't be satisfied when I know how lucky I am. Think of those poor miserable teachers I left behind at St Winifred's. Yes, I am grateful and I do love James – so please, if we can't manage it on our own then please just make it happen, help us to find that joyous union I know must be there.*

'Are you all right? Whatever kept you so late?' James said by way of greeting.

'Yes, I'm fine. James, I've had such a lovely time this evening. I want to tell you all about it.'

He looked at her with the sort of tolerant affection that might be bestowed on an excited child.

'Eat while you talk. You must be starving.'

She shook her head. 'I've had supper. James, I wish you could have seen me! They were almost queuing up. But I'll start from the beginning. I suppose it all stemmed from those illustrations for Fisherman Freddie – and, do you know, I made more money in two hours or so than in a whole week at the gallery.' She took a cigarette from the box on the side table and put it between her lips while he held the flame from his lighter to it. 'I'll tell you.' She sat on the settee and took his hand to pull him to sit at her side. 'This is nice,' she said, wriggling closer. 'Where's Muriel?'

'She went on up to bed. You were going to tell me about your evening. What had the illustrations to do with it?'

'Well, they came about because Mrs Fraser saw my sketch pad and the caricature type drawings I often do; doodling like that is how I amuse myself when I'm alone in the gallery. That's when she suggested I might take on the illustrations for *Freddie the Fisherman*. Then I thought, well, if she liked what I did, why wouldn't other people?' It wasn't quite true, but by that time Georgie had more or less persuaded herself that the original thought had been her own.

'I wish you'd get to the point.'

'Don't you see? Sketches of people, not proper portraits, more like caricatures. With the mess Europe is getting itself in, even if holidaymakers had the money to spend on a proper oil painting they'd think twice, but a few shillings on a sketch is a lovely souvenir of a holiday.'

'You mean you kept the shop – gallery or whatever it is these days – open all the evening for that?'

'No, I locked up dead on six o'clock and took my easel over the road so that I sat in front of the pier. That's where people are in the evenings. You should have seen the way they were drawn to see what I was doing. It was so exciting. I put my notice up with the prices on and . . .' She stopped speaking. Did she imagine the sudden change in him? 'James?'

'You're telling me that you sat out there in the street, plying your trade to any Tom, Dick or Harry who was prepared to part with a shilling or two?'

She laughed before she could stop herself. In James' eyes this was no moment for levity.

'You make it sound as if I'd been selling *myself* on the street!'

'Georgie, dear, dear Georgie, how is it that I fail you? How is it you can't be content with the life I provide for you?'

'James, dear, dear James,' she mimicked his tone, 'I could never be content as a stay-at-home wife. You knew that long before we were married. Would you want to be stuck here all day long?'

'That's nonsense,' he answered, his grip on her hand tightening. 'I have a career, one I trained for. So, too, did you while you were teaching. But this – yes, you have a talent, a God-given gift, you might say. And so you are throwing away the years you wasted acquiring a degree that would open the door to something so much more worthwhile. Now that you are married, don't you see how different you would feel? I know how you dreaded turning into someone like your older women colleagues – not that you ever could!'

She turned to look at him, shaking her head and afraid to speak in case her voice betrayed the misery that was welling up in her. If he'd been angry she could have fought her corner, but his complete lack of understanding made the gap too wide for her to breach.

'Please, Georgie, promise me you won't do it again. Can't you see how I feel, to think of my wife out there in the street selling her talent to strangers for the sake of a shilling or two?'

Disappointment was giving way to anger now, the threat of tears gone as she answered him. 'Then instead of sitting at home imagining I'm some sort of prostitute, why don't you get in the car and come and see for yourself? Bring Muriel. You've never even shown enough interest to come and see the gallery. James, I'm more than just your wife – I'm *me*. It wasn't beneath Dominic Fraser's dignity to come across to the pier head to see how the evening was going.'

'That boatman fellow who bought the property? Now you're talking nonsense.'

She knew from the set of his jaw and his clear, quietly spoken words that his anger was rising.

'Yes, he's a boatman. But being a boatman just means he has a talent that neither you nor I possess – and a joy in living, too. Apart from being a seaman, he had as good or probably better education than you or me, and got a First at Cambridge, which is more than either of us can boast. Not that any of that makes a scrap of difference to what we were talking about.'

'Perhaps I misjudged him; perhaps his thoughts were much the same as my own and he knew it was no way for you to spend your evening and was keeping an eye on you to make sure you were all right.'

She could tell from his more relaxed manner that he was relieved that Dominic had been 'keeping an eye' on her. Georgie's spirit seldom dipped to such depths as it did then, even though reason told her there was no logic in this feeling of hopelessness. She had come home resolved that the day would end on a high note, and that the elation of the evening would carry her to the final scene of the day. She shunned the memory of that hour with Dominic; that had no place in her life. James was her life; James was her love.

'Let's go to bed. I honestly don't want anything else to eat.' She teased his mouth with her lips and found herself pulled close into his arms.

'You think I'm old-fashioned,' he whispered. 'But I am as I am; I can't change the way I see things.'

'And neither, my darling James, can I change the things I do. Marriage shouldn't take away freedom. You have evening meetings and—'

'They are my work,' he cut in. But the battle had gone out of his tone and he spoke softly, rubbing his chin against her short curly hair.

'And painting is mine – sketching, painting, all of it. My life is with you, but I need the challenge of working as well.' The subject was closed and their near quarrel put behind them as she moved her face against his. 'Let's go to bed, James. Let's forget everything but loving each other.'

He would have been less than human if he'd not felt a rush of excitement at her words. Yet when, clad in his maroon silk pyjamas, he found her lying naked on the bed he knew a moment's self doubt and hated himself that it should be so. Small boned, there was nothing angular in her thin figure, yet she was slender to the point of being almost shapeless. Who could have imagined her sensuality? He knew that tonight she wanted the light left on; she wanted him to know the desire that drove her. As he came to the side of the bed she pulled the cord of his trousers and pushed them to the ground then, raising herself an inch or two from her prone position, she drew him close, her tongue moving sensuously, first around her own lips then lightly touching him, caressing him, then her mouth encircling him. Tonight must be so wonderful that it wiped every other thought from her memory.

And that night her mounting passion drove her to a climax that stripped her of all thought, save for the wonder of what was happening. Surely this was the miracle she had yearned for? It was only later, lying with the light still on while James slumbered peacefully and contentedly at her side, that she faced the truth of just where her imagination had carried her in those final seconds.

So the season of that year of 1938 brought the customary visitors to Tarnmouth. No one wanted to admit to the underlying fear that peace was fragile; instead they seemed intent on grabbing their days of freedom with two eager hands. In the gallery, Georgie even sold two or three oil paintings and, as for the *objets d'art* brought in regularly from the local craft workers, they were sold as quickly as replacements could be made. Yet, despite the determination with which the holidaymakers threw themselves into enjoying everything that came their way, there was an underlying fear of looking to the future. When, in the spring, Hitler had marched his troops into Austria, most Austrians had wanted union with Germany; that was the thought people clung to, telling themselves that it was only warmongers who looked on it as an act of aggression. Yet, even though few would admit it, everyone was aware that they were living in a time of instability and that peace was to be treasured but never taken for granted.

Through the summer months Georgie became a familiar sight on the pavement in front of the pier, and through the long evenings it was seldom there wasn't a model eagerly waiting to see the end results of her labour. And each sunny day – and even some days of sunshine and showers – Dominic took a party out in *Blue Horizon*, while Clifford Hunt, a retired naval man, took the anglers to sea in *Tight Lines*.

Neither the booking office nor the gallery needed constant attention, but often after a dull half-hour both would need attention at the same time. Dominic called it 'Sod's Law' and decided he'd offer employment to Barry Soames while the season lasted. He had an ulterior motive: Alice would have to push the wheelchair and so why not leave her to man the gallery for a few hours?

'No one booked to fish this morning,' he told Georgie, coming into the gallery carrying the oilskin jacket and leggings nearest to her size. 'Alice and Barry will be here – isn't that so, Alice?'

'I'd love to look after the place for you, Georgie. You know you can trust me.' And put like that it would have been difficult to refuse. These trips were only possible on the days *Blue Horizon* wasn't due to go to sea until early afternoon so, when there were no fishing bookings, there were many mornings when Georgie and Dominic escaped on to the water. No mention was ever made of that brief moment of seriousness after their fish and chip supper in Dominic's kitchen. At sea they each had tasks: Dominic was skipper, Georgie was skipper's mate. James' spontaneous, unspoken thought might often be that she had no more sex appeal than a young lad, and certainly out on the water with Dominic that's exactly what she might have been. And that was the way he treated her. So she relaxed, she loved the fun they shared, the ever-growing bond of friendship, the excitement as they reeled in their catch, the salt spray on her lips, the cry of the gulls as Dominic whistled and then threw them their tasty delicacies after he'd gutted the catch. In all her life she had never known such happiness as she did that summer. In her heart she knew that it was based on the freedom of her friendship with Dominic, and the feeling of relief she clung to that they had established a relationship that presented no threat to her marriage. For, come what may, marriage was for life. Of course one read about divorce – it often happened in the glamorous world of theatre and films – but amongst *real* people, who lived by the rules, she knew of no one whose marriage had ended that way.

She wouldn't consider that she might be living in a fool's paradise. Then one morning early in September when they were out in *Tight Lines*, the wind changed and with it so did the mood of the sea. By the time they reached shore her bubble of happy contentment (if that's what it ever had been) had burst, and nothing could ever be the same again.

Six

On that September Monday morning, Alice and Barry had arrived early. The holiday season was petering out just as it always did once August was over and as there were only two bookings for the afternoon outing on *Blue Horizon* the trip was to be cancelled.

'On a day like this don't you think there may be some last-minute people?' Barry ventured as he saw the notice Dominic was about to put in the window.

'A brilliant morning, Barry, but the Met Office forecast storms by early evening. One mention of the word "storm" and the open sea is the last place visitors will venture. It's the picture house where the trade will go. The two who have booked are sure to be in to get their money back – unless they'd rather change the date to later in the week. It's forecast to be rough for a couple of days, then settle again.'

'Well, I suppose these weather people know what they're talking about, but to look out there now it's hard to believe. No more than a ripple on the water. No takers for *Tight Lines* this morning, either. Are you off with your rods?'

'I surely am. Maybe I'll bring your supper home. I'll do my best. Will Alice be around all the morning if I winkle Georgie out to come with me?'

Alice and Barry were always glad to man the establishment. Coming there so regularly had added colour to their restricted lives, quite apart from bringing them in extra cash. When the place was quiet they worked with their crafts, Barry whittling his wood until it became a recognizable shape while Alice made lampshades. They worked within view of anyone who cared to gaze through the window, so they attracted plenty of attention and brought visitors and locals alike into the gallery. Seeing how keen the couple were to be left in charge, Georgie was able to leave the place without her conscience troubling her. So by half past nine *Tight Lines* was out to sea, leaving the shore behind while Dominic turned off the outboard motor and Georgie hoisted the sails. She loved this moment when the throbbing motor was silenced and the only sound was the dull crack of wind in the sails as the boat cut through the waves. On that morning the waves did no more than wash gently against the side of the wooden craft.

'No panic to get back today, so we'll go further out before we cast our lines,' Dominic said.

'Aye, aye, skipper,' came Georgie's reply, accompanied by a laugh she couldn't hold back. 'Don't you feel sad to think summer's nearly over? It has been so . . . so *special*; and that's quite apart from the fish suppers it has provided.'

'Let's hope we get a catch today. I want us to take some back for the Soames. It was our lucky day when Alice brought her decorated eggshells in – ours and theirs too. They work there as if it were their own.'

She nodded. If she spoke it might break the spell that was giving her this sensation of perfection. An old tub of a sailing boat, the prospect of handling messy bait and finally going home smelling of fish (if they were lucky), what was so wonderful about that? Perhaps Dominic read her thoughts, for he was watching her and when her glance met his neither of them spoke – and yet the moment printed a lasting image on their memories.

Looking out to sea, they saw a patch on the water that could mean only one thing: a shoal of mackerel. Keeping their eyes on their prey they set the sails in the direction of the dark patch that moved on the water, which seemed to sparkle as the fish leapt. Before these trips with Dominic, Georgie's fishing experience had been no more adventurous than standing at the end of Hastings pier, baiting her hook with a lugworm, casting – and waiting. As they travelled they re-prepared their tackle. Today there would be no worms or small fish for bait; today brightly coloured feathers disguised the series of hooks on each line. On that morning as they cast their lines amongst the mackerel, almost at once the fish leapt to take the feathers. They were bringing them out of the water not one at a time but three or four.

'Let's hope everyone likes mackerel!' Dominic called to her. 'How are you doing?'

'It's a bit like the story in the Bible. If we had a net we could just scoop them up. They must be stupid fish, you know. Wouldn't you think when they see their mates caught on a hook they'd have enough sense to pass on by?'

They were putting their catch in a large double-handled wicker basket, which was filling fast. The wind changed direction and strengthened but both of them were good sailors and for a while neither were perturbed. But as the weather deteriorated, *Tight Lines* was tossed around as it was buffeted by the waves.

'I think that's about it, Georgie. Too rough for them now; we shan't get any more. Thunder! We'd better start for home. We've travelled a fair distance following the shoal. You reef the main sail and hoist the jib, then right about. I'll see to the fish.'

'Aye, aye, skipper.' She made sure she answered in the same vein as when he'd called instructions on the outbound trip but, inexplicably, her spirits had dipped from the heights to the depths. Here on the sea they were in their own world; they had no responsibility to other people. But she knew there was no logic in how she felt. '*Start for home,*' he had said, and for the present Tarnmouth was his home and he seemed content with his surroundings – the boats, the harbour, the easy camaraderie amongst the seafaring men who, after a slow start, appeared to have accepted him. But he'd get the wanderlust just as he always had. Always that was at the back of her mind. They were friends now, but one day – this year, next year, whenever the spirit moved him – he would be gone. And she would be left, the rest of her life ahead of her. Her vision misted as she imagined a future without him. It would have been better if she'd never met him, or if he had remained the Sinbad or the Mr La-de-Da she had been led to believe. But that was months ago and by now even the boatmen in the harbour had come to know him for the person he really was.

With every moment the sky was growing darker and when they heard the hiss as fork lightning touched the water they knew the storm had caught up with them. Suddenly the rain came, lashing against the sails, dancing on the wooden deck. The only thing in their favour was that the strengthening wind had changed course and was speeding their progress. For all that they could see, they might have been in the middle of a vast ocean. The rain was like a solid wall of water, and through it there was no sight of the shore. Georgie loved storms, she always had. Now it cut them off from everything but the little boat that was their world. Then as the wind hit them broad side on, the boom swung, hitting the back of her head and throwing her to the ground where she lay unconscious. In a second Dominic was with her, ready to help her to her feet. But she lay still, her eyes closed.

'Georgie! Georgie, can you hear me?'

Her eyelids fluttered, then briefly opened.

She opened her mouth in an attempt to speak but her hold on consciousness was too slim and again her eyes closed. Her face was deathly pale under its suntan. Dominic had never felt more helpless. Kneeling by her side he slipped his arm under her shoulder and raised her to cradle her against him.

'Wake up. You mustn't go to sleep.' If she let herself sleep, could she drift into unconsciousness, even into a coma? He took her hand in his. 'Grip my hand, try and squeeze my hand. Georgie, stay awake. You mustn't sleep.' Her hand lay limp in his, her eyes remained shut. Even as he kept talking to her he knew she wasn't hearing him. And still the rain lashed down on them, the boat was pitched and tossed by the angry waves. This could be no ordinary sleep, for surely no one could sleep while the heavens were alive with thunder and lighting lit the sky. 'Please God, make her wake up.'

It was an odd sensation, yet her mind wasn't working clearly enough to know why she should seem to be outside her body, not knowing where she was, not knowing *who* she was. Someone was talking, she could hear a voice, but she had neither the energy nor the intelligence to want to listen. Gradually, imperceptibly, the fog in her mind started to lift. The voice was Dominic's . . . but she must be dreaming . . . 'Georgie, my darling Georgie, look at me. Please God bring her back to me, make her wake.' That her face softened into the hint of a smile was something she didn't know, as she listened to the words that she had wanted to hear for so long. 'Yes,' he was saying, 'she moved.' His hand felt real, warm with life; figures in dreams never touched you. If she woke he'd be gone; she couldn't let him go! Her hand gripped his. 'Thank God, thank God!' And this time she knew he was no dream.

'Dom . . . Thought I heard you say . . .' Talking was too much for her. Her mouth was like sawdust; her head was throbbing.

She raised her hand and touched her temple where already a lump was appearing. 'Must . . . up . . .' She was trying to struggle to her feet as she retched violently.

He half carried her to the side of the boat and when she leant over the side her body convulsed as time and again she retched but wasn't sick. Then, shaking her head, she gave him a weak and shamefaced smile.

'Sorry,' she muttered, panting. 'No way to behave. Think I feel better.'

'Never been so frightened in my life.' Then, in an attempt to put them back on course for their normal, easy friendship uncharged with emotion, he added, 'We'll soon be home.'

'You live there but it's not your *home*.' Her voice broke. In her present weak state she had no fight; misery swamped her as she half remembered her dream and then faced reality. 'Home is the place that gives . . . gives solace, comfort. But you don't stay anywhere, soon you'll be gone,' she sobbed.

He drew her into his arms. 'Georgie, my precious, beloved Georgie. You are the only home I want, what difference where it is? I stay here because you're here.'

'All my fault.' It was difficult to understand what she was saying between gulps, snorts and sobs as her breath caught in her throat. 'I knew I wasn't in love. I shouldn't have married. I should have waited.'

'Not in love? Not in love with James?'

'I *do* love him and he loves me. And we're married . . . that's for life . . . we promised. I didn't cheat him; I told him he was my dearest friend.' Sniffing, she wiped the back of her hand across her nose and then her eyes. 'Didn't bring a hanky.'

'Here, have mine.'

She gave an inelegant blow. Then, seeming to stand a little taller, she continued what she had been saying. 'He had lost his wife and was lonely – and he loved me, he loves me still, just like I do him. James could never have an unfaithful thought in his head, that's what makes me feel so ashamed. But I can't help it.' And again she was losing her battle against tears. 'Didn't want this to happen, Dominic. Why couldn't I have gone on not liking you? But now we're friends, that's what I try and believe. But it's no use. I've never felt like this about anyone.

When you go away there won't be any . . . any *colour* . . . any *hope*.'

This time when he drew her towards him she raised her face, her lips slightly parted as his mouth covered hers. She almost forgot the throbbing of her head as she clung to him. A sudden gust and the boat listed, bringing them back to earth. There was work to be done. *Tight Lines* wouldn't bring them home unmanned and neither would the mackerel gut themselves.

'You stay where you are,' he told her. 'We'll soon be home.'

'Home?' He understood what she meant by the single word.

'Yes, my darling, home. As long as you're there for me it will be home. We must talk, Georgie; we must work something out. Friendship alone can't make a good marriage. You know that, I know it and I bet James would agree if he knew how we both feel.'

'I'm better now,' she told him. Better perhaps, but not better enough to concentrate on the future; she wanted just to hang on to these precious moments. 'I only have a sore head where I bashed it. I can bring us home while you do the fish.'

Kissing the tip of her nose, he told her, 'Captain's orders, you just sit back on that wet deck and pretend it's comfortable.' They both laughed, their spirits soaring and for no good reason. The gulls had started following the boat but today they were to be deprived their tasty pickings.

Back in Tarnmouth they tied *Tight Lines* to its mooring at the harbour, gave half a dozen mackerel to Hector Meakes, a one-time boatman now in his mid-eighties who liked nothing better than to wander down to the harbour in the hope of finding someone to chat to. He had found shelter in the overhang from Dominic's shed, but as for companionship, there had been no one about. In fact they were all sheltering in the Jolly Sailor Inn, where he intended to track them down as soon as the rain eased a little more.

Carrying their rods and each holding a handle of the wicker basket, Georgie and Dominic bade him goodbye and started back up the hill to the esplanade and the gallery.

The violent storm had given way to heavy, steady rain, which looked set to go on all day.

'We've been worried about you,' was Alice's greeting.

'It was quite a storm,' Georgie agreed, 'but we had a lovely sail and you should see what we caught.'

'You must both be soaked to the skin.'

'The rain had no chance against these oilskins.' But Georgie gave an involuntary shiver as she said it.

'I'll go and light the geyser and you get straight into a hot bath, Georgie. After that fall it's what you need before you stiffen up. Sure you feel all right?'

Alice had wondered about them for weeks, and something in the way he looked at Georgie confirmed her fears. With all the single young women out there, why did he have to fall in love with a married woman, especially one who always spoke of her husband with such affection? When Georgie let her glance meet his, yet another piece of the puzzle fell into place, doing nothing to dispel Alice's concern. Was Georgie the sort of woman to amuse herself outside wedlock? Surely not. But one read of such things happening. No good could come of it, no good for any of them.

Steam rose out of the bath tub, the mirror over the basin was clouded, the gloss paint on the walls already running with condensation. Lying back, Georgie was comforted by the warmth; it would have been easy to drift into sleep. The fast-growing lump on her forehead was throbbing, but apart from that she was none the worse for her accident. She must stay awake; Muriel had always warned her how dangerous it was to sleep in the bath. Dear Muriel, how good it was to see her so much more confident in her new life. Clothes make such a difference to how a woman feels, Georgie thought, and since Muriel had had some money to spend on herself she was a new woman. What would Dad think if he could see her now? Georgie tried not to imagine the day he had been killed, the dreadful, cruel things he had said, designed to hurt the woman who had dedicated her life to caring for them and, in hurting her, to escape his own sense of shame. It was easier to dwell on how things were at Gregory House now. Probably James would still be home having lunch. How good it was that he and Muriel got along so well . . .

Then she faced the fact that she had been guiding her

thoughts in their direction because she was frightened to dwell on what the future would bring. The love she and Dominic shared was like a miracle . . . *miracle* . . . the miracle of a perfect union. But how could that ever be for them? Stolen hours together that would become festered by guilt? No, they must never let that happen, she told herself firmly. Yet wouldn't even stolen hours be better than a charade of wanting no more than friendship?

She looked around the steam-filled room, a man's room. There was no perfumed bath oil for the water, not even so much as a handful of cheap-smelling coloured soda crystals. She smiled, imagining Dominic using such things. He was thoroughly masculine from the top of his head to the soles of his feet; it was nothing to do with his seaman's attire, for dressed as immaculately as any sophisticated man about town his masculinity would still be there. How was it she could be so sure that loving him would give her – give both of them – that miracle of union she yearned for? With her eyes closed she leant back in the bath, her hands moving on her underdeveloped breasts. And into her mind came memories of James. Each time she had drawn him to caress her he had pulled his hand away as if because she was small she wasn't a proper woman. *But I am, I am!* And as if to prove it her hands moved on her two barely perceptible mounds, her thumbs waking every sensuous nerve as they encircled her hardened nipples. Suppose the hands were Dominic's, suppose it was he who was resting against the end of the bath with his knees apart so that there was room for her in front of him. She must stop this; she must get out of the bath; she must—

'Georgie,' she heard as he tapped the door. 'Georgie you haven't gone to sleep again? You're all right, darling?'

'Yes. No, I mean, I didn't go to sleep. I've been daydreaming. Dominic, is it all right if I use your towel? It's the only one in here.'

'I'll fetch you a clean one. Hop out and push the bolt back, then I'll pass it round the door.'

She suppressed a giggle. What if she told him she hadn't bolted the door? Instead she said, 'OK,' and heard him retreating to fetch another towel. When he came back he opened the door just far enough to push the towel into the room, but before he could even do that she leant out of the bath and flung it wide, holding her open arms towards him.

'There's room for two,' she said softly.

A minute later, his clothes in an untidy heap on the ground, he was about to climb in. 'I'll take the tap end,' he said gallantly.

'You weren't invited to join me just to sit on the bath plug. Come this end and I'll wriggle in between your knees.' Such a short time ago desire and passion had been driving her to devise a way of getting him in, but now as they looked at each other the mood changed and they both started to laugh.

'The lady is nothing short of a scheming minx,' he told her. 'But she has good ideas.'

So they sat just as she had imagined. Putting his arms around her, it was with his hands gently holding her breasts that he pulled her to lean against him. Bending his head forward he nuzzled the back of her neck.

'The world would be scandalized, but Georgie, blessed Georgie, how can this be wrong?'

'It's so *right*. I don't know whether to laugh or cry.'

'Then laugh, my darling. Today there can be no tears for you and me. For so long I've tried to run away from the truth.'

She nodded. 'Yes, and me. I wouldn't let myself face up to what had happened. Laugh, you say. But how can I when I've been such a fool? I'd said "no" to James for weeks but then . . . Oh, Dominic, I'm so ashamed. When Dad was killed . . .' And so, lying against him in the fast-cooling water, she told him about the time of the accident, James' kindness and his never failing consideration not just for her but for Muriel too, her own thankfulness that he was there for them – and her abiding love for him. 'How could I not love him? But to marry for the wrong sort of love is as big a mistake as marrying for money or any sort of convenience. He will never forget the wife who died – if he did he would be a different man. But we had friendship and . . . and . . . I feel hateful saying this even to you – but the truth was, I was sex-starved. At that school I was surrounded by women; women who were growing old and seemed content to remain spinsters. I was desperate for physical love. I believed that once we were married I would find the miracle I was looking for.'

'And you haven't?' he asked her gently, moving his chin against her head.

'How could I? We live like any other married couple, but . . .' He felt her shudder and held her even more closely.

'We'll work it out, darling. One thing I swear – I swear it for myself and believe it's true for you, too – nothing is going to change how we care for each other. And how you feel about James only makes me love you more.' Then, in an attempt to lighten the tone before tears got the upper hand over laughter, 'Now then, lady, out you get before your bath does you more harm than good. Then chuck me the other towel. Were your clothes dry? Had the oilskin kept the wet out?'

So they were back on safer ground. Only then did they consider that the Soames must have been forming their own opinion on what was going on upstairs.

'I'll dress quickly and go on down. I'll say I fell asleep in the bath and now you are going to have a quick dip.'

He agreed to the tale. For his own sake he didn't care about anyone's speculations, but he would make sure that no hint of gossip touched Georgie.

At the end of September Tarnmouth pier closed. A long winter lay ahead, but during the last week of the month one thing happened that must surely have lifted the spirits of every man and woman. Neville Chamberlain returned from a meeting with Adolf Hitler bringing a paper bearing both of their signatures and guaranteeing that Germany had no thought of invading any more of its neighbours. After his army had marched into Austria during the spring of that year, a plebiscite of its people had shown that almost all of them wanted union with Germany. Then had come his invasion of Sudetenland, part of Czechoslovakia. The threat of war had hung heavily over Europe, but with Chamberlain's assurance that there would be 'Peace in our time', the people breathed a sigh of relief and thankfulness.

In the gallery Georgie and Alice were reading the morning paper when Dominic arrived, coming there before he went into the booking office.

'Do you think we can believe Hitler's word?' Georgie asked, addressing whichever of them chose to answer.

'Oh, but we must. If we don't show him some trust, we can't expect him to keep to his promise.' Alice spoke first. Female logic, perhaps.

'James says the Prime Minister has shown weakness. Yet I don't see that he could have done more than he has.'

While Dominic had listened, he had been lighting his pipe, drawing hard on it then pressing the tobacco more firmly in the bowl with his thumb before again holding his lighter to it.

'Can we believe it, Dominic? No sane person could want war, and Britain and France have threatened that that's what it will mean if he tries to take anywhere else.'

'What do I think? I think while people are all asking the same question you are asking, they ought to be down on their knees thanking their God for the lifeline this agreement has thrown us. We all know the arsenal Hitler has built in his country – and he can only have manufactured weaponry on that scale for one purpose. War will come. Now let Britain use this respite wisely – gun for gun, bomb for bomb, plane for plane, we need to match him. Unless I'm much mistaken, that won't be possible; he's been preparing for years. But every month must make a difference.' He changed the subject. 'I'm going to have a word with Barry, and see how the seagull carving is getting on.'

The Soames had made a niche for themselves at No. 14, The Esplanade. They had a strong streak of independence and wanted no payment that wasn't earned. Each day they came to the booking office and, even now that *Blue Horizon's* season was finished, usually there would be one or two people wanting to arrange a fishing trip, mostly for Saturdays or Sundays. But taking bookings for an angler or two didn't merit a day's wage so Barry insisted that, instead, he should be paid a small percentage for each person Dominic took out. Most of his time he spent whittling his wood, trying to accrue enough for a display in the weeks preceding Christmas.

As the months of winter passed, increasingly Georgie felt removed from the events which only a year ago had added zest to her life. Every day she came to the gallery, every day she presented a face of friendship to the workers who toiled at their craft and – although seldom, once Christmas was behind them – occasionally went home with an extra few shillings in their pockets.

Alice had come to know her better than most and she was worried.

'The place doesn't mean as much to her as it did in the beginning,' she said to Barry as from the window of the booking office she watched Georgie and Dominic disappear in the direction of the harbour. 'You know the kindest thing we could do would be to tell them we can't look after this place for them. They go off down to that boat of his – decorating it, that's what she tells me. How long does it take to put a lick of paint on a boat? She's been making curtains for the cabin, if you please. You can't tell me the trippers want to draw the curtains and shut out the view!'

'It worries me too; it worries me for the sake of that poor husband. Do you think he is blind to the change in her?'

She looked at her beloved Barry and said a silent word of thanks.

'We shouldn't condemn, I suppose, when we don't know the whole story. But, Barry, Dominic is a good man, too good to be used to pander to her vanity. When she mentions her husband, she seems to go out of her way to paint a rosy picture of him. If she thinks she's blinding me to what's going on, then she's mistaken. And what about Dominic? How long will he be satisfied if she's leading him along for nothing?'

'Sometimes I think it takes a bit of adversity to sort out the gold from the dross. Trouble comes and it either makes or breaks. Alice, dear Alice. Healthy . . . vigorous . . . if only my rotten body could keep pace with my mind. When I was making myself accept how things would be for us, I felt . . . well, you know how I felt. Not just for me, but for you too.' She bent forward and kissed his forehead.

'And now?' she probed.

'Things have had to change for us both. There are times I can't face knowing it'll never be like it was for the two of us. In the beginning I secretly resented it that you could get what you wanted from . . .' Rather than use words he held his hands out in front of him. 'Perhaps time really is the greatest healer; now having the power to do that to you, it's . . . damn it, yes, it's almost like it is happening to me, too. It's something we share.' His face was working and for a moment she thought he was going to cry.

'Yes, darling, you make it wonderful for me,' she whispered, moving her chin on the top of his head. Was it true? She wouldn't even consider any other answer and, if it helped him, then it was doubly true. 'We've always been blessed – about that I mean – not every couple are so lucky, or so I've heard. But what about Dominic and Georgie? I know it's not our business, but I hate to see them storing up trouble for themselves. She never speaks a word against her husband, yet just see the way those two look at each other sometimes.'

If she could have had a glimpse of them at that moment in the cabin of *Blue Horizon* she might have been reassured. While he reached up to paint the ceiling, she was concentrating on a mural for the partition between the cabin and the engine house. Later, their work done, they went to the Jolly Sailor.

It was early yet and the only person in the bar was a one-time fisherman who, too old to go to sea, still hankered after the company.

'Hello there, you two. I saw you going aboard. From the looks of you, Missie, you've been having a busy morning.'

'We both have, Jacko,' Georgie answered. 'I hadn't realized I was such a mess. Don't worry though, most of the paint on me is dry; I've been wearing these overalls for ages.'

'So what are you up to in *Blue Horizon*? Getting her tarted up ready for the start of the season?'

'Don't know about tarted up,' Dominic laughed. 'Spruced up, I'd say, with just a lick of paint. But you should see what Georgie has done. Look in some time, why don't you?'

The old seaman beamed with pleasure displaying an expanse of gum and three teeth, two at one side and one the other. Then he pulled off his woollen hat and moved his head in something akin to a bow of respect. 'That's mighty civil of you, my boy, and you too, Missie. I'd like that. Mayhap I'll climb aboard when we kick out of here at two o'clock. That be all right?'

'Sure. Glad to see you.'

'I'm afraid I shan't be there, Jacko,' Georgie said. 'I must get back to the gallery in a minute. Most of the paint is dry, but this morning I put the pier in the picture and that will be tacky.

I'm sorry I shall miss you.' They had a soft spot for Jacko. Like plenty of others who had spent their years working out of Tarnmouth Harbour the place seemed to draw them back. 'I must fly. Alice and Barry will be wanting to get home for their lunch.'

'I shall look in at the booking office about six o'clock.' Dominic made his voice casual. 'But you'll be OK there for the afternoon?'

'Of course I will. Remember to bring your key when you come in case I've locked up and gone home.'

'I'll remember.'

Underlying their brief exchange they both understood the message: later in the afternoon, after Jacko had left, he would come to man the booking office. In fact it was about four o'clock when he arrived, finding Georgie working on her illustrations for a new book.

'The sunshine is working wonders; I've taken a booking for a trip for four anglers on Saturday morning and I see in the book that Barry has booked two for Sunday. No weekend slacking for you!'

'Thank God for that. Weekends are the hardest.'

She pushed her work to one side and got up, going to him and putting her arms around his neck.

'I know. The days are twice as long as those in the week.' She raised her face towards his, her lips parted in invitation.

'No, Georgie! Damn it, no! We've got to put an end to this nonsensical charade. Or do you drive away from here – the woman I love, *my* woman – then arrive home the woman they expect, the woman they know, *his* woman?'

She frowned. She had never heard him speak in that tone, his anger at the situation encompassing his feeling for her.

'I don't give a damn if there is gossip about *me*, but as long as you are someone else's wife I will see there's no cause for any about you either.' He held her chin in his hand and raised her face so that they looked directly at each other. 'I'm not made of stone. Night after night I think of you there with him – and where is the end to it all? We ought to have been honest from the start. If we lived here together he could petition for divorce and cite me as co-respondent. Yes, there'd be gossip, but it wouldn't matter then. It wouldn't be long before we could be married. Think of it, Georgie, imagine the life we could have.' But when she lowered her gaze and tried to turn away, his persuasive expression vanished. 'Don't play with me; don't pretend while all the time you are comfortable living there and keeping me on a string.'

'Don't, Dominic, please don't. You know that's not true.'

'So you'll tell him the truth? You must. Our lives are in limbo – worse than that. At least in limbo you don't know what you're aiming for. Who do you put first, him or me? In God's name, who do you want to spend your life with, him or me?'

She walked away from him and stood gazing out of the window, gazing but conscious of none of it. He waited, more frightened than he dared to acknowledge.

'When I was teaching at St Winifred's,' she said, speaking quietly and with no show of emotion, 'the parents of one of my pupils were divorced. The mother committed adultery and went off with some company director. The girl didn't come from a wealthy home, but she was clever and had won a scholarship place so her parents only had to pay her boarding fees. I expect the mother – a pretty, doll-like woman, I remember – I expect her rich lover swept her off her feet. She was given custody of Beth, the daughter. She was a changed girl; her sparkle had gone. At half term she went back to her father and it was after that that I found her crying in the woods at the back of the grounds. Crying? She was right at the depths. She loved both her parents; it had always seemed to be a very normal home with both of them so proud of her. But divorce changed everything. You talk of gossip and scandal, but have you the slightest idea what it can do to the people caught up in it? Her mother was all right, she and her new man moved to the south of France where Beth was supposed to join them for holidays.'

'Rotten for the kid, I can see that. But what's all this got to do with you and me? You have no family, your husband is a grown man – and you say he has never been in love with you any more than you have with him.'

'Just listen – and try to understand. Beth's father had been employed by a firm of printers. I told you they weren't rich people. Perhaps the wealthy can take divorce in their stride more easily, but living alone he was miserable – well of course he was, his world had fallen apart. And Beth's work suffered. She was just sixteen, coming up to School Certificate, and we had great expectations for her: Matric, Higher Schools, entry to a top university. She had been outstanding all through her school life. But it was as if she had lost her grip and nothing could stop her falling. I worked with her, I tried, but I couldn't get through to her. The other girls whispered behind her back. They didn't mean to be unkind, but they had never come across anyone involved in divorce. The same thing must have been happening where her father worked and the next thing we heard was that he had lost his job. Beth begged to be allowed to go home to see him and when she came back she was . . . like a lost soul. She sat her School Certificate and was sent off to travel on her own to her mother. Before she went I asked her if she was coming back to spend part of her long vacation with her father. She shook her head and said, "He says I can't. He got behind with the rent and had to move out. Don't know how he's living." It wasn't just what she told me, it was her voice, the hopelessness, the disinterest, as if all the life had been drained out of her. And him? Society isn't ready to accept broken marriage; what goes on in a marital home may not be important, or it may give a bit of pleasure to the gossiping hordes, but if the marriage breaks down they are ostracized even to the extent of what had been a seemingly secure job being lost.'

'Did the child find her own way to a good future?'

Georgie shook her head. 'She failed her School Certificate and lost her scholarship. Miss Shackleford, the headmistress, wrote to her with her results and to her mother saying that under the circumstances the Board of Governors had withdrawn her free place and suggesting that in any case she had been less than an asset to the school over a difficult period in her life. For me, that was the last nail in St Winifred's coffin.'

'And you never heard any more from her?'

'No. But I read how her father's body had been retrieved from the Thames.' For a moment they were silent, then she said, 'We can't make commitments and break them because we are too weak to keep faith. Dom, oh, Dom, please try and understand, I can't do that to him. He doesn't deserve it, he's a *good* person – and so is Muriel. If I grabbed at what I want, what would it do to them? Married to James, it's *you* I love, you I want. Every day, every night it's *you*. But if I tell him I'm leaving him and living with you, what happens to Muriel? They are good friends, she isn't just a housekeeper, and they spend hours together. But that is all right because I live there too. And you know how starchy local government can be. Would they even consider keeping a Town Clerk who was involved in divorce? I can't do it to them, Dominic. And if I did, our happiness would be soured.'

'So you think we can go on like this? You might be married for fifty years for God's sake – or when Muriel gets too old for anyone to think ill of her, and James retires on his pension, perhaps I'll stand a chance then?' Sarcasm hid his hurt; she knew it did.

They looked at each other in silent misery, and then she was pulled into his arms, being held so close that she could feel his heart beating.

'Don't leave me, Dom. One day, somehow, I don't know when or how, but things will come right for us. It can't be right if we snatch what we want and hurt people who don't deserve it.'

'I know what you say is right, I know it with my heart, but living it is hard.'

'Not so hard as it would be if you went away.' For a while they stood just as they were, then she said, 'It's funny, isn't it? When you said I could rent this place I thought heaven had dropped at my feet. The only thing that put a blight on it was that I resented it belonging to you; I looked on you as the enemy who had spoilt the way things used to be here with dear old Mr Adams. Now though, each day when I drive to Tarnmouth it's because I want to be with you. I'm so grateful for Alice and Barry.'

'Let's lock the front door and go upstairs. Coffee? Tea? There's even some of that evil-coloured Green Lady you liked in the cupboard.'

They went up to his none too tidy kitchen-cum-living room; he put the kettle on the gas ring while she turned the handle of the coffee grinder. She knew they had to keep occupied or the thoughts that were uppermost in both their minds would be too strong to be resisted. How easy it would be. Temptation whispered to her that there could be no wrong in the love they would share while the kettle boiled dry and the world was forgotten. But reason carried her imagination to what would follow: joy, oh yes there would be such joy, she had no doubt that the blessed miracle of union would be there for both of them and with it would come guilt, guilt that would tarnish their love, and furtiveness that comes with deceit.

They drank their coffee and smoked a cigarette; they talked about old Jacko and his visit to *Blue Horizon*; Dominic said he was driving up to London the following Tuesday as it was his mother's birthday and, if she liked, he would take her illustrations; they arranged to go fishing the next morning if the weather held. From one thing to another, they kept the conversation going. It was only as she said goodbye to him that they came near to acknowledging how near to breaking point that afternoon had brought them.

'Darling Georgie.' He kissed her forehead with more tenderness than passion. 'We won the battle, yet again. *You* won the battle. The hardest thing is to know that he'll take you as his right. You must want him to; you need physical love – didn't you say that was what drove you to marry?' he reminded her.

In answer she took his hand and steered it to her breast, thinking all the time of James and his barely disguised revulsion. But Dominic's hand caressed her. Her body let her have no secrets; he knew she was as aroused as he was himself.

'Go home, Georgie. Damn it, you're not playing fair.' A nervous tic at the corner of his mouth told her even more than his words.

'I'm sorry,' she muttered, turning away from him, 'sorry for you, sorry for me. I don't mean not to play fair . . . love you so much . . . such a bloody, bloody mess.'

They looked helplessly at each other.

'Then we'll bloody, bloody have to get over it,' he mimicked her use of the word that was so out of character on her lips. It broke the tension and helped them to laugh.

'I'm off,' she said, keeping her voice bright and brushing her lips against his cheek in a fashion that was more sisterly than lover-like.

Once the 1939 season started there was less chance for the two of them to go out in *Tight Lines* – in fact there was little opportunity even for Dominic to go, for custom was good for both the day trips on *Blue Horizon* and the short afternoon outings too. In the gallery for weeks on end last year's customers came to see what they could buy, for something handmade and unusual was a lasting memento. Although as they made sure they didn't let it show that they were worried, the hope given by Mr Chamberlain's assurance that the peace was secure did very little to build their confidence. The trouble was that wretched wireless; it brought Hitler's ranting right into their homes. If they could have understood the language it might not have been so worrying, but the future was unknown and it seemed to most people their future depended on the behaviour of a maniac.

On Fridays, Dominic only took passengers out for two hours in the afternoon. For those who were going home the next day, two hours was as much as they wanted to spare, for they liked the shingle beach in the morning and the pier in the evening. And this was no ordinary Friday; the holiday mood had been hard enough to keep alive all through the season but by that Friday, the first of September, it had become useless even to pretend. Already women up and down the country had been stitching heavy black material to curtain their windows; thousands of children were being transported away from areas feared to be open to danger and taken to live with strangers in the safety of the countryside; gas masks had been issued and tested. England had prepared its people for the worst and even those who had clung so tenaciously to that last straw of hope knew it was slipping from their grasp.

Having seen his passengers safely disembarked, Dominic went straight to the esplanade. Passing the gallery, he continued on to the corner by the cinema where the evening paper seller always sat calling out anything startling enough to attract a customer even though it was usually impossible to understand what it was he was calling. Whatever the news, he always attracted attention with 'Readallaboudit' then followed that with something that had caught his eye on the front page. Today there was one item that threw anything else into insignificance. 'Readallaboudit. German troops invade Poland. Readallaboudit. Prime Minister sends ultimatum.'

Taking the penny coin Dominic held out to him, he handed out the evening paper. 'Don't make good reading. Looks like we're in for it.'

At the gallery Georgie was wrapping a set of coasters she

had worked on herself, each one depicting a different scene of Tarnmouth.

'You've heard?' Dominic greeted her.

'Barry brought his wireless. We listened to the news before they went home. They have until Sunday to pull out of Poland. Surely even Hitler can't want to bring his country down with another war? He's probably calling our bluff. No one wants war – no one.'

'No one ever wants war – the German people must feel just the same. But there's no way he's going to let himself be seen as dancing to our tune. And what about those poor wretched Poles? We have given our word; there can be no way out. By this time next week the lads in our army and the French army too will know what war is all about. Christ, what a bloody mess.'

She nodded and from her expression he knew she was trying to envisage what war would mean. She would have been too young to have anything more than hazy memories of the last one. For Dominic, four years her senior, it was a little clearer.

'I was just trying to imagine how those poor women must feel: mothers of young soldiers and sailors, wives of men in the services. Will it be like last time, millions of lives wasted?'

'That, my darling, is war,' he said softly, drawing her into his arms. Then, more positively, 'But this time they won't wait a couple of years before they bring in conscription. They can't win a war without men – and we know the training that has been going on in Germany. They'll have to start conscripting right from the beginning if they want time to train lads before sending them to risk their lives. Will James be called? Or will he volunteer straight away so that he can choose the service he wants?' Did she imagine it or was there hope in the question?

'You'd like him to go to war?'

'Darling, I wouldn't wish it on James or anyone else. But logic tells me it's a mistake to wait your turn and then get drafted into something unsuitable. They'll probably start with the youngsters, eighteens, twenties.'

'James will soon be forty-two.' Her answer surprised him. 'And anyway he's far more use where he is. He has been extra busy over these last months – local civil defence, organizing public air-raid shelters and distribution of material for those ugly things we've all had to ruin our gardens with so that we can burrow underground like a lot of animals.'

'Please God you'll never have to use it.' Then, 'Bully for James! His work will go on undisturbed. I fear *Blue Horizon* has made her last trip until this fiasco is over and I shall take *Tight Lines* out of the water and tow her across to the shed. She'll come to no harm in there.'

'We're not at war yet.' She heard the snap in her voice. 'Even now it might not happen. You are playing right into Hitler's hands with your assumption that everything is going to be dreadful.'

'On the contrary, I am looking ahead so that I can deal with everything smoothly before I go.' He tipped her face towards his, his serious expression making it impossible for her to look away. 'Even though common sense tells us that there is no other way, we shan't know for sure until Sunday. After that I shall do the things I have to do here – then enlist in the merchant fleet.'

'No,' she breathed. Then her fighting spirit was back on course. 'They might not need you; you said it would be young men, really young. Dom, you're thirty years old. They'll just be boys. If you can't work with the boats there must be useful jobs you can do here. Don't they make boats at that place up the river?'

'You want me to live comfortably while other people fight my battle?'

His going to war was something she hadn't ever considered. She heard the hysterical note in her voice and realized it came from fear.

'It's not *your* battle, nor mine either.'

'It's not of our making, but if it happens then, yes, it *is* our battle. Did those poor Poles cause it? Of course they didn't. But they can't wash their hands of it and say "It's not my battle". No right-minded person can pass by on the other side. So if war comes I must fight for the cause, and then comes the question: in which service? I am a seaman, Georgie my dearest. The ships of the Royal Navy have always sounded to me like floating barracks, vast, regimented. The merchant fleet is right for me.'

'Perhaps it won't happen,' she whispered, nuzzling against him, his Guernsey sweater rough against her face. As if in answer to her words they heard an unfamiliar and eerie sound, a loud wailing cry from a hooter, the note rising and falling, up, down, up, down. 'Hark! What's that?'

'I saw a notice. At six o'clock they were going to test the air-raid sirens. This is the warning that enemy planes are approaching. They'll follow this up with the All Clear.'

In silence they waited until, after a break of no more than a couple of seconds came the single note that would be the sign that danger was past.

For months they had put off thinking about the future, seeing no hope that Fate would point them to a way of being free to be together. If war came – and in her heart Georgie was as sure as he was that there could be no other way – Dominic would volunteer. She shivered.

'You can't be cold?' He held her closer, moving his hand on her back.

They had been waiting for Fate to point a way to them. She clung to him, frightened to let the thought form and yet not able to escape it.

Seven

'How is it we haven't been asked to have an evacuee?' Georgie said as she dried the supper dishes for Muriel.

'And quite right too that we haven't. You know how late it is when James finishes with meetings lately; he deserves to have things nice and comfortable at home. War isn't just for those who join the services. Things have to be taken care of for those at home, too.'

'Yes, I know. But I don't expect the powers that be would look on that as a reason not to billet someone on us.'

'There now, that's done for another day,' Muriel said, as she made sure everything was washed. 'I'll start putting away while you finish drying. Not a reason, you say? Well, in my mind it is, but the fact of the matter was that instead of calling here at the house, Mr Rustbridge – the chemist from Wilborough Street, he's in charge of finding places for the children – well, he spoke to James after one of the meetings, asked him if we had a spare room here. So James was able to tell him the two bedrooms were slept in and the third, the little one, you use for your painting.'

'I only use it to keep my clobber in so that I don't clutter the place downstairs. He ought not to have made that an excuse.'

Muriel frowned, weighing up what Georgina had said.

'I felt it smacked of pulling rank,' Muriel agreed, 'until I stopped to really think about it. I meant what I said about James and the long hours he spends at the Town Hall. Then I thought of some poor little child who'd never been away from home and imagined how it would be for him – or her – here. We are none of us used to little people. You were a very self-assured nine-year-old, used to boarding school, when I married Cyril. Children need to be where they will feel comfortable. And, even though he never says so, I know you must think the same as I do. James is very quiet lately, as if he's never free of the things he has on his mind.'

Georgie hadn't noticed.

'You've seen more of him than I have through the summer.'

'And that's not as things should be. Georgie, you are his wife. Always you're dashing off to Tarnmouth. Sometimes I wonder you can bear to tear yourself away even at the weekends.'

'I love what I do there,' was her answer, 'and I'm sure James is happy with what he does, too. He's always taken pride in his work.'

'Yes, yes, of course he has. And it isn't my place to interfere. But your happiness, and his, means a lot to me. Try and give him more of your time, dear.'

Later as she lay in bed Muriel let her mind go back over the conversation with mixed feelings. If Georgie took to heart what she had said, her own life would be the poorer. Certainly there were evenings when James had meetings, but often he didn't hurry back after lunch. They listened to the news on the wireless together, news that always set them talking. But what she had said about his seeming quiet, almost withdrawn sometimes, was the truth and there could be no reason for that except that he was overworking. Tonight he had been in his study when Georgie had gone on to bed but, listening quietly for his tread on the stair carpet, Muriel had heard him come up a few minutes ago. She closed her eyes, despising herself that she could feel such jealousy of Georgie whom she had loved as if she were her own. *Forget Georgie, forget what had been said*, she told herself, *forget everything but this aching love you have for him. Disgusting, he's my son-in-law; he must see me as a matronly carer in the home. And if he could look at me now, would he pity me and suppose that this is how widows behave, women on their own? Or would he be disgusted and think that at my age this aching need that tortures me ought to have died?*

She might have been surprised if she could have seen into the room along the corridor. As he always did, James prepared for bed in the bathroom and then came quietly into the bedroom where the light was still on. Automatically he felt in the pocket of his pyjama jacket. He had always liked to be sure he had a handkerchief but since he and Georgie had married he never went to bed without checking he had a sheath easily accessible. With Kathy it had been different; both of them young and in love, and a child would have been welcome. But it had never happened. With Georgie he had always been careful that she shouldn't get pregnant, never really asking himself why. On that night as he went into the bedroom the light was still on but she was already asleep. Standing by the bed he looked down at her, his disappointment overtaken by tenderness. Sleeping, she looked young and vulnerable, dear Georgie. Was that why he knew it would be wrong for them to have children? In truth many women were mothers long before they were her age.

Sitting on the stool by the dressing table he gazed at her. Even though she had the covers pulled right up to her chin he knew exactly what she was like – and perhaps that was the root of the trouble. She had always been lithe and slim, he had known that right from the first; her slim straight build had given her the appearance of chic sophistication. He loved her dearly, now no less than when he persuaded her that what they shared was a good basis for life together. In the darkened bedroom, without what he believed they called foreplay, she never failed to satisfy him. But what about Georgie, did she sense that something always held him back? In the two years they had been married their relationship had grown no closer. Still they were friends, truly fond of each other – of that he was certain – but did she realize that marriage should be so much more than that? The guilt was his, and he was ashamed. What would he think of any other man who married an attractive, intelligent young woman and then lost his desire for her? His mind slipped back to where it had been a few minutes before and he faced the truth that the reason he had no desire for them to have a child was that now, as never in the days before their wedding, he was aware of a difference in their ages. To say he looked on her as a child would be ridiculous, but certainly she wasn't his equal. By the time she'd started school he'd already had his law degree.

Times with Georgie were the high points of his week. But since they'd lived here, the three of them . . . He pulled his mind up short as he moved to the doorway and switched off the light, then in the total darkness of the blacked-out room groped his way to open first the curtains, then the window. Careful not to disturb Georgie he climbed into bed. *She sleeps like a contented child*, he thought. If only he could switch off his thoughts as he had switched off the light.

Dominic wasted no time in applying to join the Merchant Navy and, if Georgie had been hanging on to the hope that the wheels of bureaucracy would turn slowly, she was disappointed. His medical confirmed that he was A1 and by the last week in October he had his joining instructions.

There had been so many changes in the seven weeks since the start of war. Everyone whose work wasn't considered essential to the war effort had had to lay up their cars, and that applied to James, Georgie and Dominic, too. It seemed quite out of character for James to go to the Town Hall each day on a bicycle, but with everything changing around them it was just part of the new pattern they must learn to live by. Georgie's journey was more complicated; she walked to the end of the road, waited for a bus to the railway station and then caught the train to Tarnmouth. In the car the journey from door to door would have taken less than half an hour, but with the new arrangement it took more than twice as long.

'Why don't you have another thought about what you want to do?' James suggested. 'I was talking to Clive Bryant, headmaster of the grammar school, after the Air Raid Emergency meeting last evening, and he was bemoaning the fact that already some of the younger staff members have enlisted. I mentioned your background and qualifications and he was most interested. There would be a place there for you, Georgie – no waiting for buses and trains, but a ten-minute cycle ride to work and the freedom of the school holidays.'

'The man's deaf,' she said, turning to Muriel with a laugh. 'Either deaf or lost his marbles. Don't you remember, James, my joy when I took myself out of teaching?'

Trying to fit his mood to hers, he too managed to laugh as he answered, 'There now, and I thought your delight was that you left to marry *me*.'

'Seriously, I don't know what the future of the gallery will be. Already I know the war has altered things for two of the workers. One's husband was a Territorial so, of course, he's in the Army already, and another has got a job at Hoopers, the boat builders up the river. But I'm going to keep open as long as any of them need the outlet and as long as things still sell. Perhaps the war won't last long.'

'People said that with the last one,' Muriel put in. '"It'll be over by Christmas," they said in the first weeks. But it was four years.'

'I remember,' James said. 'I only got in towards the end. Never thought to see it again.' He and Muriel looked at each other, both remembering.

They think they know; just because they remember the last war they think they know the dreadful sick feeling of being left behind. Four days and he'll be gone, I don't want to think . . . But four days, we've still got four days. And each time his boat docks he'll come home. Please, please keep him safe. As a background to her thoughts she was aware that Muriel and James were reminiscing, but it meant nothing to her. That had been *their* war; this was *hers*, hers and Dominic's.

'I'll leave Barry's glass case on the wall with the boat in it, shall I?'

For both of them, this was a task filled with sadness. They were stripping the booking office and stacking everything connected with the fishing expeditions and the summertime boat trips in the small back room.

'Yes, leave it. And those two pictures.'

The smile he threw at her might be forced, but sounding cheerful helped them both.

'Make sure you put *Not for Sale* stickers on all of them. I want to be able to move back in when I get home and find it all as it was.' Then, turning to look at her and holding his hand for her to take, 'Understand?'

'Aye, aye, Skipper.' Yes, she understood what he said and the underlying need for him to say it. There must be a future; the crazy things that were happening all around them could never change the rock they built on. Faith, trust, hope, determination, all these things had become the stepping stones that carried them safely through each day. Each day . . . Monday was over, and already it was Tuesday afternoon. 'We still have part of tomorrow; today isn't the end.'

He held her shoulders, forcing her to meet his gaze. That forced cheerfulness had given way to a depth of seriousness he seldom plummeted.

'Today isn't the end; tomorrow isn't the end. However long we are separated, and for whatever reason—'

'No. Dom, no.'

'Yes, Georgie, yes. We neither of us have any real idea of war, and this time I don't believe anyone really knows what to expect. Perhaps I'll come sailing home unscathed to find that some stray bomb has fallen in Winchford. It's not only those who serve in uniform who are in danger. God knows what is ahead for anyone – generals, privates, civilians – there are no rules any longer.'

'It's crazy; the whole thing is crazy and wicked. I'm sure people in Germany are torn to bits with misery just like we are. The glorious allies and the enemy – just *people*, all of us, wanting to love and be loved.'

She was shaken by silent sobs she could no longer force down and gently he drew her into his arms.

'Here, blow,' he said as he passed her his handkerchief.

'Sorry.' She made a mighty effort to overcome her outburst. 'I feel I'm being pulled in two. This is *me*, the real me, but later I have to go home just as if this day is the same as every other. I'm sorry, Dom; I'm just making it harder for you. I don't expect your mother created a scene when you said goodbye.' She made a great effort to regain composure, then in a tone such as she might have used to a troublesome pupil at St Winifred's she said, 'I've no time for histrionics. It's simply self-indulgence.'

'The Georgie I love has never been good at hiding her feelings, even in the beginning before I found a way into her affections. And as for Mother, of course she didn't create a scene, as you put it; she has become used to my comings and goings over the years. She knows I'm like the bad penny; I always turn up again. And now we have a lot to do and not too long to do it in. Can you give me a hand with this desk? It's pretty heavy, so we ought to take the drawers out first.' So the task of emptying the booking office continued.

Already the words 'after the war' were being bandied around, as if the return of peace would bring everyone's personal Utopia.

Just after six o'clock they locked the door and, in an effort to retain some sort of normality, went their separate ways, he to the harbour to check *Blue Horizon* for the last time, then spend an

hour or two in the Jolly Sailor, and she up the hill to the station
in time for the six twenty-five train which would get her to
Winchford about twenty minutes later. Waiting on the platform
where two dim blue lights turned complete darkness into shadowy
gloom, she turned up the collar of her coat. Only days ago they
had been enjoying Indian summer, but now even the elements
were in tune with her private despair.

'You'll be waiting for the six twenty-five, ma'am.' The tall figure
of the Station Master appeared through the darkened doorway
from the building, 'I've just heard it's been cancelled. It'll be
another hour before the next. You'd best go into the waiting
room, you'll catch your death out hear. Turned bitter, you'd think
it was January not October. There's an electric fire high up on
the wall in there; just pull the cord to turn it on.'

'I'd better go out to the phone box first and ring home to say
I'll be late. Thanks for telling me.' Wasn't the cancelled train as
much in keeping with her aching misery as the bitterly cold
wind?

It was James who answered her call.

'Is there anywhere warm for you to wait? I don't know why
you don't close early now the evenings are dark. I don't like you
to be waiting by yourself on the station.'

She tried to make her laugh sound mirthful, but it wasn't easy
while in her thoughts she was in *Blue Horizon*, hearing the wind
buffeting and feeling the gentle rocking of the boat. Perhaps by
next season the war would be over. Reason told her it was impossible, yet standing in the phone box with a pile of pennies in her
hand to feed into the machine if James was still on the line when
her three minutes ended, it was luxury to imagine the happy
holidaymakers walking up the plank on to the boat, Dominic
greeting them in his characteristic way, with the courtesy of a
host receiving guests except that before he started the motor he
went round taking the fares. She smiled, picturing it all.

'—that I would get home early this evening. She has a lovely
fire going in the drawing room. Damn this war. There's a car
sitting in the garage and you waiting about on a night like this.
Why don't you take a taxi home, Georgie? If you haven't enough
on you to pay him, I'll be here when you arrive.'

'I think the station taxi is out. You and Muriel eat your meal and get it cleared away. If I hop off now I can get something to eat at the Bay Hotel; it's right by the station. And don't worry, James darling, I'm OK. There's a heater in the waiting room.'

She had no intention of eating at the Bay Hotel. Even on an ordinary evening she would have to be really hungry to want to sit there alone having dinner, and on this evening food was the last thing she wanted. But it was a good many hours since she had fried sausages while Dominic had gone to the fish and chip shop to buy chips to save them cooking potatoes. Thinking about it, she was ashamed at her lack of expertise. Muriel delighted in preparing meals, serving them so that everything looked attractive and appetizing, and she had been more than willing to leave it to her. But fried sausages, chip shop chips and a tin of baked beans could hardly be looked on as a culinary delight – and that had been the last lunch she and Dominic would share until he came home. Her stomach rumbled, reminding her just how long since she'd eaten. There was no chocolate in the machine on the platform, but on her way to the waiting room she turned the handle of the station cafe and, to her surprise, found it was open. The blackout was so good it was a wonder they ever had a customer once daylight faded. Despite the tea being stewed and the Eccles cake having sat on the counter since morning, she felt better for them. And when she finally got back to Winchford station she found a taxi and arrived home in style.

'You two look cosy,' she greeted them, going straight to the drawing room. 'Fancy needing a fire. It was only two days ago we were gardening in the sunshine.'

'You must be frozen, dear,' Muriel said. 'You feel it when it changes suddenly like this. And what a shame you're late when James has an early night. He was home here just after five.'

'Take your coat off and come by the fire,' James told her. 'I'll pour you a drink. Sherry?'

'Have we any whisky? I'd like whisky and a cigarette, followed by a hot bath. Is that OK?'

He passed her his cigarettes and lighter. 'Whisky it shall be,' he said, 'and you, Muriel, what can I get you?'

'A sherry would be lovely. Shall I get the drinks while you two have a chance to talk?'

'No, no, you stay where you are.'

Georgie watched him go out of the room and thought as she had a thousand times what a truly nice man he was.

'While we were sitting here waiting for you, James was saying he wished you would close the gallery earlier now the days are short. There can't be customers wandering along that seafront once the streets are in darkness and there are no lights in the shop windows.'

'Perhaps I will, Muriel, I'll think about it.'

It was all a charade: the pretence of being happy to be home, the pleasant smile on her face, the look of concentration as James told them of talk he'd heard that the local buses were to cancel their service at half past seven each evening.

She finished her cigarette, drained her glass and escaped to the bath. Economy was the new order of the day; it even extended to bath water, which wasn't supposed to be deeper than five inches. On that evening she cheated. Then, having crumbled a lilac-scented bath cube in, she lowered herself to lie down, closing her eyes and savouring the luxury. Downstairs they would be talking amicably or, with her occupied upstairs, they would probably be playing cards. No, she heard the wireless; that must be the nine o'clock news. They never missed that. Then they would discuss what they'd heard as if the ghastliness of what was happening – or what was expected, feared, anticipated to happen – would honestly touch their lives. Her illusions about the merchant fleet being safer than any other had already been dashed. *Keep him safe,* she begged silently. *Even if he never settles down in Tarnmouth afterwards, even if he stops loving me, please, please keep him safe.*

Half an hour later, wearing her nightdress and dressing gown, she went back down to the drawing room.

'Three can play, we'll start the game again,' Muriel said, immediately scooping up the cards she had been dealing.

'No, you two go ahead. I haven't even seen the newspaper today. You're both always one step ahead of me. I must try and see what's happening in the world. I won't interfere with your crossword, James.'

'You can give some thought to four down if you're feeling clever. It's beaten us for the time being.'

'I bet you a pound to a penny you won't come to bed until you've got it.'

How empty the conversation was, and how easily they were fooled into seeing no further than the cheerful front she presented. She picked up the paper, gazed unseeing at the words while her mind went on a journey of its own. She and Dominic still had one more morning before the one thirty train carried him away . . . one morning and in her imagination she saw it so clearly. She wanted the night to be over.

He heard her arrive and came down to the gallery immediately.

'There's coffee in the jug upstairs. Are you coming to collect it or shall I bring it down.'

'Dom.' She came to him and raised her face to his. 'Good morning, Dom. And it will be; it must be. I'll put a notice on the door that this morning the gallery will be closed. It's all we have. All . . .' She hesitated, knowing what she wanted to say but dreading that by putting it into words the wonder of it might be lost.

The staircase was narrow, but with arms around each other they went up side by side. She believed his thoughts must have moved on the same lines as her own through the night, for she saw his holdall was ready in the passageway; there would be no last-minute rush of things he had to do. It was just nine o'clock; the morning lay ahead of them.

They drank their coffee, they even smoked first one cigarette and then another, reminiscing, rekindling never-to-be-forgotten moments, revelling in the knowledge of what was to come. It had started to rain, spattering the windowpanes and rolling down like teardrops.

'It looks cold and cheerless,' she said softly. 'Remember how well we fitted into the bath?'

His expression was hard to read.

'I remember everything, Georgie, every hour of joy, every hour of longing.' He took her hand and drew it to his face.

'You know something?' she said in a voice that held more laughter than seductiveness. 'I'd never touched a beard until yours. I'd expected it to be prickly, but it's soft.' She leant towards him, moving her cheek against his. 'With two of us sharing we would be keeping to the rules if we had ten inches of water. Yes?'

'And then? What are you telling me?' he whispered, knowing the answer and yet frightened to believe.

'I've fought and fought against it, but . . . but Dominic I was wrong. I put other people first, never you and me. Just at this moment, it makes us sinners – well, me, not you. You are free, you don't have to be plagued by guilt and shame – but if it makes me a sinner, then that's what I'll be. I know, I just *know* that love can never truly be a sin.' He felt as though his Adam's apple filled his throat; he was frightened to trust his voice. 'Dominic?' she prompted when he was silent.

'Love is God-given,' he said huskily. 'My blessed Georgie, I love you.' For a few seconds neither spoke, both awestruck by the mysterious solemnity of the moment. And then he said what in normal circumstances would have been left unspoken. 'If we believe in an omnipotent God – as we do, we *must* or there's nothing – then we must know that if we live by love, not self-ishness and greed, but love, then there can be no sin.' He felt the movement of her head against his neck as she nodded. Heightened emotion had let him speak straight from his heart, but they both needed to get their feet back on the ground. 'Shift yourself, my darling, I'm going to light the geyser.'

Five minutes later they were facing each other through the steam in the bathroom. Their moments of solemnity had passed and yet because of them they felt closer. Neither of them were people to bare their souls easily; yet now, about things that formed the foundation of their code of living, they had no secrets.

He unbuttoned her blouse and slipped it off her shoulders; she unbuttoned his shirt and raised it to pull off over his head. She unfastened his belt and unbuttoned his trousers so they fell to his ankles and he stepped out of them; he undid her bra and slipped it off her arms, then unbuttoned her French knickers so that they fell to the floor. Next, kneeling in front of her he un-fastened her suspenders, and then took off the narrow belt that supported them. Now all that remained were her stockings and so, one by one, with hands that were a caress, he pushed them down and lifted her feet out of them. Still he knelt. She could hear him breathing and knew his heart must be beating as hard as her own as he leant against her. Only at the back of her mind was she aware that nothing like this had ever happened to her, just as following that thought came another that couldn't be repressed: of course it hadn't; this could never have been part of James' love-making. She pulled Dominic's head closer, feeling the movement of his tongue against her.

'Yes . . . yes . . . yes . . .' Did she speak the word or was it only in her mind that she cried out to him?

'I want you now,' he breathed, struggling to his feet. If it were possible for her to become even more aroused, then the sight of him was all it took. Woman's intuition and urgency guided her as she grabbed a towel and covered the cold, closed seat of the lavatory then pushed Dominic to sit on it.

What was she doing? For a second he thought she was about to kneel in front of him, but instead she straddled him and guided him to penetrate deep into her. Together, both with their eyes closed, they let out a half sigh, half moan, neither of them moving. Then, as she eased herself firmly on him, hardly more than clenching and relaxing her muscles, they opened their eyes and looked at each other.

'My darling, my blessed love,' he murmured so quietly she might have dreamt it. And when he moved his hands on her underdeveloped breasts, teasing her nipples, she knew that coming to her, within her grasp and getting closer with every second, was the miracle she longed for. She heard herself whimpering with joy as she started to move, raising herself up, pushing down hard, up, down, up, down, her actions as out of control as by then were his.

Then it was over, but breathless and filled with joy she knew that they had found that miracle. She leant against him. Only seconds later she started to laugh.

'Share your joke,' he murmured into her hair.

'I was just waking up to where we are. That pipe from the cistern can't be the most romantic resting place.'

He chuckled, ruffling her hair. 'When we're old and grey and looking back, we'll say to each other, "Where were we the first time we made love?"'

And she took up the story, 'On the lavatory!' Their abandoned laughter went far beyond its cause, but their heightened emotions had to find an outlet and to laugh was better than to cry. The minutes were racing by; so soon he'd be gone.

Together they bathed, the water doing much to revive them.

But they couldn't dry, dress and go back to the kitchen-cum-everything-else room they'd left; they weren't ready for that. It was nearly half past ten; he would have to leave for the station in about two hours. By silent mutual consent they scooped up their discarded clothes and went to his bedroom. It was cold, the wind gusting and blowing the rain to hit the window.

'In you hop,' he said, holding open the covers. She did as he said, noting that he set the alarm on the bedside clock. Tick-tock, the sound wouldn't let them forget the passing seconds.

They lay close to each other, the warmth seeming to shut them away from the outside world. When they spoke it was in little more than whispers.

'Dom, I can't live with James, not after today.'

'God! But why have I got to leave you, today of all days. I ought to come with you to talk to him.'

'No, it wouldn't be fair to him. I must talk to him on his own. And you needn't be scared for me; James would never create a scene. He's kind and understanding. I'll tell him I'm in love with you and want a divorce. I just wish I didn't have to hurt him. And Muriel, too. She'll feel she can't stay in his house once I've gone. It's what I've dreaded. But there's no other way. I can't put them before *you*. You're . . . you're my whole life.'

Again his Adam's apple was playing tricks. Then something else came to the forefront of his mind, something he had thought of earlier and then events had left no space for it.

'Georgie, earlier . . . I didn't use anything. Suppose you find you're pregnant?'

She nuzzled closer against him. 'I'm due on Friday and you could use me as a calendar. This is a safe time, I read about it in a magazine.' *We still have an hour before we have to get up*, she thought. *It's different now, lying here, warm, close to each other right down to our feet.* And as if to prove her point she wrapped one leg across his.

For a while they savoured the rightness of simply lying together, and only gradually did their hands move on each other. The uncontrolled passion that had led them to the unconventional setting last time was replaced by something more tender, aware of the ticking of the bedside clock and of the uncertainty of what lay ahead. This time each movement was a slow caress, their eyes were open and lying above her he raised himself on his elbows so that they looked at each other as they moved. Soon the day would catch up with them but for these moments there was nothing but *this*, their farewell. And the miracle was there for them, uniting them.

She watched him set out for the station, his holdall slung on his shoulder. Not once did he glance back as he went past the cinema, past the Bay Hotel and then the bank before he turned up the hill to the station. Only then did he turn and for one brief second they raised their hands in farewell. Then he was gone. She felt sick; her jaw ached in the effort to hold it steady. Turning back into the gallery she seemed to hear the ghost of the girl she had been that wild and stormy day on the sea. *'Without you there would be no colour, no hope.'*

The 'closed' sign was still on the door. She was alone, utterly alone. Uninvited an image flashed into her mind of Gregory House where James and Muriel would be having lunch. At the thought of food she tried to swallow the lump in her throat, but her mouth felt like sawdust. She must pull herself together. What good would she be either to herself or Dominic if she went to pieces like this? With forced determination she went back up the stairs where, along the corridor, she noticed the bathroom door was ajar. Following instinct she was drawn to it; she wanted to remember every precious moment. Inside the small room she leant against the closed door, her eyes shut in a vain attempt to bring him close. Again he was kneeling in front of her; she im-agined the touch of his tongue. Sensing something different in the warm moisture, she felt with her fingers. A smile tugged at her mouth as she saw the blood. What was it she had said about her being so regular that you could use her as a calendar? It was almost as if he spoke to her, telling her that he had done this to her, his love so deep inside her had brought her forward two days. Two years of married life and this had never happened before; but then nothing had ever happened before as it had on that day. James . . . After this morning she couldn't live as his wife. He deserved better; none of it was his fault.

At two o'clock, knowing that already Dominic's train would have carried him miles away, she washed her face and re-did her

make-up then went downstairs to unlock the front door and turn
the sign to read *Open*. He was starting out on the challenge of
his new life, one that had never been part of his pattern, and so
she would accept her own challenge. This evening she would
wait until Muriel had gone to bed and then talk to James. She
tried not to imagine the interview ahead of her; it had to be
faced. She wanted to get it over, but she hated to imagine the
look of hurt surprise she would see on James' face; and she hated
too the knowledge that she was throwing him back into his life
of loneliness. Then there was Muriel: if she'd been simply an
outsider employed as his housekeeper she would have stayed. But
she hadn't worked for a wage; she had been part of the family.
Being James, always kind and caring, he would suggest she carried
on as they were; but Muriel would refuse, seeing it as charity. So
he would overlook the rights and wrongs and write her a glowing
reference. But for neither of them would things be the same, and
they had become good friends over the eighteen months she'd
run the house.

The rain showed no sign of easing and, not surprisingly, no
one came into the gallery until at about a quarter to six Georgie
heard a car draw up outside.

'Shine the torch over here,' she heard a woman say. 'OK. I've
got the door open.' Then a couple pushed open the inner door
of the gallery and came in.

'What a day to choose,' the woman greeted her. 'We've driven
all the way from Guildford and when we left home the rain had
cleared up. Anyway, we're here now. You may recognize me; I've
been in here quite a few times looking at all the treasures you
have.'

She was a plump woman of some sixty years, smiling and rosy
cheeked.

'Come along now, m'dear,' the man, presumably her husband,
said. He was a tall, thin man, quietly spoken and, Georgie suspected,
used to taking a back seat. He took his wife's arm and turned
her towards the wall covered with paintings. Then, smiling at
Georgie, he said, 'There'll be no peace till she gets what she's
after. She's been on and on about this place. Twice she's come
on the coach with parties: the WI was one and the Stanton Singers
– she's front-row soprano – they came just at the tail end of the

season. Each time she's come home full of chatter about this place. It's a picture she's after, something to hang at the head of the stairs.'

Georgie replied smilingly enough, giving no indication of how aware she was of the passing of the seconds and the uphill wet walk ahead of her to the station.

'We've come today because it's my birthday and Sid's half-day closing.'

'Had you seen something you liked when you were here before? What sort of picture are you looking for?' Then, her mind catching up with what she'd been told, 'Oh, and a very happy birthday to you. I hope you find something that will always bring you a memory of your day – rain and all,' she added with a laugh. Her customers both had the same thought: what a delightful young woman, so attractive and not a bit stuck-up like some of them would be in this kind of trade. 'If you'd like to go through to the other room you'll find some more in there.'

'In there, too? When I was here before that was where we all bought our tickets for a ride on the boat. All day we were out on the water on my first visit, and my word what a lovely day we had. That was with the WI. The second time, well I dare say none of us were in the mood for throwing ourselves into holiday fun. It was just before the war started. It was very nice though, the same young man took us out, but that time it was only for two hours, no getting off and looking around town further along the coast. So you say you've taken over what was the booking office.'

'It stands to reason,' her husband pointed out, getting a word in where he could. 'There'll be no call for sea trips until this little lot gets sorted out. I wouldn't mind betting the young chap who took the boat out will be off into the Navy. Once a seaman, always a seaman.'

'He's in the Merchant Navy.' She felt a strange relief in talking about him.

'Dear, oh dear. What a dreadful business it all is.' The man shook his head, his thin face a picture of sorrow. 'Well, we must hope. I'm no seaman, but I know that given the choice of a battleship or a cargo vessel, I know where I'd feel safer.'

As he said, he was no seaman, but his comment made Georgie

think again about her belief that a merchant ship wouldn't be a target. False or true, his comment had made a deep dent in her hard-fought-for facade of cheerfulness. She wished the couple would make their decision about a painting and go.

'I've found it! Come and see, Bertram,' the rosy lady called from the doorway of the erstwhile booking office. 'It was on the other wall when I was here at the end of August.' Then to Georgie, who walked across the corridor to see which picture she was so excited about, 'You've been changing them around, you naughty thing. This was in the other room.'

'I change them round all the time,' Georgie told her with a bright smile. 'It wouldn't do to look as if nothing ever moved. It's the rustic cottage you fell in love with, is it? I wonder it hadn't gone before this, but I find most people look for something related to the sea when they come in here.' She imagined Edna Hopkins' pleasure when she heard that her first offering to the gallery had been sold.

Husband Bertram took out his wallet; he even smiled as he laid the notes on the desk. He and his Kitty had had plenty of frugal years in the past, so it was nice to be able to splash out and buy her something like this she'd so wanted. The picture was carefully wrapped and then, at last, Georgie led the way along the unlit central passageway to the outside door, holding it open for them. At that same moment the clock on the church at the eastern end of the esplanade struck six. She still had to lock the cash box away and book the sale, then run up the stairs to put on her hat and coat and collect her handbag. It would be a rush to catch that train and the last thing she wanted was to spend an hour in that dingy waiting room. The rain was dancing on her umbrella, the wind was bitterly cold and, to make matters worse, the evening was so dark that she couldn't see to avoid the puddles on the uneven surface of Station Hill. But at last she arrived at the station: dimly lit, eerie − and empty.

'You missed it by not two minutes.' The Station Master's voice surprised her from where he stood in the shadow of the building, then added with a ring of pride, 'Weather like this, leaves coming down all over the place in this wind, but we got it off right on the dot.'

'It would be punctual for once the very night I got held up,'

Georgie answered, taking no pains to hide her irritation as she thought of the hours she had stood on this platform. It was only seven weeks since she had laid up her car, but to think of the comfort and convenience of it seemed like looking back at some former life.

'You've got a long wait tonight. The seven forty stopping train has been cut, so the next one isn't due out until eight fifty-five.' He wasn't a vindictive man by nature, but he'd been a railway man all his life and he wasn't going to be spoken to like that by some young know-it-all. *Serves her right, too, sarcastic young madam,* he thought as he turned back into his room closing the door behind him. These last weeks had put a lot of pressure on the railway service, what with people not having petrol – very likely she was one of those – all the special trains laid on for those poor little kiddies in the beginning, all of it extra work and all taken for granted, men chucking up their job with the railway and getting off for a bit of adventure in the army. *People just don't know, and some of them – like her most likely – don't care.*

Walking out of the station, Georgie was met with a blast of wind that turned her umbrella inside out the moment she put it up. She got it straight again and started off down the hill holding the edge of it with her second hand to save it happening again, and feeling the rain trickling up her arm. She had more than two hours to kill before her train. The obvious thing would be to go to the Bay Hotel, but this evening of all evenings she couldn't face sitting alone eating. She'd go back to the gallery and phone Muriel – or James, but he probably wouldn't be home yet.

To her surprise it was James who answered the phone.

'James, I missed the train. And the next one has been cut.' What she had meant to say was that she wouldn't get back to Winchford until well after ten so the buses would have stopped. She'd get a taxi from the station. That's what she had meant to say – she even considered saying there was something they must talk about. But in fact what she said was, 'So I've come back to the gallery. I'll stay here tonight.'

'My dear girl, you can't do that. Where will you sleep? Get a taxi all the way home.'

Please, James, don't be kind, don't make it harder than it is.

'There's a settee in Dominic's quarters. I'll be quite comfortable.'

'You can't do that, Georgie. Whether or not it's comfortable isn't the point. He's been very kind taking you fishing, I dare say, but you can't expect him to accommodate you like that. Get a taxi. I'll watch for it to arrive and go out and pay the driver. You must be soaked if you've walked to the station and back in this weather.'

'A bit moist, certainly. But, James, don't worry about me imposing on Dominic. He isn't here. I told you he was joining the Merchant Navy, don't you remember? He's already gone, so there's no one here.'

'And you think he wouldn't mind? It's certainly more sensible than walking back to the station. You'll have to wear the same clothes in the morning. Have you any means of drying them?'

'Don't worry, my Mac is waterproof. I didn't get wet underneath. But it was really beastly walking in it. I'll see you tomorrow.'

'Can you get something to eat?'

'If you'd ever been to see the gallery you would know there's a fish and chip shop a few doors along.'

'Well, put the fire on, take care, and sleep well.'

'James . . .'

'Yes?'

'Nothing. Just goodnight, James.'

'Goodnight, darling. I hope that settee is as comfortable as you expect.'

She put the receiver back. Not going home . . . what had made her say it? Wind and rain wouldn't stop her. It was something she didn't want to admit: she was putting off the moment when she would have to tell him – tell both of them, for Muriel would be affected too. If only James were different, if he were less kind, less considerate. If he weren't still her dear, dear friend.

Upstairs she made a pot of coffee and lit a cigarette. Her mind was racing and yet settling nowhere. She wanted to close her eyes and relive those morning hours with Dominic, to relive hundreds of hours with him, times when she had been aware of happiness that is rooted in being utterly natural, just her plain unadulterated self. As if by contrast, so much else crowded in on her. St Winifred's and her longing to be free; the dreadful day when her father died and she made up her mind she would be responsible for Muriel. Her fleeting thoughts came to rest, not on Muriel but on her father. It was almost as if he was there with her and she knew that he of all people would understand her confusion. She felt the tears roll down her cheeks and didn't wipe them away. *You must have been so unhappy, Dad, so worried and frightened. Didn't you know that you could have shared it with me? Or is it easier to share when a person has died? Could I talk to you if you were sitting here with me? Probably not – and yet I can talk to you now, because you listen with your soul and you care. I've got to hurt them, Dad, and they don't deserve it. I love both of them but I have to do it. I've put it off until tomorrow. Is that right, Dad? After this morning I can't share a bed with James, dear James. You understand. I know you do. And as late as that I couldn't get back. So I'll have to wait until tomorrow. Am I making excuses? There's a bed in the little room with my painting things. What ought I to do?* If I took that train tonight, by the time I got home it would be about half past ten. Perhaps Muriel would have gone to bed and I could talk to James by himself. Then I'd tell her in the morning.

With her eyes closed she tried to listen for his answer. And perhaps she heard it in the acceptance that by leaving James she would be losing the comfort and security she had taken for granted. But why should she think that? Dominic was no pauper unable to provide them with a home. But the thought was born of something she was frightened to face, something too dreadful to contemplate: what if Dominic's boat was lost, what if he didn't come home? She seemed to hear her father's voice warning her. He had been so proud of her position at St Winifred's; how he would hate to see her alone and scraping a humble living. But it wouldn't be like that! One day the war would end and Dominic would be there with her; for the rest of their lives they would be together. It was that warning voice that decided her. She would go tonight. To put off telling James would be tempting fate not to bring Dominic back to her.

The nine fifty-five was ten minutes late and by the time she walked out of Winchford station the dark street was empty – empty of traffic, empty of people. There was nothing for it but to walk, which even in daylight would have taken about twenty minutes. Of course the windows of Gregory House gave no indication whether anyone was still up, but in that it was no different from any other blacked-out building. She felt for the keyhole then opened the front door, finding the hall in darkness as she expected. They must be in bed. In a way she was glad. She would have to talk to James in the bedroom, but at least they would be on their own. She was too fond of him to want Muriel or anyone else to see his look of bewildered hurt. But how could she talk to him in their bedroom and then spend the night on the unmade-up bed in the little room? She ought not to have come; she ought to have waited until the next day. Then she remembered her reason for not waiting; in coming tonight she felt she was keeping Dominic safe. Logic played no part in her thought processes.

That's when she realized there was a faint light coming from the drawing room where the door was just ajar. Not bright enough for the electric light, so perhaps there had been a power cut. But surely they would have gone to bed; they couldn't read or play cards by candlelight. So it must be from the fire – the coals must have slipped and made it flame. What instinct made her tread carefully and quietly across the hall she didn't ask herself; in fact she wasn't aware that she was creeping any more than she was that instead of flinging the door open in her usual way she pushed it just an inch or two so that she could look in.

She felt paralysed of all movement; she couldn't take in what she was seeing. It was like looking at two strangers. Muriel, whether in the dowdy clothes she had worn in her days at Sycamore Cottage or the more up-to-date fashions of recent days, had always managed to look well-groomed in a prim way, and the thought of her flaunting her body would have been unimaginable. Now she was neither groomed nor prim as, wearing just her nightgown, she clung to James. And James? Much more familiar to Georgie in his silk pyjamas than Muriel was in her nightgown, he was crushing Muriel to him with a passion Georgie had never suspected of him.

Her only coherent thought was that they mustn't know she was here; they must never know she had seen them. Later she might ask herself what stopped her walking in on them. Surely that would have turned the situation to her advantage. But for the moment she wanted just to get away . . . Taking the handle she pulled the door almost closed and then crept back across the hall and out of the front door, closing it with her key so that they wouldn't hear. She was grateful for the noise of the wind; it helped her reach the road without any risk of their hearing her treading on the path.

Just for a moment she stood there looking at the scarcely discernable shape of the house. Never had she felt so alone.

Eight

Upstairs Muriel got ready for bed, listening for his step on the stairs. Yes, she heard him go to his room. And then silence. It was strange there being only the two of them in the house. After such a perfect evening she knew exactly where she wanted her thoughts to lead her, but through the hours as they'd talked, listened to music, talked again, how could he not have been aware of what she felt for him? If, now, she were to follow her instinct and reach to fulfil the craving of her body, she felt that surely he must guess. Filled with shame and embarrassment, she plumped her pillows and turned on her side, determined to sleep.

What was that? In an instant she was sitting up listening. A knocking sound! There it was again. Never a nervous woman, she got out of bed and picked up her unlit candle. She could walk down the stairs safely in the pitch darkness of the blacked-out house. She was sure she knew what the noise was: just by the drawing-room window there was a hanging basket and when the wind was in a certain direction it swung to hit against the bricks of the house. It hadn't knocked during the evening; the direction must have changed suddenly. In the daytime the sound almost passed unnoticed; in the silence of night it was irritating and disturbing. She would have to draw back the heavy curtain to open the window and get at the basket, so she mustn't put on the electric light. In her mind she knew exactly how she would reach out and lift the hanging basket from its hook. Inside the drawing room, she lit her candle and put it on the occasional table right away from the window. It could do no harm to open the curtain just for a moment, and then push the bottom sash window right up. She had to stretch as far as she could to lift the chains of the basket off the hook, but she managed and gently rested it on the ground. Feeling pleased with her success she shut the window, thankful that on such a night the Air Raid Warden hadn't been on his round looking for cracks in the blackout. With a flick of her wrist she closed the heavy curtain, then heard something fall to the ground. One of the hooks had come out of its ring, leaving the corner of the curtain hanging down and letting light escape.

She could have left it until she could get the steps from the shed in the morning, but having moved the basket successfully she wasn't going to be defeated now. So she fetched the chair that stood in front of the escritoire and climbed up to fix it back and close the gap. The window was tall; she had to stretch and was concentrating on what she was doing so she didn't hear James come into the room. The knocking had disturbed him, and then he'd heard what he thought was a window being opened. Like Muriel he had come down the stairs in the dark, concerned not just by what he'd heard but also by what appeared to be a dim light from the drawing room. Could it be an intruder? Or was he only *trying* to believe that, while in his heart he knew that the knocking had disturbed Muriel too.

He made no sound as he walked barefoot on the carpet and when he spoke he was directly behind her.

'Let me reach that for you.' In the shock of hearing his voice, Muriel lost her balance. She didn't fall, but she might well have done if he hadn't grabbed her to steady her. 'Down you get.' Still holding her, he half lifted her to the ground. 'Pass me the hook when I'm on the chair.' And in a second it was done, the night was shut out and they faced each other. There was nothing to stop them switching on the light now, nothing except instinct. To be there together in their nightwear would have made strangers of them in the bright light of electricity, but one candle and the flames from the burning coals made the scene unfamiliar and dreamlike.

'It was the hanging basket,' she said, as if by talking about something so normal she would be able to overcome this strange, uncertain feeling.

'You've been leaning out of the window.' He reached to feel the damp sleeves and shoulders of her nightdress. 'You're quite wet. Come by the fire.' He was speaking softly as if he didn't want to break the spell. They both knew that what she ought to do was go back to her room, put on a dry nightdress then get back into bed. But rationality had no place there in the dimly lit room. Both of them moved towards the fire. When James took

away the guard he'd put there before going to bed, then added
two or three small pieces of coal, neither of them appeared to
find it an odd thing to do. Dreams are full of odd things.

But there was nothing odd about what happened next; it was
natural and spontaneous. As he stood up from tending the fire
he again felt her damp shoulder, and of its own volition her hand
covered his.

'Muriel, my dear, dear Muriel,' he breathed, the words so quiet
that she might almost have imagined them.

'I've never seen you with your hair ruffled before.' She said
the first thing that came into her head, anything to fill the void
and spoken in a whisper as if sound would destroy the wonder.

'I love you, you know that, don't you?' If she'd not been
standing so close to him she wouldn't even have heard.

'I think I knew. But we can't. I'm almost your mother-in-law.'

'And is that supposed to make me stop loving you? Oh God,
Muriel, what have I done?'

'You've married Georgie, dear Georgie, who I truly love as
though she really were my daughter. And you're her husband.
Yes, I love you, and not as your wife's mother should. I'm ashamed
that I have stayed here when I knew what was happening. I may
feel like Georgie's mother, but I'm a woman too, with all a
woman's needs, desires.'

'For months Georgie refused to marry me. Friendship could
never be enough, she said. But I believed that once we were
married everything would be different for both of us. But it hasn't
happened. We go through the motion of being lovers—'

'No, James, don't tell me.'

'I must tell you. You're the woman I want.'

Into her mind flashed the thought that for the first and perhaps
only time, they were alone in the house for the night. Married to
Georgie, and with something lacking between them, was he trying
to use *her* to get rid of his sexual frustration? At the thought she
fell from the heights to the depths. How could he possibly be in
love with her? She was older than him, a woman already in the
menopause. He was a handsome man in the prime of life; one
who was disappointed in his love life with a younger woman. But
that woman was Georgie, that darling child she had loved since
she was nine years old. *Remember all those things Cyril said about*

you, she told herself in an effort to find the courage to do what she knew was the right thing. *Remember his angry sneering voice saying I was old and dried up; that I was dowdy, that he didn't want me in his bed; he couldn't satisfy himself with me, he knew what it was like making love to me and he didn't want me.* The confidence that had been growing in her since she had lived with Georgie and James was slipping out of her grasp; she felt middle-aged, frumpish.

James couldn't have known her thoughts but he was aware that she was confused, uncertain.

'Don't look like that, darling. You're far away. Come back to me.'

She shivered. 'How can I? I want to, more than I can ever tell you, I want to. But how can I?'

She turned away from him, fighting to hold on to some sort of dignity while her conscience was telling her she ought to leave; she couldn't stay after all they'd said to each other. She couldn't cheat Georgie.

Standing behind her his hands were warm on her damp shoulders. Then she felt his face against the back of her neck. And his hands, his warm hands, they were moving to touch her over-large breasts, breasts that had nothing to protect them except the thin cotton of her nightgown. She was driven by the clamouring need of every erotic nerve in her body. Her breasts were too large for him to cup one in each hand, his fingers were moving over them, she could hear him breathing. Then, in that same second when everything else was pushed from her mind she was brought down to earth again by the image of Cyril. In the early days of their marriage instinct had made her carry his hands to touch her just like this and always he had pulled them away, seeming to be repelled. Her bosom was too big, too heavy, and too ugly; she had known it then, she knew it now. Pulling away from James, she turned to face him, and in the next second she was in his arms. She couldn't fight; her arms were around him drawing him closer, her hungry body pressed to his, her lips parted as his mouth covered hers.

And so it was that neither of them heard Georgie coming towards the slightly open door; neither of them heard her creep away and leave as quietly as she had come.

★   ★   ★

By morning Georgie might be able to think rationally, to see a way forward. But as she walked back into town her mind wouldn't settle on any one thing long enough for her to take a strand of the tangled web and try to unravel it. Dominic . . . the wonder of their morning . . . Muriel, who had been woven into her life since she was a child . . . Muriel who must be in love with James, truly and wholly in love with him or she would never have acted as she had . . . James, dear steadfast, unchanging James . . . and yet was there a side to him she had never seen?

Suppose the last train had been cancelled? Nothing could be relied on. Would there be a taxi at the station or at this hour would they be off the road? The night in the station waiting room would be the alternative, waiting for the early train bringing bundles of morning papers, milk and post to be left at every station. *I can't think straight . . . so much to decide . . . Dominic, if only you were there waiting for me, we could talk about what we have to do. I know what he'd say, I should petition for divorce citing Muriel. Would he really say that? No, not if he knew them; not if he'd known Dad. Oh look, a taxi putting people down at the Marlborough Hotel!* She started to run, waving wildly to attract the driver's attention.

Minutes later she was sitting in the dry, speeding towards Tarnmouth – at least, as near to speeding as was possible on roads that were awash and with a combination of shielded headlights and torrential rain adding to the driver's problems.

'Not fit for a dog,' he commented.

'Am I your last fare?' She made herself sound interested. 'You'll be glad to get home.'

'That I will. And not just because of all this lot. No, I don't like leaving the missus longer than I have to. Our boy – just eighteen he is – he joined up, keen as mustard. Last time round I did the same thing, added six months to my age so keen I was. I soon learned, buggered if I didn't. Please God it won't be like that for the boys this time. Damned wars. Not the likes of you and me who cause them or want them; no, we just have to pick up the pieces of the mess made by the politicians. The same whatever side you fight on. You got a husband likely to get called up?'

She was about to say no, he too had been in the last war. Imagination can play tricks and in that moment it was as if

Dominic were with her, smiling, half closing one eye in acknow-
ledgement of the secret they shared.

'He volunteered straight away. He's in the merchant fleet.'

'Is he, by Jove? If I had to go I reckon I'd want the Army. Air
and water are fine for some, but I always reckon you've got a
better chance if your feet are on the ground. Well, lady, may his
God go with him, aye, with them all, poor bastards.'

They covered another mile or so before he spoke again, apparently following the same train of thought.

'Tell you one thing: friend Roosevelt over there in the US of
A, I reckon he's got the right idea. They took their time coming
into the last lot and it looks like they mean to keep clear this
time. And who can blame them? Thousands of miles away, even
though plenty of them have roots this side of the ocean. What a
country though, eh? The land of the free, isn't that what they
call it? Precious little freedom for anyone once you start looking
around and taking up the cause to help some downtrodden lot.
Where did you say you wanted to be dropped off in Tarnmouth?'

She had hoped for a driver who would concentrate on the
road and not want to talk, but when she got out of the taxi she
realized that not only had the journey gone quickly, but it had
been good for her. It had brought home to her that for people
everywhere across the length and breadth of the land – this land
and beyond – there was no life cocooned from anxiety. From
admiral to able seaman, from duke to dairymaid, no one could
live untouched by the chaos unfolding in Europe.

Dominic's first night in his new life . . . *Keep him safe . . . I must
think . . . Muriel and James . . . how long has it been going on? . . .
No, I don't believe it has . . . James, unchanging, kind and good; what
is the best thing to do now about James? Tonight I had meant to tell
him that I was leaving him; he would have to divorce me for desertion
. . . but that was before I knew about them.* Round and round it
went in her head, always coming back to the same place: should
she accuse him of committing adultery with Muriel? It may not
be true; she had no proof. But James wouldn't lie about it. There
would be a court case, and it was the sort of story some of the
Sunday papers would delight in: *WIDOW IS CITED IN STEP-
DAUGHTER'S DIVORCE. When her husband, Cyril Franklyn,
was killed in a motor accident, his widow went to live with her daughter,*

recently married to James Bartlett, Town Clerk of Winchford . . . There would be innuendos about her wanting a younger man, and then there was James and the damage it might do to his future. Divorce was legally possible, but it was sufficiently rare that it was a gossip-monger's delight. So what if she told James that Dominic was her lover? Would any court take her word or would there be someone watching them when he came home on leave? It made everything so sordid and beastly. If James and Muriel really loved each other – and she knew them both so well that she was sure what she'd seen tonight couldn't have happened if they didn't – then, for their sake as well as her own and Dominic's, she wanted to find a way to untangle the mess they had all made.

Coffee and cigarettes were her supper as the situation went round and round in her mind. If only Dominic were here, he would see a way forward. And it was with thoughts of Dominic that she finally stubbed out her cigarette and went to his bedroom. Could it be not much more than twelve hours ago they had lain there together? She undressed quickly, turned off the light, opened the thick curtains and then got into his bed. Purposely she lay on his side, resting her head on his pillow. And as she lay between waking and sleeping she knew exactly what she would do. The image of James and Muriel was vivid, and she was thankful for it. It took away much of her feeling of guilt. Tomorrow as soon as she closed the gallery she would go to Winchford. But she wouldn't stay; even before she'd seen the two of them together, she had known she could never share a bed with James again. Tonight she hadn't let herself be tempted to put off telling him until tomorrow; it had been her illogical belief that if she didn't do it tonight, Dominic would be the one to suffer, that had made her go to Winchford.

I'll go as soon as I close the gallery tomorrow, she promised silently. *And I won't wait until Muriel has gone to bed. This concerns us all. But I must be careful not to let them suspect I know about them.*

If only Dominic were here. She wanted to tell him what she was doing; she wanted to give him the same hope to cling to that she had found. New-found hope and the sick worry that nothing assuaged filled her mind, but sleep was winning the battle.

The coals James had added to the fire had burnt through into hot embers but as he and Muriel talked they hadn't even noticed. Certainly they were getting cold, but sitting close to each other on the settee, his arm around her, they were too engrossed to be aware.

'What have I done to her?' Muriel's long face was a picture of misery as she thought of the little girl she had first loved. 'I say I love her like my own daughter, and it's true, James. So how could I let this happen? If I get a job and move out, you and she could have a new start.'

He shook his head. 'You make it sound too easy. You love her, I love her, and neither of us wants to hurt her. But, darling Muriel, she is a strong-minded woman. And don't we insult her to imagine she would want us to . . . to sacrifice what we have found together so that she is protected as if she were a child?'

'Then there's your career, James. If you were divorced, especially if you were seen as the guilty party – you and me, too, but they wouldn't care who the woman was, you're the one they'd have the guns out for – do you think they would even let you keep your job? I can't do that to you, James. That wouldn't be love; that would be selfishness.'

And so, just as it did with Georgie, the situation went round and round, always coming back to the same place.

'Things will look clearer in the morning. The fire's going down, we ought to go up.'

As he said it she willed him to meet her gaze. Neither put into words what they were thinking but as they reached the corridor at the top of the stairs, with one accord, they both turned towards her room. Then he stopped, remembering that knowing Georgie wasn't coming home, all he had in his pyjama jacket pocket was a handkerchief.

'I need to get something. You go on in.'

She understood his meaning and was quick to reassure him. 'We shan't need anything, James. It's more than two months since my last period; I seem to have finished with all that.' She hated saying it; it made her sound old and unfeminine. Tonight she longed to be desirable, beautiful, but she couldn't be less than honest, especially with James.

Going to the chest of drawers she took out a clean nightgown, then standing by the bed with her back to him she took off the one which, now they were away from the fireside, still felt cold and damp. She knew he had moved closer, she knew he was going to hold her, she knew his hands would move on her as they had downstairs. Joy surged through her. She leant against him, his hands were warm, and his thumbs moved, encircling her nipples. With closed eyes she followed her instinct, instinct that was to carry her to what she had longed for as long as she had known sexual desire. With her hands covering his, carrying to him a silent message that she didn't want him to stop, she bent right forward so that her two heavy breasts hung before her. He felt the weight of them in his hand just as he had in every sexual fantasy. They were both breathing fast, excitement coursing through their veins. She moved her hands from his and, reaching behind her, guided him to enter her. Never had she been penetrated so deeply, never had she felt anything like this. It couldn't last; for both of them this was the culmination of years of desire. There are some dreams that can never be matched by reality; this wasn't one of them. Their climax was simultaneous. For them, let the future bring what it may; there could be no turning back.

Although she had no train to catch, Georgie was up at her usual hour in the morning and she knew just what she meant to do. The telephone operator seemed less wide awake than she was herself and she had to repeat the number for Gregory House before the girl started to make the connection. Then she heard the bell and a moment later James' voice. 'James Bartlett speaking.'

'James, it's me. I wanted to catch you before you left home. This evening I have something important to tell you. You won't be at a meeting, will you? You will be home early?'

'Important? Yes, I'll be home. But you can't just tell me that, and no more. Can't you at least say what it's about?'

'No. I want us all to be together. I'll get there as quickly as I can. Tell Muriel – not that she'd be out, but I want her to be there to hear.'

'Yes, of course I'll tell her. Anything that concerns us, concerns her. Georgie, tell me . . .' But he couldn't bring himself to say the words. Was she wanting to tell them that she was pregnant? But she couldn't be. Always he'd been so careful.

'See you this evening. Bye, James.' He heard the click as she hung up.

There were two taxis outside the station when she arrived at Winchford that evening, so she got in the first one and gave the address of Gregory House. This wasn't her usual mode of transport; she usually waited for the six fifty-five bus, and even though it was almost time for it she was glad to break with routine. This evening was like no other. She wished Dominic could know what had happened. He had been at the forefront of her mind all day as she wondered where he was, on land or sea, and whether he'd had a chance to write. All day she had listened for the phone to ring, imagining picking up the earpiece and hearing his voice. But no call had come.

'You arrived in style this evening,' Muriel greeted her. 'Was the bus cancelled, dear?'

'I don't know; I didn't wait to find out. I wanted to make this evening special.'

'Why's that? Have you sold a special picture?'

'No.' Georgie shook her head. 'Muriel, has James not told you? I've come home to tell you both something important.'

It could only be one thing. Georgie must have had confirmation that she was pregnant. What else could give rise to this talk of something special? Muriel never wore her heart on her sleeve, but the evening would put her to the test. She smiled brightly as she said, 'James hasn't said a word. I expect he thought you would want to tell us yourself. Supper's doing nicely; let's go in by the fire for ten minutes. He's in there with his crossword.' All she could think about was how different it had been last evening. And James, how must he be feeling? He'd given no hint when he came home, and yet Georgie spoke as though he knew.

The one thing Muriel never doubted was James' genuine love for her. Last night had meant as much to him as it had to her, she was sure it had.

'Have we time for a sherry before we eat, Muriel?' he asked when they joined him.

'Yes, it's a casserole so it'll sit happily in a low oven. Georgie has news – something special, she says – so pour the drinks first,

James, and then we can raise a glass to whatever it is.' *If it's the promise of a child, that must be the missing link in your lives, the link that will hold you together. And I must look for a housekeeper's job somewhere else.* Her imagination was running away with her: from housekeeping in some dreary house to working in a canteen in a munitions factory, it carried her on a journey of loneliness. But she should be rejoicing; she loved Georgie and she loved James, she wanted their happiness. If last night had never happened she would be looking forward to Georgie's baby. She hadn't realized how she had been standing holding her glass just as James had passed it to her. She must do better than this!

'Come on then, Georgie, aren't you going to tell us your news?'

'There isn't an easy way of saying this. James, dear James . . . I'm leaving you.' It was the last thing Muriel expected to hear. She put her untouched drink on the table, ashamed of the give-away shaking of her hand.

'But why, Georgie? You always seemed happy. Have you met someone else?'

Georgie shook her head. 'Now how could I? You know exactly how I spend my days.'

'Then I don't understand. It's a big decision to make; you must be quite sure – both of you. James?' She looked at him for support. Here they were being offered what they wanted above all else, and that was what made it so difficult. Georgie was a grown-up woman, but to Muriel she would always be the little girl she had first loved, and she couldn't snatch eagerly at her own happiness and then find Georgie's sudden quest for freedom was no more than reaction from all the upheaval of this dreadful war. She may have been talking to people who are joining the women's serv-ices. She talked of freedom but perhaps what she really meant was 'change'.

'I knew Georgie was coming home to talk about something important this evening,' James said. 'She phoned me earlier in the day. Whatever I expected, it wasn't *this*. Georgie, I well remember, before you agreed to our marrying, when you were at St Winifred's, you talked of leaving there to find freedom.' He looked at her, his expression less than a smile but certainly something akin to it and bearing no malice, nor yet the shocked hurt which only twenty-four hours ago she had expected. 'So let's drink to your

future, my very dear Georgie. I do honestly believe you are doing
– can I say the *right* thing? It's not so much that, as I believe
what you are asking is that we put right the wrong we committed.
I honestly believed that our friendship was a sound basis for a
life together, but there was a missing ingredient. Magic, I think
you once called it.'

'Don't be too nice to me, James.' It would have been so easy,
and such a relief too, for Georgie to cry. And yet she had nothing
to cry for; she ought to be rejoicing that everything was working
out so smoothly. James would go to a solicitor and petition for
divorce; she would have to find a solicitor. She supposed they
would have to go to court and some dreary judge would ask
personal questions, but it would soon be over. Perhaps even by
the time Dominic came on leave she would be well on the way
to being single again.

But as they ate their meal James talked to her about the process
of ending a marriage because one party deserts the other. She
learned that freedom couldn't be granted in weeks or months.
Even if the wheels were set in motion straight away, it could be
quite 1943 before the divorce was granted – if not longer. He
needed a letter from her telling him that she refused to live with
him as his wife, and then he would see his solicitor. Marriage to
James had been uneventful, no heights of joy and no depths of
misery, but, listening to his unemotional description of what lay
ahead, she felt sad and even ashamed for a failure that must have
been largely her fault. She must be the one who had changed;
she knew she had. Until she'd met Dominic, freedom had been
just a dream; but with him she had found freedom of spirit.

'You look disappointed,' James was saying. 'But if there is no
one else in your life at the moment, does it honestly matter too
much? Divorce is only a piece of paper.'

'I wasn't really thinking of that, I was just sorry that our personal
life will have to be dragged through the court. But . . . but James,
we'll still be friends, won't we?'

James was very tempted to tell her that they would still be
more than friends, that when he too had that piece of paper and
could marry Muriel, he would be . . . what? Surely not her step-
father! But instead all he said was, 'We were friends before and
we shall be friends after.'

'But there's one thing that does worry me: if I'm not living here you won't get silly, either of you, and think it's not right for the two of you to live in the house? I mean, James, you couldn't go back to living on your own like a bachelor, and it's Muriel who has made this a home, not me. If she went you have to employ a housekeeper . . .'

Despite Muriel's look of embarrassment, James was laughing.

'I've never had any illusions about who makes this a home. Of course Muriel won't leave.'

It was all working out just as Georgie wanted. So why did she feel so sad? For the last time she took the tea towel to dry the dishes, more aware of the atmosphere of comfort and security that evening than she had been when it was all part of the daily routine. She dropped a dessertspoon; it fell right by her foot and when she stooped to pick it up all she seemed to see were her shoes and she felt a rush of tenderness for James. She'd have to get back in the habit of cleaning them herself now, something she had never minded doing; in fact when she had first come to Gregory House she had been irritated by his nightly routine.

'Have you found somewhere to live in Tarnmouth? You can't spend your life sleeping on someone's settee,' James said when they came back into the drawing room.

'For the time being I'm OK. I was talking on the phone to Mrs Fraser, the publisher you remember and Dominic's mother. When I told her what I was doing she said – speaking for him – for me to use the rooms. When he has leave he'll stay with his parents, I expect.' She didn't expect any such thing. Those last hours with Dominic had been too precious for her to want to discuss him, especially with James. If she had to wait as long as James said for her freedom, then everyone would know about them; but for the moment it was private and precious.

A little later, pushing his bicycle, James walked with her to the station, where with a light kiss he bid her goodbye, then waited as she made her way along the unlit corridor to a compartment on the train. Then with a brief wave to each other, he left her. Had any other marriage ended like this, she wondered? It was a crazy situation, and yet none of them could have acted differently. She imagined him pedalling home to find Muriel waiting for him. Then she thought of the cheerless room above the gallery heated by a small electric fire. The train steamed on its way. There were three other passengers in the compartment, two of them sitting with their eyes closed and the third, an elderly man with the evening newspaper on his lap, but with no hope of reading it in the dim blue light, all that was allowed in any train despite the blinds of the compartments being kept firmly pulled down.

By the time they were two miles out of Winchford, like the other two passengers, her eyes were closed, not in sleep but so that her thoughts could carry her where they would. And where better than to *Tight Lines* . . . she was with Dominic, above them the sky was blue . . . she could believe she heard the cry of the gulls . . . soon it would be like that again, soon he would be home . . . she had to believe . . . and even if the war went on for months and months, one day they would be together again. *Keep him safe, I beg above all else that he will be safe.* And so the journey passed, taking her back to the gallery and the rooms above, which were to be her home.

The next day she received a brief note from Dominic. He was about to start his first voyage when he wrote it, but could tell her nothing: no hint of where he was bound, no hint of how long he might be away. The words that mattered were simple: he would phone her as soon as he had an opportunity during the daytime when she was at the gallery. He had faith in their future and would love her always. After that the days passed without her even knowing where he was or how long he might be away.

Leaving Alice and Barry in charge of the gallery, on the following Monday morning she went back to Winchford. It was easier to collect her personal things while James was working.

'Are you sure you're all right there?' Muriel asked anxiously. 'I keep thinking of how miserable it must be for you, all alone in those upstairs rooms. Even if the Fraser man isn't likely to return until we are back to peace again, it can't be the sort of comfort you have grown up with.'

Georgie laughed. 'Muriel, you really are a goose,' she said affectionately. 'The best thing you could do would be to come and see for yourself how comfortable I am. But you're right; I want some of my personal things round me. When I've collected things together I'll phone for a taxi; I'm not taking all that painting clobber back on the train.'

'Can I help you, or shall I get some coffee ready for when you've done?'

'That sounds good. I'll scoop up my clothes and sort things out when I get to Dominic's. He has a second bedroom, unfurnished, but that's a sort of storeroom. So I shan't be short of space.'

Upstairs in the bedroom she had shared with James, she stripped her wardrobe and drawers, then in a very uncharacteristic way she crushed everything into the two outside cases she had used in the past. Packing them carefully between two layers of clothes she laid photographs that were precious: one, small and faded, had been taken by a street photographer in Hastings when she and her father had been carrying their fishing rods to the pier; another, again with just the two of them, had been on her graduation day; and the third – one she had never liked but it had meant so much to him – was one Muriel had taken of them at the annual fête at St Winifred's. To Georgie they were a permanent link with all they had shared.

She hadn't looked forward to coming to the room that had been the background of so much of the life she had shared with James, frightened of the ghosts of his ever-considerate kindness. Yet looking around she felt *nothing*; it was no more personal to her than a hotel bedroom. She was glad to close the door on it and bump her heavy cases down the stairs to stand them in the hall.

It was nearly a fortnight after Dominic's short note, at about half past one on a Tuesday afternoon, when Georgie left her lunchtime poached egg on toast and rushed down the stairs to answer the telephone.

The line was poor; Dominic sounded a million miles away.

'Darling, are you all right?' he said through the crackles. 'God, but it's hard to say what you want to say talking into this thing.'

'Dom, I have to tell you, the day you went I knew I couldn't go back to James . . . not after . . . after . . .'

'You've done it? Oh, thank God. This time next year you'll be my wife.' Then, his chuckle on the fading line making him sound like a stranger, 'I ought to plight thee my troth – I will, when I come home. I'll kneel before you.'

'Promise?' she teased, chuckling, remembering and above all rejoicing that though he was thousands of miles away, nothing could divide their spirits. Then, more seriously, she said, 'But it can't be as soon as that.' And so she told him that it would be at least three years until her divorce was finalized. 'I can't explain more than that now, but soon you'll get some shore leave and we can talk. Now tell me about you . . .' The minutes went so fast and soon the line was dead.

Once Georgie had brought all her personal belongings to the gallery she didn't attempt to visit Gregory House again, but spoke to Muriel sometimes on the telephone. Always they had had such an easy relationship, but now they were both conscious of things they couldn't say. And apart from that, Muriel was worrying about Christmas; she couldn't bear to think of Georgie alone in those miserable rooms – for even if they had been decorated and furnished to a high standard of comfort, never having been up the stairs she had a fixed image in her mind and she didn't like what she saw. And in the first week of December, as the festival drew near, she couldn't hold back her anxiety.

'Surely it wouldn't matter if you were to come home just for those few days. I'd get the bed ready for you in the little room. How can any of us enjoy it if you are there all by yourself?'

'It must be telepathy somewhere along the line,' Georgie answered. 'I was going to tell you: I've had a letter from Mrs Fraser – you know I've often mentioned her to you – and she has invited me to spend Christmas with them. There will just be her and her husband, for it's unlikely that Dominic will get home; the transport of cargoes can't stop so that the men can all spend Christmas with their families. They live in Buckinghamshire. I'm really looking forward to it. She and I get on so well and it'll be nice to meet Mr Fraser, too.'

'Oh, Georgie, I'm more pleased than I know how to say. I've been lying awake at night worrying about it.'

Georgie laughed. 'Then don't, Muriel. I'm far, far happier living here than ever I was in that really good flat at St Winifred's. In any case I shouldn't have been on my own for Christmas even if the Frasers hadn't invited me; I have made friends here. I shall see the New Year in with Alice and Barry. A new decade.

But what a state everything is in.' Then, making her voice sound more cheerful than she felt, 'But we're getting morbid, let's talk about something better. When are you coming to see me?'

'I will. I promise I will. I think the winter must have got into my bones; I seem to have slowed down.'

Georgie didn't take the remark seriously. Muriel was hardly old and in all the years Georgie had known her she couldn't remember her ever being ill. So she supposed it must have been an unnecessary excuse.

'Well you know where to find me. Take care of yourself and of James. Give him my love.' Then with a laugh, 'But don't tell the solicitor. And talking of solicitors, I went to see mine, a Mr Boyd; his office is just by the church. I asked him if during this time of waiting for the divorce I could . . . could sleep . . . well not sleep, make *love* . . . or would that upset the case.'

'But why should you worry about that, dear? You're there by yourself.'

'I know that, silly. But it's going to be years before I can get my freedom – who knows what might happen? If romance comes my way I don't want to have to run along then and ask the solicitor!' What she really meant was, *what about when Dominic comes home?* But still something prevented her confiding in Muriel, for all her fondness of her. 'And you know what he said? He said I could sleep with anyone I liked just as long as it wasn't with my husband. And I suppose the same applies to James; not that he ever was a womanizer. But we ought to know how we stand. This is going to be such a protracted affair. I must go, someone is coming in. Bye. Come and see me soon.'

The Frasers were more liberal-minded than most people of Georgie's acquaintance and Dominic had told them the situation between her and himself. Secretly they hoped that his ship might dock just before Christmas, that he would collect his mail and know that she was with them in Buckinghamshire. But Priscilla Fraser didn't hint at such hopes when she and Georgie spoke on the phone. Yet, on Christmas Eve, as the taxi turned into the drive of Woodwaye, their house in the Buckinghamshire countryside, Georgie's imagination was carrying her on a journey of its own. Suppose that when she rang the doorbell it was Dominic who answered it. She knew from talking to people who came into the gallery that plenty of servicemen would have Christmas leave. That plenty more wouldn't was something she didn't want to consider.

The driver took her right to the house and as he fetched her case from the boot she heard the front door open behind her. *Let it be him, please let him be home.* She turned, hope immediately stripped from her by disappointment. There was no doubt that the man who came down the three steps to the forecourt was Dominic's father, Malcolm Fraser.

'Welcome, my dear,' he called as he approached, his genial tone hiding his own disappointment that the arrival of a taxi hadn't meant that Dominic had returned in the unpredictable way they had grown used to. As if to make amends for his disappointment he thrust a note into the driver's hand, took the suitcase, and steered Georgie towards the house where a smiling Priscilla was waiting.

'So,' he said as they came into the wide hallway, 'let me have a look at you. Yes, yes, you'll do very nicely.' His teasing smile was so like Dominic's that she felt at ease with him immediately. 'I like to know I approve of the daughter the boy's giving me.'

'Don't embarrass the poor girl, Malcolm,' Priscilla told him.

'He's not,' Georgie laughed, taking an instant liking to the man who, at least in appearance, was so much an older version of Dominic. 'He's just honest, aren't you, Mr Fraser?'

'Never mind the Mister. My name's Malcolm. From bits I've gleaned when that son of ours pays us his occasional flying visit, I believe Father or Dad wouldn't come easily to you.'

She liked him more and more.

'No one can have more than one Dad in a lifetime. And I don't see you as Pop. I'd love to call you Malcolm.' And, after all, she had called Mrs Fraser Priscilla almost from their first meeting.

'While Malcolm pours us a drink − and I'm not going to ask what you'll have; these days things are getting so tight it's a question of what is there to offer − I'll take you up to your room.'

It was a double bedroom. On the bedside table was a photograph of Dominic and on the dressing table an arrangement of Christmas roses. Was there significance in the double bed? Could they know something she didn't? She knew it was crazy that her imagination could so easily bring hope alive. Perhaps he had landed while she was on the way from Tarnmouth; perhaps soon he would be here. But her hopes were dashed when Priscilla asked her if she had had any recent news of him.

'He telephoned about ten days ago. I'm sure he rang you, too. But goodness knows where he was or how long he'll be away. I did so hope – we all did, I know – that he would get home for Christmas. But I suppose being on the sea, carrying supplies, it's not like being stationed at a land-based camp. We shall have to be patient until he has shore leave.'

Downstairs they gathered by the log fire and sipped their drinks, but the thought of Dominic was at the forefront of all their minds.

'Georgie hasn't heard since that last time he phoned, either,' Priscilla said, reading Malcolm's thoughts.

'He's been gone two months; he must get a few days soon,' Malcolm said. And if his voice was a little too confident and cheerful, they were prepared to go along with the sentiment. Yes, he must soon get leave. None of them were ready to ask exactly how he would divide his time when that leave came.

Brenda, the cook's daughter who came to help when help was needed, tapped on the drawing-room door and told them lunch was ready. It occurred to Georgie how different life was here from the way Dominic chose to live. Brought up to take a comfortable home for granted (Mr La-di-Da, Sinbad the Sailor, she could almost hear the mocking voices from his early days in Tarnmouth), and yet he was completely at home at the kitchen table above the gallery, eating fish and chips, or even frying his own catch. He was the product of two loving, well-adjusted parents.

Over lunch she tentatively put forward something that had been forming in her mind.

'I've brought some illustrations to show you, if you think it might be worthwhile. I know this must be a bad time – things are in short supply and it will get worse – but I just had the idea I might like to write something myself, write and illustrate, I mean. You wouldn't let it make any difference that I know you; promise me you wouldn't.'

'Business and pleasure are two different things, my dear,' Malcolm told her. 'I don't interfere with Priscilla's side of the business, but I know she agrees with me over that.'

'Good. That's what I hoped. I've never done anything like it before, and it may be no use at all. But I enjoy what I've been doing for *Freddie the Fisherman*. The world could do with a little more childlike innocence, don't you think?'

'Indeed it could,' Priscilla agreed. 'I promise I'll be a hundred per cent honest with you, Georgie. This afternoon we'll have a look at what you've done.'

As good as her word, Priscilla read the short book about the adventures of Mrs Squirrel and her bushy-tailed family. When she finished she told Georgie she thought the characters were delightful, guaranteed to become loved by small people, especially when brought to life by the illustrations. They were just about to start talking business when they heard the front door slam. Looking at each other, with one accord they were on their feet. He was home! And if Georgie didn't think of it in those terms, then at least he was here, he was safe, and a moment later she was pulled into his bear-like hug.

That evening the four of them walked to the village church for the midnight service. It was something Georgie had never done before, but it appeared to be part of the Frasers' accepted Christmas even if they didn't go inside the building at any other time. Sitting between Dominic and his father she was filled with a sense of peace – peace and something she couldn't name. Closing her eyes she let the words of the vicar wash over her, and in her heart she felt she was close to her own beloved father. Could he see her here? She had so wished he could have known Dominic and what they felt for each other. 'Sing choirs of angels . . . sing all you choristers in heaven above,' the Christmas-swelled congregation chorused in one voice. She felt her hand taken in Dominic's. Her eyes stung with unshed tears, tears that had nothing to do with sadness. *Yes, Dad knows. Dad knows and he's pleased.*

It was late in the morning towards the end of January when Muriel arrived unexpectedly at the gallery. She had taken extra trouble to look her best; a touch of rouge on her cheeks, lipstick and even mascara, which always enhanced her eyes, her one good feature. Yet Georgie's first thought was that she didn't look well.

'Lovely surprise!' Georgie accompanied her words with the usual hug.

'I've been meaning to come for ages, but before Christmas I thought you'd have customers coming in and out all the time and we wouldn't have the chance to talk.'

'Well, we shan't get that problem today. By January people forget we exist. But it's a good chance to get some painting done. I'll just look up the road and make sure no one is haring down on us, then I'll lock up for lunch. We'll go to the Bay and celebrate – my treat. Come upstairs while I get tidy.'

It was really good to be with Muriel again.

With the front door locked they climbed the stairs and Muriel had her first sight of Georgie's Spartan quarters. The bedroom looked comfortable enough, but the one and only living room with its gas cooker and what could only be termed a kitchen table was anything but.

'Is this where you spend your evenings?'

'No. I eat in here, that's about all. I have a portable wireless in the little room behind the gallery, and I've bought another heater like I use in the front so it's never cold down there. I paint in the evenings, so it's really quite comfy.' *And it's nearer the telephone*, she added silently, thinking how she constantly listened in case there was a call from Dominic. 'Are you hungry? I hadn't thought about food, but come to think of it I'm looking forward to going out to lunch.'

What was different about Muriel? She'd gone to such lengths to look smart but it was as if her mind was only half here.

'Are you all right? You seem quiet. Nothing wrong with James?'

Muriel turned her head away, something in the movement telling Georgie that all wasn't well.

'Surely you can tell me. We've never had secrets.' But that wasn't true! Never until lately had they had secrets. She put her arm around Muriel but even then she wasn't prepared for what happened. Muriel, always straight-backed and upright, seemed to sag as if all her strength had deserted her. She gave up the battle as a sob escaped her. Georgie steered her to the settee at the back of the general living room and turned the electric fire to face her.

'I think I must have a tumour . . . mustn't say the other word, it would be tempting fate.'

'A tumour? Where? What makes you think so? Do you feel ill?'

Muriel shook her head, but this time she looked directly at

Georgie and made a supreme effort to stop crying. 'Not really ill, but not *right*. Glad I've told you.' She got the words out before the snort she couldn't hold back.

'Have you seen a doctor? What does James say?'

'No. If I go to the doctor and he tells me I'm right ... no ... no I can't. Everything was so good, now ... now this ...' Forgetting about her mascara she rubbed her hands across her eyes. 'It might be just the change. I keep trying to think that's all it is. Could it be, Georgie? I told you, some months back, don't remember when, I told you that I'd been all over the place, dates didn't mean anything. Nothing for two months or more, then I'd be so flooded that I was almost frightened to go out, then nothing again.'

'And is it still the same? You ought to see a doctor, Muriel, and he could tell you what we have to expect. How long is it now?'

'Since my last time? Months. It was back in the summer, the evening of August Bank Holiday it started, when the fair was in the field behind the house. Nothing since then, so it must all be over for me now. I get so tired. Is that what happens in the change? I just don't know.' She hesitated, as if it took all her courage to say, 'And then there's this hard sort of lump – do you think after all these months I'll get another period and it'll go? Just feel it.' She unfastened her coat and drew Georgie's hand to her stomach. 'Can you feel? I was always quite flat down there.' Yes, Georgie could feel it. Surely this didn't happen to every woman? James was always so careful; surely he hadn't made her pregnant? But she couldn't even voice the thought.

'Perhaps women always put on weight with the menopause. Now listen, it's no use us wondering and probably worrying for nothing. I'm going downstairs to telephone the doctor and ask if he can see you this afternoon – either here or in his surgery.'

She made the appointment. Dr Halsey would come to the gallery at about half past three.

'It's such a relief,' Muriel said when Georgie told her. 'I've been frightened to go, but now that we've talked about it I feel he's going to say it's nothing unusual. Can I wash my face and borrow some of your powder and things? Can you hear my tummy rumbling? I really am hungry. Oh, Georgie, I've been wanting to come and talk to you. But I've been too frightened.'

'Chump!' Georgie gave her an affectionate hug. 'You know I'm always there for you.'

'I suppose worry takes it out of one, but I really have been feeling a bit rough. Some days I don't want to look at food – although of course I always see there is a good meal for James.' Then, with a sudden smile, 'But today I could eat a horse. Perhaps not having anyone to talk to about it, I've been worrying for nothing. Let's go and have a nice lunch. I feel better than I have for weeks; don't they say a trouble shared is a trouble halved?'

With something akin to girlish excitement they got ready for their outing, taking extra pains with their make-up, examining the end result like two conspirators. And the Bay Hotel didn't let them down. Muriel's confidence was growing by the minute. The 'closed' sign remained on the front door that afternoon and just after half past three Georgie went down to open it in answer to Dr Halsey's ring.

In the far from comfortable living room he listened to Muriel's tale of woe, nodding at each piece of information but saying little. Then he took her into the bedroom for an examination while Georgie was left to wait. Minutes went by. More worried than she liked to admit, she crept to the closed bedroom door and tried to listen, but their voices were low so it got her nowhere. Then footsteps; they were coming out. She hurried back to her place on the settee and waited.

'Now, when you get home, the first thing you must do is see your local doctor. At this stage he will tell you no more than I have been able to myself, but he will want to keep an eye on you. We mustn't delude ourselves; you are at a difficult age for a first child.'

Nine

Leaving Muriel upstairs, Georgie went down to show Dr Halsey out.

'Will she be all right, Doctor? She's been so worried; she was sure there would be no chance of her conceiving at her age.'

The doctor seemed to be scrutinizing her, weighing up the situation before he replied. 'You know her well?' he asked at last.

'She is my stepmother. She and my father married when I was nine years old, and we've always been close.'

'Well, I'm glad she had the wit to come to you over her problem. And there's no denying that at forty-seven she can't be expected to sail through it like a twenty-seven-year-old. She tells me she has always been healthy. You know that to be true?'

'I've never known her to be ill.'

'And may she continue that way. I asked her if she'd talked to her husband and she said no, she hadn't. Too many women seem to think husbands have to be shielded. In my view it's not right. Now, mind you see that she goes straight to a doctor. A twenty-year-old can often give birth with no trouble at all; young bodies are made for childbearing. Well, my dear, I wish her well. Now, can you tell me her address for the bill? It's Mrs Franklyn, she did tell me that, but I haven't taken the address.'

'Send the bill to me here – my name is Bartlett, Mrs Bartlett.'

She watched the doctor walk away in the direction of his surgery, and then started back up the stairs. She remembered Muriel telling her on that day her father died that when they had first been married she had longed for a child, but he had always been careful it wouldn't happen. So would this be joyous news to her? And what about James – he who had never come to bed without checking that he had a sheath in his pocket? He might be five or six years Muriel's junior but neither of them were young to have their lives changed by a baby. How would he react? He'd been married before and never had a family; add that to the care he'd taken to see that it didn't happen when she was with him, and the future for Muriel looked bleak. Those were the thoughts that rushed helter-skelter through her mind as she climbed the stairs and went into the living room where Muriel was standing gazing out of the window, her hands cradling the bulge she had feared and hated.

Hearing Georgie come in, she turned, not moving her hands. 'Not a tumour. A baby, something I've longed for all my life. But not like this.'

'How far gone are you? You said your last period was in August; but that's five months.' Georgie couldn't believe that it had been going on before the evening she had seen them together. Surely, she would have known?

'That doctor said he thought about fourteen weeks. He examined me; he took ages, outside then inside. I just lay there wanting to die. I knew he'd found something; I tried to make myself ready to hear what I'd been dreading. Then he said, "Mrs Franklyn, how long have you been married?" I don't know what stopped me saying I was a widow. But I didn't. Instead I told him I was married in 1920. I don't know why I couldn't have said I was a widow. Then he told me I was pregnant. An illegitimate baby! But what am I doing, telling you, *you* of all people?'

Georgie shook her head. 'We don't have secrets, you and me.'

Dropping to sit on the settee, Muriel started rocking backwards and forwards, backwards and forwards, as if she were trying to escape from something that had a hold on her. 'I'm so ashamed. I let it happen – I wanted it to happen. He's your husband – *yours*, of all people!' It was hard to understand all she said. She was crying and talking at the same time, her voice bordering on hysteria. 'I thought of him all the time – and when you left I was *glad*. You hear what I say? I was glad, because there were just the two of us. Not married, but now it's as if we are. Late October, that's when I conceived. I know it must have been then. It was the first time. It's my fault; I told him it was safe, I said I'd finished with all that. I thought I had; it had been so long.' When Georgie put her arm around her shaking shoulders Muriel didn't seem to be aware. 'I must go away, somewhere where he can't find me. I'll lie; I'll tell people my husband has just died. You see?' Her voice rose into a high-pitched squeak. 'It's all lies. It's my punishment for stealing him away from you, from *you*, my darling little Georgie. What have I done, Georgie? Soon this lump will show, talk will get back to the Town Hall—' She broke off mid-sentence, suddenly aware of what she was saying.

'Muriel, do you imagine I couldn't see that James was in love with you?' Perhaps it wasn't the wisest thing for Georgie to say, but it was meant to try and calm her. It did the reverse.

'That's awful! You knew what was happening – to me and to him. Georgie, oh, Georgie, I never meant to hurt you. I should have looked for another place. I drove you away.'

'That's not true. I left him because we should never have married in the first place. I love James, truly I do, but I was never in love with him, nor he with me. We both knew that. But we thought marriage would bring us closer. It didn't. I wanted my freedom. We must think, Muriel. We have to find a way.'

Muriel was biting at her bottom lip without even realizing she was doing it. Her forehead was puckered in a worried frown and her long, narrow nose shone like a beacon. At that moment she looked her age and more. But she made a supreme effort to regain control.

'If you told the solicitor about how I am, how long would it take for the divorce? Surely not as long as they say it will now?'

'I don't know. But that would certainly put paid to James' career. It won't do him any good going through a divorce, even for desertion. In his sort of position it doesn't do to break the rules even if it wasn't his fault that I left him. Adultery would be far worse. The Council would never condone that. And apart from James, I wouldn't divorce him for adultery; I wouldn't do it because of Dad. Think of what a field day the papers would have when the case was heard. Imagine the smutty-minded people drooling over the story; imagine the sniggering there would be that Dad's daughter's husband was the father of his widow's child. People wouldn't understand; they'd read it as enter-tainment.'

'Don't know what to do.' Muriel seemed to speak to herself; she wasn't expecting an answer. 'God, why didn't you let it be a tumour? I can't do this to James.'

'Talk to James, tell him everything. He might be so delighted at the thought of a child that nothing else will matter to him.'

'It's my fault. I told him I'd gone past conceiving. I thought I had,' Muriel repeated. Then, as if she were suddenly back to the real world, 'I must go or I'll miss the five twenty train.'

Georgie had suggested that James would find a way forward although she had no idea how he possibly could. *Damn all the stupid conventions*, she thought. *They're both good people, how dare the rules of society rob them of their chance of happiness?*

'I'll walk with you to the station,' she said. 'If you want to be home before James you mustn't miss that one. Did he know you were coming here?'

Muriel shook her head. But when she answered, her voice was more than just calm; it was expressionless, as if her bout of crying had drained her of all emotion. 'I made up my mind after he'd gone this morning. He phoned and said he couldn't get home for lunch. I'll get my coat on. Don't you bother to come with me to the station, you stay in the warm.'

'I'm coming with you.' In ordinary circumstances she would have let her go alone, but there was nothing ordinary about that day and even a little thing like being seen on to the train might make Muriel feel less alone. Not that she *was* alone, of course, Georgie reminded herself, for this evening James would share the problem. Need it be such a problem? If they loved each other – and Georgie had no doubt that they did – they could overcome anything. There was another cloud though, one Muriel hadn't even mentioned: having a first baby at forty-seven years old could bring problems of its own.

They hardly spoke as they walked briskly to the station. Georgie made one or two attempts at starting a conversation – avoiding the thing that was at the forefront of both their minds – but she received no more than a monosyllabic reply. When Muriel had arrived in the morning it had been apparent that she had taken pains with her make-up; she had looked groomed and attractive. Before the homeward journey she hadn't so much as washed her tear-stained face, but had put on her hat and coat without looking in the mirror. The result was a middle-aged woman, plain and dull. They reached the platform as the train was signalled, so any long and difficult farewells were avoided. A light kiss on Muriel's cheek and Georgie saw her into the compartment where the blinds were already pulled down. She told herself that Muriel's hysterical outburst had probably done her good, acted like a safety valve, but telling herself and believing it were two different things.

Walking back to the gallery the situation went round and round in her mind. She felt helpless; it was something the two of them had to sort out for themselves. But she couldn't escape the memory of Muriel's uncontrolled crying.

Once home the first thing she had to do was close the heavy curtains, then she switched on the light in the one-time booking office. She told herself she ought to keep out of it and not interfere, but instead she lifted the earpiece of the telephone and into the speaker asked for James' number. Miss Webster recognized her voice and put her through without question. Just for a second the sound of his voice was reassuring. But the feeling didn't last.

'James, I want you just to listen. Don't interrupt, don't say anything.' And so she told him the whole story from Muriel's fear that she had a tumour to the outcome of the doctor's visit.

'Christ!' Just one whispered word, but one that spoke volumes. James never blasphemed.

'I had to speak to you. I'm so worried about her; she was in an awful state – and then so calm it was almost worse. Be gentle with her, James.'

'Gentle? Of course I shall. Ring off, Georgie. I must get home.'

It was quite dark by the time James pushed his bicycle into the shed. That he saw no lights in the house was no different from any other evening; Muriel was always very careful about the blackout. But the back door was locked; when she arrived home she must have forgotten to open it ready for him. He tapped on it, expecting to hear her footsteps. Nothing. She couldn't be in the kitchen or she would have heard. He walked round to the front of the house and used his key.

Once inside the dark hall, he was struck by the silence.

'Muriel! Are you upstairs?' No reply. 'Muriel!' In the dark he went up the stairs, stopping to close the curtains on the landing and then going towards what was officially *her* bedroom although he had shared it for weeks. Would he find her sitting there in the dark, hiding from him, hiding from something she was frightened to face? He had a strange empty feeling in his stomach, frightened of what he'd find. He'd thought recently that she'd looked pale, although she assured him she was well. Why couldn't she have told him what was frightening her? Again he felt his way to the window and drew the curtains before turning on the light. The room was tidy, just as it always was.

At Winchford station she must have found a long queue for the bus and she would have been one of those left to wait for the next one. Perhaps she was still queuing or else she could have decided to walk. He decided to walk that way and meet her.

When he reached the station a bus for their route was just approaching, but there was no sign of her. To get home as quickly as he could he joined the end of the queue, watching out of the window all the way in case somehow he had missed her. Putting his key in the lock of the front door he found himself muttering, 'Let her be here.' Then reason took control and he knew that if she had been waylaid between the station and home – gone into a shop perhaps – soon she would arrive. That's all he asked, nothing but that she should come home to him. At the back of his mind was the knowledge that ahead of them would be problems, but until she was with him again those problems had no significance.

The house was as he'd left it. If he hadn't had that call from Georgie he would have concluded that Muriel had met someone while she was shopping; he would have lit the drawing-room fire and poured himself a drink and looked at the crossword while he'd waited for her to come in. But he *had* received the call from Georgie, and now he was gripped with fear that was beyond reason.

On his bicycle he rode back to the station then up one dark street, down another, behaving in a way that was completely out of character as every time he saw the dark shape of a figure walking alone he slowed down, praying that in the dim light of his bicycle lamp he would recognize her. No one can disappear in streets as familiar as these. Was that her? No, hope gave way to disappointment. He ought to go home; by some miracle she might have missed her stop to get off the bus and had to walk back from the other direction. Making himself believe that that was what had happened, he pedalled hard in the direction of Gregory House.

There was a figure in the front garden. She must have gone without her key . . .

'Mr Bartlett, sir?' It was a man's voice and, pushing his bike up the driveway, by the light of its lamp, James recognized it was a policeman. His throat seemed to close; his mouth felt like sandpaper.

'Mr Bartlett?' the policeman asked for a second time.

'Yes. What's happened? Where is she . . . been searching . . . was there . . . accident?' A coherent sentence was beyond him. His hold on the handgrips of his bicycle tightened as if his life depended on it.

'I believe there is a Mrs Franklyn living here – your house-keeper?'

'Muriel Franklyn lives here, yes. What's happened, for God's sake?'

'Sorry, sir, but it appears she was seen on Wellington Bridge in Otford, climbing over the parapet. It being dark, the gentleman couldn't tell if it was a man or a woman, but he knew what he saw and tried to get there before she jumped. You've seen the sign on that bridge, keeping the youngsters off in summertime. Danger: Submerged Rocks. You've seen it, I'm sure. The gent who saw her jump—'

'Where is she? She's not . . . not . . .' James couldn't form the word.

'This gent knew better than to jump from the bridge, what with the rocky bottom and no great depth of water. So he went over the stile and down to the water that way and half waded and half swam, I reckon, till he could find her. That was the message that got phoned through to the station. He got her and dragged her to the bank and did all the right things, turned her on her side and pumped at her to get the water out. Then he went back—'

'Where is she? Where is she, for God's sake?'

'In Otford Cottage Hospital. He went back to the road and collared the first person he could to go and phone for the ambu-lance. Ambulance, police, no time was wasted. Poor soul. Is there any relative, children perhaps, we have to contact?'

'Is she going to be all right?'

'I'm no doctor, sir, but that good Samaritan who fished her out saved her life, if it was there to save. Now, about family . . .?'

'A stepdaughter. Write down her number. Tarnmouth 594.

I must get to the hospital.' Then, as he started on the path to the shed a thought occurred to him. 'How did you know where she lived?'

'The ambulance men picked up her handbag. She dropped it on the road when she climbed the parapet. They found her identity card.'

'Yes, of course. Thank you, Constable.' Already James' mind was moving to the next stage: a taxi to Otford, the next town down the line, to the hospital where by now Muriel must be aware of where she was and how she got there. If she had been distraught this afternoon, how much worse she must feel now. He had to get to her; nothing else mattered except to reassure her.

What the policeman hadn't told him – because he hadn't been told himself – was that when she leapt into the water she had hit her head on a submerged rock and had been brought out unconscious. She came round while she was being lifted into bed, her wet clothes replaced by a hospital gown. Her mind was only half with her, so she wasn't ready to wonder why she was there. She was tired . . . so tired . . . It was habit rather than reason that made her murmur, 'Thank you,' as the Sister tucked the covers. 'So tired . . .'

When the Sister was confident that Muriel had no lasting damage from the 'accident', she came to tell James and Georgie they could go in. James had been waiting for the longest hour of his life, but Georgie had only joined him a few minutes ago.

'She is very tired; don't try and make her talk.' Then, the Sister's brusque manner softening, 'Just let her know you are there with her.'

'You go first, James. I'll wait here for a minute or two then join you.'

Muriel was in a side cubicle, for which he was thankful. There was so much he wanted to say to her. But her eyes were closed. Surely, even if she were asleep she would hear his voice. He bent over her, taking both her hands in his.

'Muriel, hear me, darling. You, the child, our child and me. None of the rest matters. Can you hear me? Please God, let her hear me.'

There was a flicker of her eyelids, and just for a second she looked at him, her mouth softened, wanting to smile. Then she was asleep again.

The reporter from the *Winchford Times* prided himself that no scrap of local gossip slipped through his net. Each day he went to the Police Station for reports on road accidents, chimney fires, lost dogs – all of it was grist to his mill. But seldom was there anything as newsworthy as some woman going into the water from Wellington Bridge. In his most businesslike way he jotted down the details: a Mrs Franklyn, residing at Gregory House, Maitland Road. The young constable on the desk was in a chatty frame of mind and enjoying the drama of the situation every bit as much as was the reporter.

'I dare say she works there. The house belongs to the Town Clerk, so they tell me.'

'Do you know anything else about her background – any family?'

'Yes. PC Giles went to the house and he was given the telephone number of her stepdaughter. It was me who got on the blower to her and told her where her stepmother had been taken. She said she'd go there straight away.'

So the reporter was hot on the trail. As James and Georgie came into the reception area on their way out, they were waylaid. It was his good luck that he had seen the Town Clerk often enough when he'd been attending the monthly open meetings of the Council, so the boyish-looking young woman with him must be the stepdaughter. He'd trained himself to be observant and he noticed she wasn't wearing a wedding ring.

'Miss Franklyn?'

'Yes, do you want me?' she answered quickly, before James had a chance to say something they might regret. She had no idea who the man was, but some premonition told her it was wiser to be Miss Franklyn. 'You go on, James. I'll ring you tomorrow.'

The reporter waited patiently while James protested and she overruled him.

'Now then, what did you want me for?'

'This tragic accident with your stepmother. I shall be writing a report – a short report – for the local paper. I wondered if you could throw any light on what made her take such a step?'

The question was music to Georgie's ears. Here was a way to stop the gossip before it started.

'She is a very reserved person; she tries to keep her feelings under wraps. But I know her so well. My father was killed in an accident. She has tried to pick up the threads, but his death was a dreadful blow to her. When it happened I couldn't see how she was going to make a life without him. He had that sort of personality; losing him killed something in her. Perhaps she tried too hard, refusing to let her grief come out.' Georgie wondered whether she might be over-icing the cake, but her reporter friend appeared to be lapping up the romance of the story. 'She went to live at Gregory House, keeping house for Mr Bartlett. Sometimes I thought she was winning her battle, but then she'd let the mask slip. Broken hearts don't mend easily. As soon as they let her out of hospital she'll come to stay with me until she is fit to go back to Mr Bartlett. What she did today was wrong; we all know that. But when you write about her, please do it with understanding. She's the best stepmother in the world.' Well, at least that much was true.

Muriel was kept in the hospital for two nights and then Georgie collected her and they went by taxi to the gallery. That James loved her she didn't doubt. But she still wouldn't let herself risk ruining his career; that had been her thought from the start and it hadn't changed. Yet his words echoed constantly and comfortingly. '*All that matters is you, me and our child. Stay for a week or so with Georgie. I'll phone you every evening. Whatever the future holds, as long as we face it together it will be good.*' So how could she be frightened? The world was an unkind place for an illegitimate child; and although James was held in great respect in the town, once he had the label 'adulterer', that respect would be gone.

James paid his first-ever visit to the gallery after he finished work at the end of that week, coming to take Muriel home to Gregory House. Georgie spent the evening with Alice and Barry so that they would have space to talk by themselves. And that's when James described to Muriel their road to a future.

When Georgie arrived home they had already left. On the

table she found a note in Muriel's writing – at least, it had started as a note but had filled two pages written in a hand that was running more out of control with every word.

> *Georgie, all that misery is over. You said James would know what*
> *we had to do. If there were just the two of us we would go on*
> *as we were until the time when he is free to marry; but with the*
> *baby coming we must be able to put the same name on the birth*
> *certificate. So I am going to change mine by Deed Poll. James*
> *has long-standing friends who are willing to give the application*
> *priority; I won't be kept waiting. It means we must leave Winchford,*
> *but I don't think I have ever been so excited. A new beginning!*
> *And Fate is trying to look after us – in the Local Government*
> *paper he has seen an advertisement that a Clerk to the Rural*
> *District of Deremouth in Devon is needed from 1st May. He has*
> *applied. My fingers are crossed. They must make a quick appoint-*
> *ment to give time for a period of notice. Just imagine, we shall be*
> *known as Mr and Mrs, right from the start.*
>
> *That's one thing. The other is that, a minute or two ago, while*
> *I was writing this, the telephone rang. James went down to answer*
> *it. It was Dominic Fraser. He is in England and will be here either*
> *very late tonight (if there is a train), or first thing in the morning.*
> *A good thing I'm going. It wouldn't do to have a strange woman*
> *in his bed! You'll have another night on the settee I'm afraid.*
>
> *Ring me tomorrow. Georgie, be happy for us, pray that James*
> *will be appointed and – I'm so thankful. Just think of us – James,*
> *me and our own child. James is as pleased as I am. I'm so thankful.*
> *xxx*

Georgie found room in her heart to be thankful too, even while above all else was the thought that within hours Dominic would be here. She hadn't seen him since he had surprised them at Christmas by arriving on the doorstep unannounced, making their festive season complete.

By that time of night there was no one walking along the esplanade, so at the sound of footsteps she knew he had come home. Running down the stairs she reached the outer door just as he stepped inside the dark passageway and as he kicked the door closed with his foot he held her against him. This was real;

this was no dream. His beard against her face was like a caress; his mouth on hers sent her senses reeling.

In the first half-hour their thoughts went no further than themselves. He felt travel-soiled and 'not fit to share a bed with a lady' as he told her, so adding her five-inch allowance of hot water to his, they climbed into the bath together. It was a glorious start to the first night of his leave. It was only as he pulled back the covers to get into bed that he said, 'Sheets! What luxury. Not only sheets, but *laundered* sheets.'

'There's a story behind that,' she answered. 'But for that you might have had to put up with the ones I'd slept in.'

'I can think of nothing better. I'll leave the light on for a while. But what's the story? No, tell me tomorrow.'

'I want to tell you now, Dom. Thinking about it all makes me want to shout "Alleluia". I'm so thankful for all that we have.'

Eager for what lay ahead of them, he had said, 'Tell me tomorrow,' but, as he listened, he understood why she hadn't wanted to wait until the next morning. He, too, was moved by pity, thankfulness for Muriel and for themselves and where life had brought them.

'Alleluia.' He repeated the word she'd used. 'There can't be a better word to express my thankfulness that we are as we are. Georgie, my blessed Georgie,' he whispered, his mouth against her short hair. 'To say I love you is only half of it. It's as if we are one.'

'I know. One soul, one body . . .' And minutes later in that magical, mystical union, so they were.

Each day of his leave seemed to pass in half the time of a normal day. The Soames willingly looked after the gallery, partly because they were glad of the chance to earn and partly because they were so happy to see Georgie and Dominic together. Not that they saw very much of them, for most of the days were spent in the harbour, working on one or other of the two boats. 'Working' might be an exaggeration, for *Tight Lines* had been lifted out of the water before Dominic went away and was in his large shed at the bottom of Quay Hill. Certainly they found jobs to do on *Blue Horizon*, but they both knew they were looking for work simply because being there linked them with the past and pointed them towards the future.

In the middle of his leave his parents came down by train.

'Don't hang around waiting for us,' his father said when he phoned the evening before their visit. 'Rail isn't always the most reliable form of transport – another inconvenience of this damned war. You say you and Georgie are working on that boat of yours down in the harbour, so when we arrive we'll come straight there. We've got a room for the night in the Bay Hotel, but we'll be away again next morning. A brief visit.'

Georgie was no natural homemaker but she made an effort to see the cabin in *Blue Horizon* was comfortable and welcoming. Food for a picnic lunch was more of a problem. She took her ration book and Dominic's dockets to Basil Geary, the butcher further along the esplanade, and asked him what he could find for her that would be easy to cook and yet seem like a celebration without using up their week's ration.

'Nothing that needs skill, Basil. I'm not much of a cook.'

'Then here's just the thing. I made it myself last night. To be truthful I made two; I wouldn't dare let you have one if it was all I had. The missus'd skin me alive. But yesterday when Mrs Maidment from Dean Farm came to pick up their meat ration, she brought a rare treat – half a hare and a pheasant. Said her husband had been out with his gun. So how about a nice game pie? That'll turn Dominic's parents' visit into a celebration right enough.'

He was proved right. The best Dominic could manage to find was a bottle of third-rate white wine, and for dessert Georgie used her points to acquire a tin of raspberries. No hope of cream so she had to use half her milk ration – with a splash or two of tap water added – to make custard. But no banquet could have had a better atmosphere than there was that day on the *Blue Horizon*. Talk of the war wasn't allowed, although 'when this lot's over' crept into the conversation more than once. Watching Dominic with his parents, Georgie let her mind move ahead another thirty years. If his wanderlust was inherited from his mother (not that she had ever been able to chase her own rainbows, but she had always understood the urge in him that prevented him settling), his appearance came from his father. At sixty Malcolm Fraser had still kept the same build, tall, with a slim frame that managed to give the impression of strength; his

wiry hair was completely white, as was his beard; there were deep
lines around his blue eyes, lines that in Dominic were hardly
visible. But the years would change all that and, looking at
Malcolm, Georgie had a comforting feeling that this was the way
their future would take them.

James' legal background, and the friends he had never lost contact
with, proved to be an asset and the formalities for Muriel's name
change were quickly and painlessly dealt with; then she had to
obtain a new ration book and identity card. Only she and James
were aware of that growing bump that had so worried her –
or if anyone thought she was putting on weight they certainly
didn't suspect the reason. When James was offered the post of
Clerk to Deremouth Rural District in south Devon it seemed
their troubles were all behind them. With notice given that he
was leaving Winchford at Easter, he took three days' leave and
the two of them travelled westward by train to look for a home.
The Deremouth region was looked on as a safe reception area,
so accommodation was difficult. The agent had nothing on the
books for sale suitably close to the Rural District Council offices,
which were situated a mile or so north-west of the coastal town
of Deremouth. Public transport was unreliable, especially as
James knew he would often have evening meetings. He needed
to be near enough to come and go on his bicycle. This was
where they hit their first hurdle: the agent knew of nothing for
sale in the right area.

    'If you would consider renting, then I have the keys to Downing
Cottage in Otterton St Giles just across the other side of the
estuary, virtually due south of your place of work. It's the only
property within cycling distance. But I can't see it being suitable.
The previous tenant was an old lady; she'd lived there for seventy
years and died only last week. I doubt if it's had so much as a
lick of paint on it for half a century. There's mains water and
that's about all. No drainage, a chemical closet, a bathtub in the
kitchen with a cover that turns it into a table (too low to be
much use) and bath water heated on the kitchen range in buckets.
No, it's out of the question. I don't know of a farm worker's
cottage so badly equipped. Three hundred years old – and not
much different from how it was built. The only thing in its favour

is that it's very sound structurally and I understand the owner had it re-thatched about eighteen months ago. But there's no point in taking you there, it's not a bit suitable.'

'We'd like to see it,' Muriel said. 'We could at least get it repainted.'

'Even that's not easy. Shortages in everything you ask for these days. And as for having a septic tank put in – not that you would want that expense with a rented property – but it would be out of the question. You need a permit to breathe these days.'

Despite the agent's unenthusiastic view of the cottage, they said they wanted to see it. He made no secret of his unwilling-ness to take them there. Although he had a petrol ration, he saw no point in wasting it on such a fruitless outing.

'Is Otterton St Giles on a bus route from Deremouth?' James asked. 'If so, and as you say the place is empty, we could find our own way there and wouldn't need to take your time or your fuel.'

So that's what they did and as soon as they set eyes on Downing Cottage they knew it was right for them – even though they also knew their hearts were ruling their heads. The house was three hundred years old, with a thatched roof, a front door as solid and heavy as on many a church, a heavy iron front door key like nothing they'd ever handled and a neglected garden crying out to be cared for. As they walked from room to room their future was taking shape before their eyes.

'Are we crazy?' James asked, having seen from Muriel's expres-sion that she was as drawn to the ancient house as he was himself.

'No, but we would be if we didn't take it,' she replied. 'It may lack all the amenities the agent warned us about, but people have lived here for generations. We aren't any less capable than they were. And it's only down the lane to the village and the bus stop.'

He put his arm around her as they stood in the living room looking out of the window at the overgrown wilderness of a garden.

'I wonder if there's any chance of buying it,' he mused. 'This war won't last forever and we could make this something really special. The small fourth bedroom could be turned into a bath-room; we'd have a septic tank. There's electric light nearby; it wouldn't cost a fortune to have it installed.'

She nodded. '*You* can't move until after Easter, James.' They had already agreed that when they found somewhere, she would come down ahead of him. With a newly issued ration book and identity card she was now officially Mrs Bartlett, something that would be difficult to explain to the Winchford butcher and grocer where she was registered for rations.

'It's not an easy house, Muriel – cooking on that range, heating water on it in buckets to carry to that little tub of a bath, a chemical closet. It'll be too much for you as the weeks go on. We ought to find a flat, even a couple of rooms in town.'

'Oh, James, James.' She laughed affectionately. 'Don't let the cottage hear what you say. For generations, people have lived and died here; women have had babies, men have chopped wood and grown vegetables. Are we any less capable than they were? No, of course we aren't. One day we'll make it as beautiful as it could be, but if you always wait for "one day" nothing gets done.'

They looked at each other in solemn silence, and then he lightly kissed her forehead.

'I love you, Muriel Bartlett,' he said softly. 'This will be our new beginning.' He was gripped by sudden fear: most women had finished childbearing long before they were her age. Their new beginning . . . *Please God let it be.* 'Let's get the next bus back to Deremouth and surprise the agent by telling him we want to rent it as from now. Then we'll get the late train home to Winchford Tomorrow we'll contact the removal people.'

The days of Dominic's leave went so fast. Surely that was the cry echoed by all those who waited at home, watching for the post, counting the weeks and days until life could be normal again. After that week's shore leave he managed to get home briefly almost each time he docked, and even though he didn't always have the luxury of a seven-day leave, just a seventy-two-hour pass made them so much luckier than those who were serving overseas.

In June 1940 the British Expeditionary Force, or those of it who were able to escape, were driven out of France by the advancing German army. With no word from Dominic, Georgie gave consent for *Blue Horizon* to join the convoy of small craft that, manned by volunteers, ploughed the channel collecting those

stranded on the beaches of Dunkirk. There were plenty of experienced seamen on Tarnmouth Harbour willing to take the pleasure
boat to sea.

No one wanted to admit to fear for the future, yet there were
moments when it couldn't be overcome. When Winston Churchill
sent out his rallying call that, 'We shall fight them on the beaches,'
he stirred national pride across the country but in the still watches
of the night it wasn't so easy to believe. And then on those
beaches, coils of barbed wire were installed and concrete tank
traps erected.

Then in the middle of July came the news that Muriel had
given birth to a healthy son, weighing in at just over seven pounds.
Surprising everyone, his entrance to the world had been 'easy';
he had been born in that ancient cottage like many children
before him. The future had new promise. A first-time mother at
an age when for most women caring for a baby was a distant
memory, never before had Muriel felt so joyously in tune with
her body. Her figure seemed unchanged by childbearing, she was
still erect and slim, and the bosom that had been an embarrassment all her adult life had found its purpose as she suckled her
precious son . . .

On an evening in late August, with no Council meetings, James
was home just after six o'clock. He opened the heavy front door
with the key they kept under a flowerpot and stepped straight
into the sitting room where, on the settee by the open window,
five-week-old Christopher was sucking hungrily at his mother's
bountiful breast. For a moment James looked at them, wanting
the picture to make a lasting impression. He swallowed, his Adam's
apple suddenly seeming too large for his throat. Muriel tapped
the settee by her side and he crossed the room to sit by them.
Christopher continued to smack his lips, attacking her right breast
with gusto. The day was still warm and she had taken off her
blouse and bra to feed him for, being of a practical nature, she
would rather the baby threw up on her bare shoulder when she
winded him. James' hand moved to the left breast, always large
but at that moment so full that at his first touch the milk spilled
out.

Muriel clenched her teeth. Did feeding a child do this to every
woman? But it wasn't just that, it was the caress of James' hand,

the unspoken message passed and received. Making a supreme effort she made herself laugh as she covered his hand with hers.

'This is only his first course; that's his dessert I'm losing. Come on, young man. Time to change over before it all gets spilt.'

She had pulled herself back from the edge of desire and James made an attempt to do the same as he wiped his hand on his handkerchief. In all his life he had never known such contentment as they had here. Always he had lived in houses that provided up-to-the-minute convenience. Downing Cottage had nothing; and yet it had everything.

As the months wore on, there were changes at the gallery. It was only open from half past nine until one o'clock each day, in the care of Alice and Barry. Instead of being paid a wage they kept ten per cent of the takings just as Georgie had, and Mr Adams before her. They paid no rent (but then neither did Georgie any longer pay rent), and neither were they responsible for heating or lighting. Items of craft were still brought in, and still they sold; so too, more rarely, did a picture. It was as if, in a world so changed with war, people tried to hang on to what was normal and precious.

About half a mile upstream from the estuary was Hoopers, a firm of boat builders, and it was there that Georgie found a job as an assistant to a skilled worker. She could have earned more money if she'd gone to Palmer's Metalworks, a factory just inland of Tarnmouth engaged in making all types of wire fencing but these days mostly barbed wire. But Georgie wanted to work with boats. She didn't spell out her reason even to herself, but in an environment of boats she felt near to Dominic. In fact Hoopers were building landing craft, something quite new to her. Sometimes as she pedalled to work at half past seven each morning she would look back to her days at St Winifred's and wonder what had become of that austerely groomed young woman with her up-to-the-minute attire and well-manicured nails. Were those poor stifled, aging and yet ageless women still there just as they had been then? In her workman's overalls and with her hair tied up in a turban-like scarf they probably wouldn't even recognize her now.

*   *   *

To look back to the days when Dominic had first told her he meant to join the Merchant Navy was like remembering a dream. In her ignorance she had believed he would be safer there than in the Royal Navy. But she had learnt her mistake. Reports of attacks on convoys of merchant ships constantly haunted her.

Even in a small town like Tarnmouth there were young women who were unattached and intent on milking each day for every bit of fun – and with the coming of the Americans in 1942, 'fun' took on a whole new meaning. They had more money to spend than the British; they had about them an air of confidence, even glamour, akin to what could normally only be found on the silver screen. When a British Tommy put his arm around a girl she was conscious of the harsh material of his uniform and its distinctive smell. Was it disinfectant? Was it something to kill bugs? To some women, like Molly Curtis whose husband was stationed at an Ack-Ack Battery on the south-east coast, the smell represented romance, thankfulness.

'Bill's home for seven days,' she told Alice when she brought in her latest set of crocheted chairbacks. 'When the children came in from school yesterday, you should have heard their excitement. "Dad's home, Dad's home, I can smell that funny smell." I must run. I've got his ration card so I'm going to see what the butcher can let me have on it. Last week he had some lovely chops, but you get more mince than anything. Funny life. I've started some doilies but I'm not going to get anything done this week.' Alice watched her go, hoping that Basil Geary would find something better than mince for her. Funny life indeed!

'Poor lassie,' Barry said. 'I dare say no life is all beer and skittles, but these days I think we've got off lighter than most. Not so bad, is it?'

'Pretty good, Barry love,' Alice replied. 'No, I wouldn't change places with a living soul.'

In a world turned so upside down, the fact that Georgie and Dominic were living together (at least when he had shore leave) created no gossip. Five years earlier eyebrows would have been raised; she would have been seen as a woman without morals. But if war had done one thing it had given people more to worry about than other people's ways of finding their happiness. In fact

as time went on those who didn't know them very well probably assumed they had married, and those who did know them
well respected them both. Towards the end of 1943 James and
Georgie returned to Winchford for the hearing of their divorce
and nothing felt more natural than when they left court they
should have lunch together.

'It's just like it used to be,' she said as she took up her knife
and fork to attack the pigeon pie which they were trying to
persuade themselves was a delicacy although, in fact, it was the
only meat on the menu. 'Like it used to be before we were
married, I mean.'

'Of course you were right. Friendship – even *real* friendship
like we shared; not just companionship – is no basis for marriage.'

'No, but divorce is a good basis for friendship,' she answered
with a satisfied chuckle. Really it was surprising that she had never
been able to persuade herself that she was in love with him, for
he must certainly be the best-looking man she'd ever seen.

Lunch over, she took the train back to Tarnmouth. In six
months she would be free, and on Dominic's first leave after that
they would be married.

The nearest Tarnmouth came to an air raid had been a stick of
bombs which had been offloaded as an enemy bomber approached
the coast returning from some less fortunate inland target. These
had fallen, one on a field, one on the allotments and a third just
out to sea. A small, quiet seaside town, but on the flight path to
targets of far greater importance, the sound of the sirens was
familiar. Usually the alarm was followed by the All Clear within
less than half an hour, although there would be a repeat performance on their return flight. By early 1944 people had become
almost blasé and took it for granted the pattern wouldn't change.

One afternoon in April, Georgie had been in the boatyard
since just after seven in the morning and everyone was working
overtime. There was a buzz of excitement; the pressure of work
must mean that the much talked of invasion wasn't far off. Hoopers
was a small firm; there were others, some much the same and
many larger and more important. Everywhere there was a feeling
of hope. Soon the army would be back in France pushing the
Germans back to their own border and beyond.

That was only half the reason for Georgie's permanent under-lying sensation of excitement. It had been with her since Dominic's last visit home, for at that time her Decree Absolute had been almost due. Now it had finally arrived, and when Dominic came home again they would take the train to London and, with his parents as witnesses, would be married.

'It's going to be another late night tonight,' said Teddy Hoskins, her mentor who worked alongside her. 'Good job we're not party animals. Aye, and good job there's no beer in the Crown and Anchor till next week – at least we don't have to fret that some lucky bugger's quaffing while we're hard at it. Now then, young Georgie, just plane this down nice and smooth.' She had always been 'young Georgie' to Teddy, who'd worked at the yard for nearly fifty years. She took up her plane and concentrated on what she was doing. The siren had wailed its warning a few minutes ago, but so it often did. Soon there would be the All Clear.

'Planes?' Someone stopped work to listen. 'Bugger me if it isn't. Watch out – duck – get down – quick—'

Georgie heard; she saw men throw themselves to the ground and did the same, but everything was lost to her in the sound of the explosion.

Ten

Georgie was floating through a strange and timeless mist. Who was she? Where was she? Rather than coherent thought, it was instinct that made her raise her hand and touch the bandage on her head. Voices . . . and again it was instinct that made her listen even though she couldn't relate to the words or how they were connected with her.

'Can you reach the bell? Ring for the nurse. She's waking, oh thank God, she's coming round.' Muriel's voice was familiar; it seemed to give Georgie something to hang on to in her drifting world.

Footsteps . . . then strange voices . . . something cold against her chest – the recognition of a stethoscope was out of her reach, as was the tight band on her arm as her blood pressure was taken.

'Wake up, my love,' a kindly voice urged her. Consciousness and curiosity returned at the same time. Opening her eyes she was aware of a portly and motherly looking nurse. Where was she? But no longer did she ask herself *who* she was.

'What happened?

'There was an air raid. You got thrown in the blast in the boat yard. But you're going to be as right as rain in no time. No bones broken, just a nasty wound on your forehead. But it'll soon heal, my dear. You were lucky. Another day or so and you'll be home.' And, compared with so many that the busy hospital staff were coping with on that day following the raid, Georgie was indeed lucky. 'There now, you just lie comfy and I'll let your visitors see you for five minutes.'

Visitors! Her heart was racing. Had Dominic come? She struggled to sit up as the nurse disappeared between the closed curtains that surrounded her bed. She heard whispering voices, then the curtains moved again.

But it was Muriel who appeared, followed by Priscilla Fraser.

'You poor darling! What a thing to happen to you. But thank God it's not serious.' That from Muriel while, mystified and not quite able to keep up with events, Georgie looked from one to the other.

'What happened? What day is it?' Life seemed to have gone on without her.

'The raid was yesterday afternoon. Alice Soames got James' number from enquiries and telephoned him at work. He dropped everything and came home and I caught the train yesterday evening. I've been here all night. So has Mrs Fraser.'

Priscilla said nothing; she simply took Georgie's hand in hers and held it in a firm grip. Was she giving support or looking for it? Still drifting on the edge of reality, Georgie was assailed with a feeling of dread.

'Dom?' She mouthed the word; the sound was lost.

Priscilla nodded. 'The telegram came yesterday. I was on my way to tell you. I didn't want to do it on the telephone.' Her grip became even tighter; she closed her eyes as if that might take away the horror. For Dominic's sake she must be strong and support Georgie. 'Muriel and I have been sitting here all night,' she said, making a supreme effort to keep her voice normal. 'You're going to be all right, Georgie.'

'Dominic?' There was no escape, it had to be asked; and no escape for his grieving mother either, who had to tell her.

'So many boats in those Atlantic convoys: merchant boats like his, naval boats escorting them. And under the water, under the water,' she repeated it as if she were reliving some dreadful nightmare, 'U-boats. Dominic's luck ran out. If this war goes on and on, in time luck will run out for all of them.' With one hand she still gripped Georgie's while with the other she shielded her eyes.

Muriel felt helpless. She was filled with pity for Georgie and Priscilla and yet she was too far removed to share their heartache. Into her mind came the image of what would be happening at home. Had she the right to so much when for them, and for many thousands like them, their world was falling apart? With her guilt was a sense of dread; there wasn't anyone whose life couldn't be touched by tragedy. She wanted to get home, to be with James and Christopher, to Otterton St Giles where they had become part of the community. James would be at home with Christopher as much as he could while she was away, but if he had to attend meetings there were plenty of people who would be willing to look after Christopher. He was a very grown-up little boy, perhaps because his parents were older and he had never been 'babied', and he had found a place in the hearts of all their local friends. Looking at Georgie and Priscilla, Muriel had never been more conscious of her own blessings. A day never passed – and she vowed, it never would pass – without her being aware and thankful. She pulled her thoughts back to what Priscilla was saying.

'They anticipate your being out of here in a day or two. Georgie, I want to take you home with me. That's where you should be. If there is more news, it will come to us. Another few weeks and *you* would have been his next of kin. Come home. Please. It's what Dominic would want – and it will help Malcolm and me to have you there. You were his future.'

'Don't say "were", say "are".' Georgie's firm, surely almost aggressive, tone surprised them. The news had pulled her back from wherever her wandering spirit had been. 'He *must* have a future. I don't believe he's gone. I *won't* believe it.'

'Then come home with me.'

Georgie shook her aching head. 'I want to be in our own place.' As she said it she looked earnestly at Priscilla, wanting her to understand and not be hurt. Suddenly she was aware of a silent message passing between the two older women.

Muriel was the first to speak. 'We hadn't intended to tell you yet, dear; you've had shock enough without this. But the thing is, you can't go back to the gallery. Just be thankful the raid was in the afternoon, that no one was there.' Georgie looked at her in silence; there was only so much that her mind could take in. 'It wasn't a direct hit,' Muriel said, trying to ease this further blow. 'The nearest bomb was on Mrs Briggs' shop, but you couldn't live there. Alice Soames came down to try and clear up the glass and some of the boatmen have boarded up the windows, but the kitchen ceiling is down and the gallery ceiling plaster is on the verge of falling. It will have to come down and be re-plastered. She was lucky the police let her through. The esplanade is cordoned off.'

'You've seen Alice?'

Muriel nodded. 'Yes. She came there to find out about you, but you hadn't come round. She had to get home to Barry.

Mrs Fraser and I are staying at the White House on Station Hill. When they let you out, dear, come down to Downing Cottage, somewhere quite different. We'd love to have you there. It may be ages before the repair work is done.'

Just as suddenly as energy had returned to Georgie, so it disappeared. She lay back with her eyes closed. Muriel and Priscilla looked at each other helplessly.

'I'm not going anywhere. Dominic will find me in Tarnmouth.' Her eyes shot open, defying them to dispute what she said. 'Until the repairs are done I shall live on *Blue Horizon*.' They knew it was no use arguing with her in her present mood. Muriel thought that when the shock had worn off she might see the logic in what they suggested; then either she or James would come and fetch her. Priscilla hung on to Georgie's words and longed to believe.

Two days later Georgie was discharged from hospital, her bandage being replaced with a large plaster. No one asked her whether she had a home to go to. Taking a taxi to the harbour, Muriel and Alice intended to see her settled in *Blue Horizon*. She knew they meant kindly, but to her it was vitally important that she went aboard on her own. Luck was with her. As always there were men on the harbour and, seeing her arrive, to a man they left what they were doing and came to speak to her.

'Don't let the taxi go,' she said. 'There's no means of phoning for another from here when the pub's closed.'

'I don't like leaving you, dear,' Muriel said. Then she imagined James and Christopher at home and was grateful that Georgie was amongst friends here on the harbour. What a moment for her to remember Cyril's pride when she got her degree, and again when she was made housemistress. What would he have made of the way her life had changed? But at the forefront of her mind was the image of home. 'But we both have trains to catch. It'll be ages before the gallery is fit to be lived in. Give yourself a little time here, then come to Devon.'

Priscilla had been speaking to the taxi driver. She was relieved not to be going on board; for her it would be full of ghosts. If Georgie could find comfort in them, she envied her; for herself there was no escape from the stark words on the telegram.

She wanted to get away from the coast, to try and clear her mind of the image of her son lying there on the seabed. She wanted to immerse herself in work, anything to escape the devils that plagued her.

There was something unreal about the days immediately following Georgie's return to Tarnmouth. She made herself climb Quay Hill and, walking on the opposite side of the road to the cordoned-off wreckage of the general store and its immediate neighbours, she looked at the devastation. Dennis Holbrook, the baker, was standing gazing just as she was and it was from him that she learnt that Mrs Briggs had been killed when the bomb fell. Bert Crisp had been moved from Tarnmouth hospital to a burns unit where he would be for some time; his wife was still in a critical state in Tarnmouth Hospital. The fish and chip shop had been destroyed, not by a direct hit, but by fire when the deep fat in the fryer had been thrown by the blast and had ignited.

'And then there's Dominic,' Dennis said, his gaze firmly on the row of damaged shops. 'Hearing about him after all this . . . I dunno, Georgie, sometimes you think things can't get any worse. Mr Sinbad, remember that's what we called him? You never know a person, do you, not by appearances you don't. I'm sorry – oh but sorry, that doesn't say the half of it. It's rotten for you and you haven't even got your work to keep your mind busy.' But then, neither had he. Would life ever be the same on the esplanade?

Back on *Blue Horizon* Georgie reached her lowest ebb. For how long could she delude herself that he was coming home? Yet, it hadn't been a delusion; she'd been so sure. Now, as if the sight of the wreckage of the esplanade had brought her face to face with reality, she was stripped of all hope. Sitting on deck on the long wooden bench she closed her eyes and felt the gentle rocking of the boat. If he was gone, what was there left for her? *Dom, Dom, help me . . . I don't know what to do . . . no point in anything . . . I wish that bomb had taken me.*

'Georgie Bartlett,' a voice from the quayside called, bringing her back from the depths to which her misery had dragged her. 'Telegram for Georgie Bartlett, *Blue Horizon.*'

'Georgie Bartlett, that's me.' Hope . . . dread . . . She was fright-ened to hope and yet to be prepared for bad news was to tempt fate . . . All these emotions crowded in on her as she hurried to the gangplank and reached for the envelope.

'Shall I wait for an answer?' the lad asked as she tore open the envelope. Then, impatiently after waiting while surely the stupid woman could have read it half a dozen times, 'Well? Any reply.'

'Sorry! Yes. Write this down. Simply say, "Alleluia – stop – Didn't I tell you – stop – Georgie".' Then she told him Dominic's parents' name and address.

More slowly she returned to the bench and reread the telegram, which by that time she knew by heart. 'Dominic picked up by another boat in the convoy – stop – landed in England – stop – broken arm and shoulder – stop – ring us –stop – Priscilla.'

If Georgie lived to be a hundred, could there ever be a moment of such thankfulness? So much was packed into the next hour. Outside licensing hours she hammered so loudly on the door of the Jolly Sailor that it brought Jack Dunne, the licensee, hurrying from his afternoon nap to open it. And the news she gave him raised his own flagging spirit as he took her through to the telephone. First a call to Priscilla, who told her where Dominic had been taken, then another to the taxi firm. Within an hour she was on the train to Dover, where he had been taken. The future was golden.

As the train steamed on its way the initial excitement receded sufficiently that more coherent thought had a chance. War had taught them so much: at one time a broken arm and damaged shoulder, even her own head wound, would have seemed like disaster. Now all of it was joy beyond belief. Alleluia . . . She seemed to hear him saying the word that expressed so much.

Epilogue

1949

There was an atmosphere of excitement on the quayside.

'Look! Here, take the binoculars and you'll see the sails. Then pass them on, let everyone have a look.'

Not everyone needed to borrow binoculars; there were some, like James, who had brought their own.

'May I see, Dad?' Christopher gave a jump of excitement, something as uncharacteristic as was his forgetting to say 'please'. On that special occasion James let the omission pass unchecked. At nine years old, Christopher remembered Georgie and her husband Dominic, but they had never been part of his life, so he hadn't really missed them during the two years they had been away. But on that September afternoon he was caught up in the excitement. To be truthful, his thoughts of Georgie were of the books she wrote. There were those with illustrations – they were just for babies, he thought now from his advanced years – but when he had been small his parents used to read them to him. Since he'd read them for himself he had looked forward to those she wrote about the Howard twins and their friends, a group of children about his own age who lived wonderful lives of adventures. There were no illustrations in those; they were written for older children who liked to see the characters with their own imagination.

There was a hum of excitement amongst the waiting crowd. Next to James stood Malcolm and Priscilla Fraser and, further along but still in the front line of viewers, Alice and Barry Soames. People had made a space for them so that he had a view from his chair. The boatmen were there; the shopkeepers from the esplanade were there (Bert Crisp's appearance changed by the burns despite the patient work of the surgeon); those who brought their crafts and paintings to the gallery were there and many of the gallery's regular customers too. Never before had two local people set off as Dominic and Georgie had, free to travel the world, to go where their spirit led. It was as if every one of those waiting to greet them home felt themselves to have been part of the adventure.

On one occasion Georgie had written to Priscilla and Malcolm that they had memories enough to last a lifetime. The couple had looked at each other with laughter just beneath the surface. They thought of the years when Dominic had roamed fancy-free. 'Dominic with memories to last a lifetime?' Malcolm had chuckled as he read. 'I'll believe that when it happens.'

By the time they had left Tarnmouth in 1947 the esplanade had been restored, not quite as it had been in the past for, where the general shop had once been, there remained a rough gap in between the shored-up buildings. 'Like someone with a front tooth missing,' had been Dominic's opinion. The Planning Committee had been undecided whether a more modern building should be put there, or whether it might be concreted and made into a play area with swings, a see-saw and perhaps even a slide. A new kiosk had sprung up in front of the pier, so that visitors wouldn't be deprived of ice-cream now there was no Mrs Briggs to make it.

The gallery had reopened at No. 14 and, for the 1946 season, so had the booking office. But with the coming of peace Dominic and Georgie had been restless. All they had been sure of was that, whatever they decided to do, they would be together. They couldn't slot back into the routine they had known before the war. Too much had happened in between. The call of adventure had been loud – so loud that not only had Dominic heard it (he whose ears had been ever attuned to it), but so too had it called to Georgie. Letting the upstairs rooms so that the expenses for the premises were covered, they had left Alice and Barry to run the gallery, which once again took the whole of the ground floor. And just as he had in 1939, Dominic had brought *Tight Lines* off the water and housed it in the large shed, then sold *Blue Horizon* to a recently demobbed sailor who'd had dreams of his own.

Carrying only what they could cram into huge rucksacks, he and Georgie had set out on their Big Adventure. In France they had bought a barge and travelled south on the canals, selling it when it had served its purpose. Then they took a train to Barcelona where they had bought a boat, their home for the next two years. Idleness didn't agree with either of them, but neither did being tied to a regular routine. So, as they sailed the Mediterranean, they worked, not for other people, but for themselves. She painted and she wrote; her pictures were carefully stored on board but her manuscripts were sent off to Priscilla. Dominic kept a daily log, not just of the miles sailed but also of every small detail of their time aboard and ashore; with that as his basis he started on a series of travel books, with a human aspect. Work and freedom combined. Yet they found themselves being drawn towards Tarnmouth and home. Hadn't Dominic said he always turned up in the end, 'like a bad penny'?

'Dom, look at this!' She passed him their binoculars. 'There's a crowd on the quay. Something must have happened.'

'Time to take in the sails. I'll bring her in on the motor now,' he called to her a few minutes later.

'Aye, aye, skipper,' she answered, and heard the excitement in her voice. Obeying instructions, still she stared towards the crowd wondering what could have happened. Not for a moment did she imagine the crowd to be connected with their arrival home. Only as they came towards the familiar and treacherous sandbar just outside the entrance to the harbour did they realize the reception was for *them*.

For one frightening moment the adventure of a lifetime seemed to be over; they were being drawn back into yesterday's world.

'We'll go again,' Dominic called, reading her thoughts. 'Tomorrow, next year, sometime, whenever and wherever the spirit moves us. What do you say?'

With the sail safely secured, she moved to his side by the tiller. 'I say yes, we probably will. Yes, I'm *sure* we will. But adventure is anywhere we make it; it's not something waiting somewhere else. It's of our own making; it's *us*.'

He gave her a wink that spoke volumes. 'That's my girl,' he said.